Praise for
Sundown, Yellow Moon

"[Watson's] characters, as always, feel 'realer' than those of just about any contemporary novelist. . . . Watson's people are like the people you know."   —*The Philadelphia Inquirer*

"*Sundown, Yellow Moon* may be a dark tale, but it's one worth tackling. The value comes from both the tale itself and the chance to study the technique of a master storyteller."   —Trenton *Times*

"Quietly moving . . . Its melancholy feels earned and true."
                                           —Raleigh *News & Observer*

"A writerly study of a fiction writer at work."
                                           —*The Sunday Seattle Times*

"Watson takes on the essential question of life and the investment of meaning without becoming preachy or offering his characters an easy escape."   —Fredricksburg *Free Lance-Star*

Sundown,
Yellow
Moon

LARRY WATSON

SUNDOWN, YELLOW MOON

A Novel

RANDOM HOUSE
TRADE PAPERBACKS
NEW YORK

2008 Random House Trade Paperback Edition

Copyright © 2007 by Larry Watson
Reading group guide copyright © 2008 by Random House, Inc.

Published in the United States by Random House Trade Paperbacks,
an imprint of The Random House Publishing Group,
a division of Random House, Inc., New York.

RANDOM HOUSE TRADE PAPERBACKS and colophon are trademarks
of Random House, Inc.
RANDOM HOUSE READER'S CIRCLE and colophon are trademarks
of Random House, Inc.

Originally published in hardcover in the United States by Random House,
an imprint of The Random House Publishing Group,
a division of Random House, Inc., in 2007.

Grateful acknowledgment is made to Ram's Horn Music
for permission to reprint an excerpt from "If You See Her, Say Hello"
by Bob Dylan, copyright © 1974 by Ram's Horn Music.
All rights reserved. International copyright secured.
Reprinted by permission.

Library of Congress Cataloging-in-Publication Data
Watson, Larry.
Sundown, yellow moon: a novel / Larry Watson.
p. cm.
ISBN 978-0-375-75853-9
1. Legislators—Crimes against—Fiction. 2. Suicide victims—Fiction.
3. Children of suicide victims—Fiction. 4. Teenage boys—Fiction.
5. Bismarck (N.D.)—Fiction. I. Title.
PS3573.A853S57 2007
813'.54—dc22   2007000031

Printed in the United States of America

www.randomhousereaderscircle.com

2 4 6 8 9 7 5 3 1

Book design by Victoria Wong

To Susan

Sundown, yellow moon, I replay the past
I know every scene by heart, they all went by so fast

—Bob Dylan, "If You See Her, Say Hello"

Sundown,
Yellow
Moon

Although I have devoted much of my life to writing stories, they are all, I have come to realize, part of a single story that has shifted and swelled over time but never strayed far from my core. I will call its beginning the January day when I was sixteen years old and walking home from school with my best friend, Gene Stoddard. We heard sirens, but we couldn't see where they were coming from. Their combined howl, however, was so close that we believed police cars or fire trucks, and an ambulance, had to be nearby. We ran toward the sound, hoping to catch a glimpse of the vehicles and perhaps discern their destination.

When we came to the Will-Moore Elementary School playground, its new snow packed and rutted to bare ground in places from the boots of hundreds of children, we saw a police cruiser and an ambulance speeding up Fourth Street. Those were the last vehicles in the procession.

It was obvious we'd get no closer to them and their mystery, so we stopped, our heaving, slowing breaths fogging the frigid air. Gene and I both lived a few blocks away on Keogh Street. (Our street was in a fairly new section of Bismarck, North Dakota, and the developer's wife, a student of history, had arranged to have some of the street names in that part of town named for the officers—Keogh, Yates, Cooke, Reno—in Custer's command when Custer and the Seventh Cavalry left Fort Abraham Lincoln, just west of Bismarck, on their ill-fated campaign that ended at Little Bighorn.) For all of our school years Gene and I had walked to and from school in each other's company. Recently, however, that had begun to change. We had a couple friends with cars, and one of them usually picked Gene and me up in the morning. They were both on the basketball team, however, and practices meant they stayed later at school. Also, Gene had started going steady with a sophomore girl, Marie Ryan, and he was often with her after school, but on that day she was in rehearsal for a choir concert. So we were walking together again, and we'd planned to go to his house or mine. We had to memorize the dagger speech from *Macbeth* for Miss Cordell's English class, and we needed to work on our recitations. For a moment we were tempted to take a detour in an attempt to find where all those sirens were going. Their wailing seemed to have stopped, and not far away. Could they be at one of the stores at the shopping center on Third Street? At the state capitol, only a few blocks north of us on Fourth Street? Or could they have been going to a private home on one of the residential streets or avenues that surrounded us?

Perhaps if we had not had that homework assignment, or if it had not been so cold—the snow underfoot squeaked when we shifted our weight—or if one of us had been allowed the use of the family car, we might have followed the trail of undulating sound that still hung in the crystalline winter air. But we did not. We turned up the collars of our wool overcoats (although this fashion would reverse itself before the decade was out, in 1961 teenagers imitated the attire of adults), pulled our stocking caps down to our eyebrows, hunched our shoulders to our necks, and moved on. Would it have mattered if we had not trudged immediately homeward? It would not. Sirens sound when deeds are done.

We went to Gene's home because it was closer, by four houses, and when we entered, we were surprised to find Gene's father home. He was sitting at the kitchen table, smoking a cigarette, and wearing his hat and overcoat. Is it only hindsight that makes me want to say he looked gray, drawn? Cold of course leaches color from as many cheeks as it fills.

"Where's your mother?" he asked.

"I'm pretty sure she works at the church library on Wednesdays."

Gene's father—Raymond—nodded gravely. "Wednesday. That's right. It's Wednesday."

My discomfort grew. Raymond Stoddard was a somber, reserved man by nature, but he wasn't usually tensely grim, as he appeared to be at that moment. That he wasn't aware of Mrs. Stoddard's schedule, something that the women in the other houses up and down the block would certainly know, struck me as unusual, but no more so than the fact that a seemingly healthy male was home before five o'clock. He hadn't taken off his hat and coat, and he hadn't greeted me in any way. And I knew from hearing my parents talk that Mr. Stoddard had once lost a job because of his drinking. I'd be willing to concede that my entire sense of unease might not have been true of the moment but was added only with the aid of hindsight, except for this fact: I didn't remain at the Stoddards' that day. Before I removed my own cap and coat, I made up an excuse and told Gene I couldn't stay. Later that evening, we decided, we'd get together and practice the dagger speech on each other.

At our house nothing suggested anything but the ordinary. My mother was in the kitchen moving from refrigerator to sink to cupboard to stove, preparing the evening meal and pausing only to take a drag from the Viceroy burning in the ashtray on the kitchen table. My sister, younger than me by eight years, sat on the living room floor watching cartoons and eating some kind of sweet that had already made her heavy for her age and that would lead to lifelong unhappiness over her weight. All was as it should be. The furnace was running, its constant exhalation heating the house until the insides of the windows perspired and the kitchen's cooking smells drifted all the way to the bedrooms and back again. Warmth, food, family—it was a scene of reassuring comfort, and although I might have felt it as such, nothing about it registered itself as rare, and that I took it for granted only testifies to how few interiors I knew well.

"Do you know what those sirens were about?" I asked my mother.

"I was going to ask you the same thing."

"Gene and I saw an ambulance and a cop car going up Fourth Street, but there had to be more than just those two."

"Police car," she corrected. "And two went past on Divide, too."

"Going east?"

"Going east."

"There wasn't anything on the radio?" My mother had a radio on in the kitchen from early morning until night.

"Haven't heard a thing."

"Well, if you hear anything from my room, it's me. We have to memorize this Shakespeare speech for English, and the only way I can get it is to keep saying it out loud."

"Let me know if you want me to test you."

I went off to my room and behind its closed door paced back and forth and recited Macbeth's words:

> Art thou not, fatal vision, sensible
> To feeling as to sight? or art thou but
> A dagger of the mind, a false creation,
> Proceeding from the heat-oppressed brain?
> I see thee yet, in form as palpable
> As this which now I draw.

To this day I remember the soliloquy, although I've had no occasion to repeat those lines. That they're sealed in my memory makes me believe that disaster has the power to cast not only every attendant fact in the sharpest relief but collateral details as well.

Over the sound of my own voice I soon heard sirens again, though faintly at first. Because of what we had witnessed earlier, I stopped speaking and listened carefully. Their wail traveled so easily to my ears it seemed as though I could map their movement in the air—up Fourth Street again, west on Divide Avenue, closer, closer, until they were right *there*.

I jumped to my window in time to see one police car and then another slide around the corner and career down our street. Their lights sliced through the early evening dusk and tinged the snowbanks and the houses on the block a pale, pulsing red. That same light found its way into our home, its presence a violation. In other parts of the city did they hear the sirens and calculate that they came from our block? I ran to the living room, from whose windows I could see farther down the street.

I didn't have to look far. Both cruisers pulled awkwardly to the curb in front of . . . the Stoddards'? Was that possible? Even more improbable was the car already parked there. In the drive-way, right behind Raymond Stoddard's dark blue Ford Galaxie was an emerald-green Nash Rambler. If anyone in town owned a Nash in that same color other than my father, I didn't know about it.

Surely there had been other moments in my life when I had been immobilized by conflicting impulses, but that was the first time I was aware of it. I was caught between the desire to flee back into the interior of our house, back to where those lights couldn't touch me or those sirens reach me, and a wish to run in the other direction—out of the house, across the drifted lawns and the snow-packed street, and down the block to where the real invasion was taking place, to my best friend's house. But per-haps it was confusion that truly paralyzed me. *Dad's car?*

In recalling the events of that and subsequent days, I'm some-times unsure about chronology, about what occurred before or after. In part, that uncertainty is a consequence of how I've learned about the events—often in fragments—and my own ver-sion of what happened is a patchwork (although no less accurate for that). Scenes and realizations have been stitched together, sometimes overlapping one another, as I have made, and occa-sionally revised, my discoveries over time. About the order of

days and hours I'm generally confident, but occasionally the seconds or minutes jump ahead or behind one another. For example,
I have the impression that my mother came to the window too,
and as she was looking over my shoulder, I asked her why Dad's
car was there, but before she could answer me, the phone rang
and she ran to pick it up. After a brief conversation, she came
back to the window and said, "That was your father. He said neither you nor your sister is to go outside. Do you hear? You're to
stay in the house." But in truth, the phone had already rung, and
my mother had talked to my father for a few minutes, long
enough for him to give her a brief account of why he was at the
Stoddards' and why the police would be there soon. True, he told
my mother to keep my sister and me in the house, but his real
concern was that neither of us go anywhere near the Stoddards',
no matter how hard the obligations of friendship or the tempta-
tions of curiosity tried to move us out the door. He had instructed
my mother to stay home as well, or at least until he phoned again
or until she saw Mrs. Stoddard return home, and then she was to
come running.

I could continue to withhold information, revealing it only in
slivers and shards, and in that way try to duplicate in these pages
the suspense that I lived through that night, and in the process in-
duce in you the apprehension and uncertainty that I felt, but
while that might be effective narrative strategy, it would not be
entirely true to the situation. I don't recall exactly how or when I
came to know what had happened in our city and our neighborhood, because to this day I am still augmenting the story, though
more now with human understanding than with factual details.

Nevertheless, when I finally went to bed, it was with sufficient knowledge—sufficient but incomplete—to allow me to fall asleep without being totally bedeviled by questions. This much I knew:

True to one of Gene and my guesses, those sirens had been heading toward the state capitol, only a few blocks from our homes on Keogh Street. I had been in and out of the capitol building so often over the years—on my own or with school groups, with relatives and friends who came to visit—that I knew its architecture and floor plan almost as well as I knew my school's, the public library's, or the civic auditorium's. I had no difficulty picturing the setting for the afternoon's incident.

In the capitol, both the senate and the house were in the legislative wing, an impressive high-ceilinged, wood-paneled, art-deco-inspired hall. Right outside the legislative chambers were upholstered banquettes, intended no doubt as places where the senators and representatives could meet, during session breaks, with lobbyists and constituents. In January 1961, the legislature was in session (worth noting because to this day North Dakota's senate and house convene only every other year), and during a recess Monty Burnham, a popular, charismatic senator from Wembley, in Cleave County in the north central part of the state, sat on one of those padded benches in the hall. At Senator Burnham's side was John Ritterbush, a Fargo attorney.

While the two men conferred, a lean, swarthy man approached them, reached into his overcoat pocket, and brought out a pistol. Without discussion or warning, he fired at Senator Burnham. The bullet struck the senator in the chest. Burnham tried to rise from the bench, but failed and slid to the marble floor. While he lay there, the gunman shot him again. This bullet went through Monty Burnham's throat. Ritterbush was not a target, but he was injured slightly when a fragment of either lead or stone struck him in the cheek.

The senator's wounds were mortal, and while he lay dying on the floor of the capitol's Great Hall, the gunman calmly walked away, exiting the building through a revolving door on the south side of the building. The fact that a weapon was in his possession may have kept anyone from trying to detain him.

There were many witnesses to the shooting and its immediate aftermath, and in spite of the inevitable confusion and panic, it was not long before someone volunteered an identification of the man in the overcoat. He was recognized as an employee of the North Dakota Department of Accounts and Purchases, whose offices were on the sixth floor of the capitol. His name was Raymond Stoddard.

Considering the span between the time when the shooting occurred and when Gene and I saw his father, Mr. Stoddard must have driven directly home after leaving the capitol.

And it couldn't have been long after I left my friend's house that Mr. Stoddard went out into the garage, secured a length of clothesline rope around a two-by-four beam, balanced himself on a stack of tires, and hanged himself. To this day I don't know what propelled Gene to the garage, where he discovered his father swinging from the rafter, but once he did, he went right back into the house and tried to telephone his sister, hoping she might know what he should do before their mother returned. The call was long distance since Marcia Stoddard was a student at the University of North Dakota in Grand Forks. When she didn't answer, Gene called the office of a Bismarck attorney, the only other person he could think of who might know what should be done. That person was my father.

My father arrived at the Stoddard residence shortly before the police, in just enough time to try to calm Gene and to get as much information from him as possible. There wasn't enough time for my father to cut down Raymond Stoddard's body or to open the envelope lying on the kitchen table, both of which he had intended to do. When the police opened the envelope, they found inside a note typed with these words: "I murdered Senator Monty Burnham. I acted alone." Mr. Stoddard signed the note, and since it was on Accounts and Purchases letterhead, the assumption was that he had typed it in his office before going down to the legislative wing to commit his crime.

And that was that. About who did the deed there was to be no doubt. But in spite of the popularity of mystery novels, is *who* the question we really want answered? Isn't *why* what we truly want to know? A name, an identity, won't fully satisfy us; in order to understand his motive we want to see inside the mind and heart of the murderer, the lover, the coward, or the hero. Barring that, we want to be presented with enough evidence that we can construct a reasonable explanation of what occurred and why. And in fairness I have to say, if you are one of those readers who must have all your questions answered, you must set this narrative aside immediately. If I could have warned you earlier, I would have, but you've spent only as much of your time as it takes to read a little more than ten pages. It can't have been more than minutes. All I can promise you, if you choose to continue reading, is enough information that you might be able to look into your own heart and mind and find an answer there for why humans behave as they do, even in moments most extreme. And although it's not likely to console you, your investment of time will be nothing compared to mine, almost a lifetime by some standards of measurement.

I said I knew enough to allow me to fall asleep that night, but of course many questions still troubled me, some of them of the obvious, profound variety that unsettled everyone, and some close to trivial, if indeed anything related to those events could be regarded as insignificant.

For example, I was curious about the murder weapon. I had never seen firearms of any sort in the Stoddard household, so I wondered if Mr. Stoddard had had the gun well hidden somewhere or if he had recently acquired it in order to shoot Senator Burnham. And why had he hanged himself—a method of suicide that struck me as torturous and uncertain—rather than shot himself?

The mystery of the gun was eventually solved, and in a way that illustrated how information was added to the basic narrative over time, just as it is for readers of any mystery. Raymond Stoddard couldn't have driven home and killed himself with the same pistol with which he shot Senator Burnham because he no longer had it. When he walked out of the capitol building, he threw the gun away. A groundskeeper found it months later when temperatures rose, snow melted, and the drift the gun had landed in gave up its secret. The event was a literal example of an expression my mother often used. *Det som gö i snö kommer fram i tö.* She learned it from her mother, who came to this country from Sweden. *That which is hidden in the snow reappears in the thaw.* One of the witnesses to the crime had said he believed the murder weapon was an Army issue .45 automatic, and the grounds-keeper's discovery verified the accuracy of the witness's observation.

A fact I had long been in possession of also troubled me, and troubled me especially because I had no way of determining its importance. Did it mean anything that Raymond and Alma Stoddard and Monty Burnham all came from Wembley, North Dakota, a small town 150 miles northeast of Bismarck? I hesitated to make too much of it because my father and I were from Wembley as well. Both of us were born there, but our family moved to Bismarck when I was five years old. Was that common place of origin nothing more than coincidence, a detail that teases us with its suggestion of significance when it possesses none beyond itself?

Throughout the evening, neighbors knocked on our door, sometimes with casseroles and questions about whether they could be of any help. The Stoddards were closer, in physical distance and perhaps in friendship, to other neighbors, but these people came to our house. I flattered myself that my friendship with Gene had given us special status, but of course they were there because of my father. The news of Monty Burnham's murder had been officially made public, but somehow the unofficial reports of my father's involvement had gotten around as well.

And that no doubt was why the police and the press also visited our home that night. They wanted what the neighbors wanted, but the reporter from *The Bismarck Tribune* and the two detectives came right out and said they were seeking information and flipped open their notebooks.

My mother did her best to keep up with the number and variety of visitors. She brewed pots of coffee, she put out plates of cookies and cups of nuts, she emptied ashtrays, and she kept adjusting the thermostat to make up for the heat the house lost with the door so often open. Strangers crossed the threshold, lights burned that were seldom turned on, snowy shoes and galoshes melted puddles on carpets that were usually kept dry, yet my mother remained a model of smiling courtesy, equanimity, and efficiency. Which is to say that in crisis, she was who she always was.

My father, on the other hand, seemed utterly transformed by the day's events. He was, in ordinary circumstances, sociable, if somewhat aloof, a calm, capable man who gave the impression of being in control of everything in his life from his gutters and eaves to his emotions. He was devoted to his family, his profession, and his community, and in return for his steadfastness, respect and admiration flowed his way.

But on that evening, my father seemed on the verge of tipping into rage. Scowling and tight-lipped, he answered questions posed to him with answers so terse I wondered if the police had cautioned him not to speak of what he had seen and heard at the Stoddard home. He tried to assist my mother with her duties as host, but his heart was plainly not in it. People barely put down their coffee cups before my father swept them up and carried them back to the kitchen. And on one occasion he was openly rude. When he walked into the living room and saw Pastor Lundgren speaking to Dolores Lemke, my father said to the minister, "Don't you think you could do more good at the house down the street?" When he finally sent my sister and me to our rooms, it was with a command that made us seem no different from the curiosity seekers who had been in and out of the house all evening. "All right," he said to us, "off to bed. Show's over."

Where had his anger come from? That question may have perturbed me more than any other. Granted, what he had confronted when he'd stepped into the Stoddard garage must have been shocking, disturbing, sickening. He knew both of the day's dead men, although his relationship with the senator was little more than a superficial acquaintance. Those circumstances, however, should have left my father shaken, grief-stricken, bewildered (the emotion most in evidence that evening). But rage? Had it always been inside him, waiting for the tiniest crack to come bursting forth? Or did he know something that the sad, puzzled rest of us didn't?

My bedroom was in the northwest corner of the house, the corner that took the brunt of the season's arctic winds. Built in the city's housing boom of the 1950s, our home was not especially well insulated, and during the coldest months, frost formed on the wall next to my bed. As I lay there thinking about what had happened in our city, our neighborhood, our block, I reached out and scraped my fingernails through the rime. Because the world's calamities had come so close, our home no longer felt like a refuge, and its walls seemed as insubstantial as that thin layer of ice. Nowhere were we protected, and only fools believed otherwise.

❧

I didn't speak to or see Gene until the following evening when he and his mother came to our house for dinner. To say I was nervous about being in his presence would have been an understatement. Could I have come up with something appropriate to say to a friend whose father had just died? Perhaps. But to a friend whose father was a murderer and a suicide? Impossible. As it was, I reacted with something close to joy when my mother woke me that morning with the news that Gene wouldn't be attending school that day. *Today?* I thought. He shouldn't go back to school *ever again.* I might have pretended that a wish to save him from the stares, whispers, silences, and insults he would have to endure brought on that thought, but my own discomfort was my first concern.

Evening inevitably fell, however, and with the dark came Gene and his mother, treading carefully up the block as if the real alteration to life on Keogh Street was the dusting of snow that had fallen that day.

When I saw them approach, I grabbed the newspaper with the intention of hiding it and its "Senator Slain!" headline and the accompanying photograph of the capitol's bloodstained marble floor. But as soon as I picked it up, I realized how futile it was to believe the surviving Stoddards could be spared anything. *The Bismarck Tribune* was delivered to their house, too. And what if it were not? Almost every newspaper in the land and many of its magazines were likely to carry stories about Monty Burnham's assassination, and even if those media could be kept out of their home, the news could still enter through the airwaves. They would have to keep their television and radio turned off as well. And if they ventured outside their door, they would have to see themselves reflected in others' eyes. Even if they remained behind the walls of their own home, they would still have to look at each other. They were Stoddards and forever after would carry the burden of that name. I was sixteen years old, and I hadn't yet learned of time's astonishing ability to diminish or erase almost anything, so it wasn't long before the iron logic of hopelessness led me to the conclusion that the only relief from their circumstances would be to do with their lives what Raymond Stoddard had done with his. I gave up and put the paper back down on the coffee table. In the black-and-white photograph it was next to impossible to tell whether a swirl on the capitol floor was from blood or variegation in the stone.

And then they were in our home. Because we couldn't do anything else, Gene and I said hi, and just like that a realization overturned all the morbid conclusions I had reached. Nothing needed to be kept from him. The television reporters could say the worst things imaginable about Raymond Stoddard, and the gossips could spread the most malicious rumors about the family. The newspapers could publish the most lurid photographs they could find. Gene had been inoculated against their pain. He would never be exposed to anything worse than what he had seen when he'd opened that door leading to the garage.

It was difficult to determine what physical toll the events had taken on Alma Stoddard because she had frequently looked weary and slightly frail. She and my mother were the same age and both were pretty women, but placing these brunettes side by side only emphasized my mother's vitality. Mrs. Stoddard was pale and thin, while my mother was ruddy-cheeked and robust. Even in the best of times Mrs. Stoddard didn't smile often, but when my mother helped her with her coat and in the process squeezed Mrs. Stoddard's narrow shoulders, she gave my mother a quick small smile that carried a world's worth of gratitude.

My father, mother, and Mrs. Stoddard ate at the dining room table, while Gene, my sister, and I were allowed to eat on TV trays in the living room. The arrangement worked well for me. Gene and I didn't have to speak much—that night's episode of *My Three Sons* did that work for us—and I was near enough to the three adults that I could listen in on their conversations.

Through the meal and dessert and the clearing of dishes, through coffee and cigarettes, I waited in vain. Would no one ever speak about what had to be on everyone's mind: *Why would Raymond do such a thing?* Instead the talk was of practical matters. The funeral would have to be in Bismarck. If Raymond had died under . . . other circumstances, the service could have been held in Wembley, and he would have been buried there, in the family plot next to the graves of his parents and a sister who had died in infancy. But Wembley was reserved for Monty Burnham. According to the newspaper's biography, he was the hometown boy who'd made good—a three-sport letterman in high school, a decorated World War II veteran, a successful businessman (he owned Ford auto and John Deere farm implement dealerships), and a prominent Republican legislator. And martyr, though to what cause no one knew. His funeral would be a public occasion in Wembley, and his murderer would be welcome nowhere near the community, even in the local cemetery.

Of the three local funeral parlors, Mrs. Stoddard had picked Metzger's—did my father and mother think she had made the right choice? I was looking into the kitchen as she asked the question, and she leaned across the table as if she were desperate to hear that in this matter she had chosen wisely.

My mother reached out and patted Mrs. Stoddard's hand, while my father nodded sagely and said, "Sam Metzger is a good man. And if you don't mind me putting in my two cents' worth: Services sooner would be better than later."

As if in relief, Mrs. Stoddard began to weep, and just at that moment Gene asked, "Can I get the homework for English and history? I'm going to school tomorrow." Perhaps he asked just to stop me from staring at his crying mother. If so, his strategy worked. The two of us went to my bedroom and my schoolbooks.

While I copied down the assignments for Gene, he said, "Do you want a ride tomorrow morning? I'm going to have the car. In fact, from now on I'll have the car a lot."

He didn't say this ruefully or ironically but expressionlessly, and my initial reaction was, My God, what a monstrously self-interested thing to say! Then, in the next beat, I reminded myself that none of the usual standards of human behavior applied to my friend.

"Sure," I said. "Do you want to pick me up or should I come down?"

"I'll pick you up. By the way, don't try to call. My mom unplugged the phone."

When we returned, Gene's mother was still weeping. And confessing, if it's possible to confess to ignorance.

"I don't know. I *just don't know.*" Her sobs twisted her face. "He never said anything to me. *Never.*"

My mother was up out of her chair and standing behind Mrs.

Stoddard, patting her back and comforting the sobbing woman as best she could. My father, meanwhile, remained seated, and his expression—stern, still on the edge of anger—made me wonder if it had been his questioning that had brought on Mrs. Stoddard's state.

"You think you know someone," Mrs. Stoddard said, "and then . . . then something like this happens. I've racked my brain . . . for an explanation. A clue. I've looked *everywhere*."

Now I saw what might have been an additional emotion cross my father's face. Was that skepticism? Did he know a place—a hidden area, a dark corner—where Mrs. Stoddard hadn't looked?

"Don't blame yourself," my mother said. "Please, Alma. Don't."

My sister ran into the room, and at her entrance the three adults tried to give an impression of normalcy. My father reached for his cigarettes. My mother asked if anyone needed more coffee. Alma Stoddard sat up straight and wiped her cheeks with the heels of her hands.

I turned away too, but Gene was right there, ready to answer the question I would never ask. "I don't know why he did it either," he said. He could not have been more straightforward and unapologetic in delivering that line if he were in Mr. Bollinger's algebra class admitting that he could not solve an equation. Gene had never been a particularly effusive boy. Neither of us were, but growing up I had always envied his placidity. I might have affected the same demeanor (ours was an especially chilly Midwestern version of cool), but I knew I was faking it. Inwardly I was often nervous—about grades, girls, sports, the proper

– 21 –

clothes, the correct companions. That night, however, as I confronted Gene's eerie serenity, I felt myself permanently cured of some of my anxiety. I couldn't imagine a life less enviable than his.

As if the real reason for coming to our house had been to make the announcement that Raymond Stoddard's behavior mystified them as much as anyone, having discharged that duty, Gene and his mother soon left.

In their absence we were, of course, as bewildered as ever, and almost immediately after their departure, my father went to the telephone. "I'm calling Burt. Find out what they're saying about this up there."

My father and his younger brother, Burt, left Wembley for college—my father to the University of North Dakota and law school and Burt to the University of Minnesota and pharmacy school—and after graduation both returned to their hometown to start their careers. But while my father eventually moved on, Burt remained, working in the drugstore that their father owned. After my grandfather's death, Burt took over the family business, and he continued to live alone in the house the boys grew up in.

My mother and I waited in the living room while the brothers talked. Their conversation lasted long enough that we knew something of substance was being discussed, and Burt was obviously doing most of the talking. My father sat at the kitchen table and smoked, nodding in understanding or affirmation, and only interrupting to inject an occasional question. When he hung up, he remained in the kitchen, untangling the twisted telephone cord. It was not in his nature to torment us deliberately, so I can only imagine he was wondering how he would convey the information he had gleaned from his brother.

When he finally came into the living room, he said, "Well, that was Burt." He looked at me and then to my mother. I understood his hesitation. He wasn't sure how much he should say in front of me.

"Go ahead," my mother said. "He needs to hear. Gene is his friend." With those words she conferred upon me a new status. Did I want it? I believed I did. It meant I would no longer have to eavesdrop or conjecture. But I also knew the time might come when I'd wish I could step back down in rank.

"Was Burt drunk, by the way?" my mother asked. She would never have asked that in my presence before, though her question merely acknowledged what was generally known about her brother-in-law.

"Not yet, but he's getting there."

My mother moved over on the sofa, inviting my father to join us. "So what did Burt have to say?"

My father sat down between us and for the first time that day loosened his tie. "Well, he said something that Alma didn't see fit to mention."

Once again, he cast a glance in my direction, but with nothing more than a hand touched lightly to his shoulder, my mother urged him on. My father cleared his throat and began. "It seems Alma and Senator Burnham used to go together. Were you aware of that?"

Shock crossed her face, and she pushed back against the sofa's cushions. "When was this?"

"High school. Or thereabouts."

"Oh. Well. Teenagers." Her dismissive tone wounded me.

"I'm simply reporting what Burt said. Do you want to hear it or not?"

"Go ahead. But I'll keep in mind where this is coming from, too."

I knew what that meant, or thought I did. Uncle Burt was not an admirer of Monty Burnham or his politics. Burt was a Democrat, a fact that put him in the minority in conservative North Dakota (although we had just elected a Democratic governor), while Monty Burnham was not just a Republican but a leader in the party and someone who had often been talked about as a possible candidate for higher office: governor, United States representative, or senator. But as my father talked—that night, and in the days, weeks, months, and even years to come—I learned of other reasons for Burt's antipathy.

In most respects, however, Burt was a good source to consult. He was intelligent and observant, he had a good memory, and, unlike his older brother, he was not averse to gossip. Burt was a Wembley resident past and present, and he was from the same high school graduating class as Monty Burnham, Raymond Stoddard, and Alma Shumate. (Betty Donfils, Monty Burnham's wife, now widow, graduated two years behind them.) My father, six or seven years older than these people, was never their peer, and he knew them as little more than the children of Wembley families and the younger siblings of friends. The Shumates were poor, and Alma grew up one of six children in what today would be known as a single-parent home. When she was a child, her father died in a farm accident; he fell into a grain silo and suffocated. The Stoddards, on the other hand, were comfortably middle class, thanks to Raymond's father's job with the Soo Line Railroad. My ancestors were among Wembley's first settlers, and while they were a prominent, respected, and well-established family in the community, they never enjoyed the power or prosperity that the Burnhams had. Monty's father served two terms as town mayor, and his uncle was state's attorney. Over the years the Burnhams owned a real estate company, various downtown buildings, and the two successful dealerships that Monty eventually took over. "Generations of glad-handers and wheeler-dealers," my father said, perhaps repeating his brother's phrase. Neither brother would have been intending the remark as a compliment.

Monty Burnham and Raymond Stoddard were both World War II veterans, having served together in the Pacific theater. Senator Burnham left the military as a decorated Army tank commander. During the battle for one of the Mariana Islands, according to one of the obituaries, Monty Burnham "resolutely carried on even when his tank was cut off from the rest of the platoon and battalion, and by taking the fight to the Japanese, he carried the day for the Allied Forces." Mr. Stoddard never rose above the rank of private, and as far as Burt knew, neither man came through the war with anything worse than Raymond's case of malaria. (My father, also an officer, fought in Europe, while Uncle Burt was in the Navy but saw no combat.) After the war, Raymond Stoddard worked for a county agency in Wembley for a few years before he and Alma moved to Bismarck. Monty Burnham capitalized on his distinguished war record as well as his family name to rise to prominence in Wembley and eventually the state.

"Maybe there's something in those war years," my mother

suggested. "Could Monty Burnham have been Ray's commanding officer? Maybe there was something unfair about Monty Burnham's promotion or—"

She hadn't finished before my father began shaking his head. "Didn't work that way. Anger, jealousy, resentment—sure, there was bad blood among the men. No shortage of it. But by the time we mustered out, we were ready to put it all behind us. Wartime grudges don't have any staying power, in my experience."

"Did you and Ray talk about the war?"

"Never."

"Never? That's hard to believe."

Not for me. Many of my friends had fathers who had been in the war, and some of them never got over it. Or wouldn't let themselves. My friend Stan Gronlund, for example, never stopped talking about his father's experiences as an Air Force bombardier, but in that, Stan was simply imitating his father, who was amazingly adept at relating almost everything to his years in the military. Jim Kieper's father had what amounted to a World War II shrine in his basement, consisting mostly of German military artifacts—helmets; medals; binoculars; bayonets; a disarmed grenade; even a singed, bullet-punctured swastika flag. But my father and Raymond Stoddard brought home no souvenirs, and they passed no war stories on to their sons.

"Don't believe it, then," my father said. "But it was so."

My mother shrugged. "What about the job that Ray drank himself out of? Was that in Wembley? Or here?"

"That was here. And to tell you the truth, I'm inclined to give Ray a pass on that one. When they first moved to Bismarck, he was doing construction work, and then during the winter when things were slow he took a job as night clerk at the Frontier. Construction picked up, but he didn't want to let go of the extra money. Anyway, he was burning the candle at both ends, and one night they had some sort of small scale emergency at the hotel—a small fire back in the kitchen or something—and Ray wasn't at the desk, where he was supposed to be. He was off catching forty winks somewhere. When the manager of the Frontier caught wind of it, he fired Ray."

"What did his drinking have to do with it?"

Now it was my father's turn to shrug. "The manager smelled liquor on Ray's breath, and the bartender said that Ray had been in the bar that night, so the manager put one and one together and got three. He assumed Ray was drunk and sleeping it off."

"But Ray was drinking then?"

My father leaned forward and with the heel of his hand rubbed the coffee table's glass top. If he had seen a smudge there, it wouldn't last long, not in my mother's home. "What makes us think he ever quit? Maybe he just got it under control."

"I suppose I just assumed . . ."

My father looked at me, the first time I had been included as more than a listener. "Well? Did you see any evidence that Mr. Stoddard was still drinking?"

"He might have been. I once saw a couple empties in their garbage can."

"Bourbon?" my father asked.

I didn't want to appear too knowledgeable. "Old Crow? It was a brown bottle. A little one."

"Bourbon," my father concluded. "Raymond once said he was too fond of bourbon."

"When was this?" my mother asked.

"I can't remember exactly," I answered. "Last summer, maybe? We were just goofing around and the garbage can tipped over."

"No, no," she said, nodding in my father's direction. "I mean, when did Ray confess this fondness for bourbon?"

My father sat back again. "A summer evening a few years back. We'd both been mowing our lawns, and Ray just wandered up the street. This was a driveway conversation, nothing more."

"But how did it come out, about the bourbon?"

"I don't know. Hot weather? Wouldn't a beer hit the spot? And Ray said bourbon had always been his drink of choice. You call it a confession. It was nothing like that. Small talk is what it was."

"Did Burt say anything about why Ray and Alma came to Bismarck in the first place?"

"Burt didn't. But I have the answer to that one. He came to build houses. Alma's brother was a foreman with the construction company Ray went to work for. He still is, for that matter. Harbring Construction has Len Harbring's name over the door, but Alma's brother runs the outfit. I'm not sure why Ray quit them. I suppose because working for the state is steadier."

"But if he was still drinking. . . ."

"Alcohol doesn't explain murder. A man in trouble with the bottle might take his own life, but not another's." He clapped his hands on his thighs and rocked back and forth. "None of it makes any sense."

"Burt didn't have anything else to say?"

"Nothing comes to mind. What he kept coming back to was

the business about Alma once going out with Monty Burnham." He looked at my mother. "Is that something you could ask her about?"

"Alma and I don't have that kind of relationship." My mother's tone was icy. "We never have."

"Could you ask Iris?" The Friedrichs lived next door to the Stoddards, and Iris Friedrich was Alma Stoddard's closest friend. "See if Alma ever said anything to her about Monty Burnham?"

"And what would that make me?" My mother answered her own question. "A snoop and a gossip." There were no worse labels that could be hung on her.

"Then we're stuck," my father said. He reached for his cigarettes—then stopped, balled up his fist, and pounded it into his other open hand. "God *damn* it! I keep thinking I should go down there and grab Ray by the shoulders and shake him and talk some sense into the man!"

My mother reached out and, as if she were playing rock, scissors, paper with my father, covered his fist with her hand before he could strike his palm again. Her gesture told me that she had long known what I had just learned—that in my father grief and rage could wrap themselves as tightly together as those fingers that were seeking something to punch.

"You don't have to take this on yourself, you know," she said gently. "This isn't a mystery you have to solve." Only my mother could have spoken to him in this way and have her words calm rather than anger him further.

In our home the living room draperies were seldom drawn, but since the traffic on Keogh Street, usually limited to its few residents, had increased significantly in the past twenty-four hours, my mother had closed the curtains just after Gene and his mother came over. Cars traveled slowly up and down the street as they would have a few weeks earlier when Bismarck residents patrolled the city's neighborhoods to look at the Christmas lights and decorations. Now, of course, they were searching for the Stoddard residence, hoping perhaps that its blank rectangles of glass, stucco, and wood might give off a unique and lurid glow.

But even if our curtains had been open, they would have revealed at that moment a tableau so ordinary that not even the most curious would look twice. Under a framed reproduction of a Constable landscape, father, mother, and son sat together on a sofa covered in a gray-green fabric. The three of them might have gathered to have a talk about the dangers of smoking—even as the parents lit their own cigarettes—or about the son's slipping grades in geometry. Perhaps they were asking him if he understood how important it was that he apply himself to his studies. On the television across the room Jack Paar spoke and gestured with a flamboyance rare among Midwestern men. Nothing—nothing whatsoever—in the scene revealed that a bomb had exploded on the block or that these people would henceforth have to live in its wreckage. If their faces were uncontorted by anguish, it was only because they had all learned the consoling power of the prayer of selfishness—*Thank God it's not us, thank God it's not us, thank God it's not us.*

There was something in my parents' conversation that night that I found especially puzzling. I couldn't understand why they— why my mother, really—had passed so swiftly over the fact that

Monty Burnham and Alma Stoddard had once dated. In my view, nothing of greater significance had, to that point, been revealed that could approach a motive for Raymond Stoddard. Yet my mother seemed to think that because they had both been teenagers at the time, the relationship couldn't have been of consequence. Had she been standing where I had been only a few weeks earlier, next to the pool tables at Midway Bowling Lanes, and had she seen and heard Russell Batt, a classmate of mine, she might have realized how easily a ruined adolescent romance can turn someone's thoughts to murder.

Russell Batt and Jennifer Oslund had been a couple since junior high school, but then suddenly—no one quite knew what the exact sequence of events was—just after Thanksgiving she dropped Russell and began to date Curt Forney. Since Russell still loved Jennifer, he blamed Curt for the breakup, and that night at the bowling alley Russell was waiting for Curt to walk through the door. When he did, Russell said, he'd kill him.

A tall, raw-boned, rope-muscled kid, Russell Batt had grown up on a farm and had moved to Bismarck as a sixth grader. He was quick-tempered and belligerent, and almost from the moment he arrived in town, he had been getting into fistfights. But it wasn't just his history and pugnacious nature that convinced those of us who listened to him that night that his rants were more than talk.

He had opened his jacket to reveal, tucked into the waistband of his jeans, a stag-handled hunting knife. Lest anyone think it was just a prop, he pulled it from its leather sheath, allowing its curved blade to glint in the overhead light meant to illuminate the green felt of the billiard tables. "I'm going to slip this between his ribs," Russell said, "before he can say a goddamn thing. I don't give a shit what his side of it is." Russell was drunk, but to those of us gathered around him, that only enhanced his credibility.

Curt Forney, however, didn't enter Midway Bowling Lanes that night, and whether that was because someone warned him in advance or headed him off in the parking lot, I never knew. Besides, there was no reason to believe that Russell's vow had any temporal boundaries. If he didn't kill Curt then, he'd do it another time.

If Curt Forney had appeared, would we—those of us clustered around Russell Batt and basking in his menace—have tried to intercede on Curt's behalf? I like to think we would have, although Russell's jealousy, anger, and murderous determination shrunk all of us; we were boys listening to a man's threats.

We were spared that awful responsibility not just by Curt's nonappearance but by an intercession. Also at the Midway lanes was the former Janice Robichaud. A coarsely pretty woman in her early twenties, Janice was married to Russell's older brother, Morris, but that night she was bowling with her girlfriends. Someone who had overheard Russell sought out Janice and told her what Russell was threatening to do. The bowling lanes and the pool tables were some distance from each other, but when Janice learned of her brother-in-law's agitated state, she headed toward him at a dead run.

She made no attempt to calm Russell with compassion or soft words. Neither did she try to mount a moral appeal. Instead, she lit furiously into him as soon as she was within shouting distance.

"You're talking about throwing your life away for what—that two-timing little twat? And you think that will bring her back to you? She'll hate your fucking guts. Now get the hell out of here, and if I hear about any more of this bullshit, I'm telling your brother, and he'll kick your ass from here to Fargo."

Her tirade awed and terrified us, and it obviously made an impression on Russell as well. No harm befell Curt Forney on that night or any other, but neither did his relationship with Jennifer Oslund last. Before the end of the school year she was dating Chuck Vogel, and after Chuck, Wes Lahr, and after Wes, someone else, but never again Russell Batt. Or Curt Forney. When Jennifer left for college, she seemed to leave Bismarck for good, while Russell married Nancy Lawler, and the two of them settled on the city's south side to raise their family.

But what if—what if Raymond Stoddard were made of the same combustible material as Russell Batt, although of the slower-burning sort? What if the passion that almost instantly burst into flame in Russell smoldered for years in Raymond Stoddard until he too was ready to kill the one who . . . who . . . Here, of course, my speculations bumped against reality. If there were once a competition for Alma Shumate, Raymond Stoddard was the winner, not Monty Burnham. But because I was reluctant to admit, even to myself, that I had nothing to offer from my limited store of observations and experiences that could explain Raymond Stoddard, I tried to invent a set of circumstances that would still involve a romantic triangle.

Yes, Raymond and Alma ended up together, but Ray worried that Monty Burnham remained Alma's real love, so when Ray had an opportunity to leave Wembley, he jumped at it. The Stoddards moved to Bismarck not for Ray's higher-paying job but because Ray wanted to remove his wife from the town where her former boyfriend was a constant presence. Ray's strategy worked. Or so he believed, though he couldn't keep from worrying that his former rival might someday reappear and win Alma back. Ray's concerns increased when Monty Burnham was elected to the state senate, which meant that as a legislator he would come to Bismarck every other year when congress convened.

And, finally, exactly what Ray feared came to pass. On a blustery winter day, Alma Stoddard took the bus downtown. Her destination was Schreiber's Fabric Shop, where she hoped to find some material with which to re-cover a chair. When she left the store, the wind was gusting so hard—little clouds of fine-grained snow billowed down the street and even the traffic light posts were swaying—that she decided to duck into the Coffee Cup Café for a few minutes of warmth. Meanwhile, Monty Burnham was also in downtown Bismarck. He was supposed to meet with an oil abstractor, but since he was early, he decided to wait across the street in the café with the frosted windows and the neon sign of a cup and saucer. When Monty, now Senator, walked in, he spotted Alma—he recognized her immediately—and without invitation sat down at her table.

Alma was not only shy but uncomfortable. No other customers were in the establishment, and there they were—sitting together at a table in the corner. It might have looked as though this had been an arranged meeting! Or maybe her discomfort came not entirely from her concern over what other people might think but from her own feelings. Over the years, she had thought often of Monty Burnham and had wondered what her life would have been if she had stayed with him. Which was *harder to imagine—being married to a wealthy well-known man or being married to a charming ebullient man who seemed to smile his way through every day? Monty Burnham was both of those.*

Alma shrank back from Monty Burnham's presence, which only made him strive harder to wrest a smile or laugh from her. Nostalgia was the tactic he chose. "Remember the night of the holiday party that ended with us marching through the streets of Wembley at two o'clock in the morning singing Christmas carols? Remember when we put sugar in the gas tank of old Mr. Pettinger's Reo? Remember when we drove to Devils Lake for the county fair, and on the way back my car broke down and it was close to dawn when we finally pulled up in front of your house and your mother came striding down the driveway and didn't say a word but damned near dragged you back inside? Remember the night you told me you feared we were becoming too serious and that we should stop seeing each other? That practically destroyed me, and the very next day I left Wembley and drove into Canada. I took a job on a cattle ranch outside Calgary, and when I returned, you were engaged to Ray Stoddard. . . ." No, no. On that day, their first reunion in years, Monty Burnham would keep the tone light. "I bent over in Mrs. Schmidt's class and split the seat of my pants—remember?" Finally, finally, he got a smile from Alma, and once he did, successful car salesman and skillful politician that he was, Monty Burnham knew he was home free.

They arranged to meet again, but Alma didn't want it to be in a place so public. When he suggested that he come to her home, Alma could think of nothing but all the windows up and down Keogh Street, and in each one she imagined a woman peering out and wondering, who could that be entering the Stoddard home? He looks like that politician. . . .

"What about my place," Monty Burnham suggested. "During the legislative session I rent a little basement apartment over on Avenue B. You can park in the alley and enter through the side door. . . ."

This plot required adjustment. Their renewed relationship moved too quickly. Perhaps they met in just this way, but years ago, and they never saw each other in the two years between legislative sessions. *But gradually over time, Alma Stoddard and Monty Burnham fell in love again. They not only met clandestinely, they also exchanged letters, and while Raymond Stoddard was searching for . . . for a needle, yes, a needle—he had a sliver that could be extracted only with a needle—he opened his wife's sewing kit. He accidentally lifted the box's top tray, the one containing all the spools of colorful thread* (I was of course picturing my mother's sewing kit), *and when he did, he found the letters Monty Burnham had been sending Alma. None of the envelopes had a return address—in case Alma's husband would be the one to pick up the mail one day—but as soon as Ray saw the signature—"Monty"—he knew. In fact, he didn't have to read more than that name and the closing that preceded it— "Love"—to realize the worst: He had lost his wife.*

But read on he did. He learned that the correspondence had flowed in more than one direction; Alma wrote as often to Monty Burnham as he wrote to her. Ray couldn't see the texts of any of her letters or how she signed them, but he didn't have to. It was obvious that she felt for Monty what he felt for her, and their rekindled relationship blazed hotter than before because now it was fed not only by the incendiary passions left over from youth but also by the slower-burning fuel of adult love. Ray deduced too that they had done more than adore each other from a distance. Plainly, they had been physically intimate, as Monty wrote that "I live for the time when once again I can hold your naked body in my arms, when I can. . . ."

As you can see, I was already practicing the craft of the novelist I would someday be, though less with language than with imagination—speculating on what lives other than my own were like, and on what forces underlay people's behavior. But in spite of what educators would have us believe about the creative powers of the young, reality hems in their minds more than it does adults'. At sixteen I couldn't imagine what I could at twenty-six, thirty-six, forty-six, fifty-six . . . so I couldn't really envision a world in which Alma Stoddard, clothed or otherwise, would lie in anyone's arms or a world in which anyone would want her to. The problem was not just that she was the mother of my best friend. I could, after all, summon up a few lascivious thoughts about Mrs. Crisp, the flaxen-haired, tanned, curvaceous mother of my friend Jeff, whereas Alma Stoddard had the appearance of a woman who tried to de-emphasize not only her beauty but her entire physical being. She didn't wear much makeup. She wore her hair in a tightly bobby-pinned, unflattering, unvarying style. Her clothes were dark, shapeless, and severe. A time would come when I would realize that ardor and austerity can coexist, but I couldn't get there when I was sixteen, not with Alma Stoddard.

Nevertheless, though I had nothing in the way of evidence to support it, I wasn't about to relinquish the idea that the relationship that had existed in the past between Monty Burnham and Alma Stoddard must have had something to do with the present, and I couldn't figure out why my mother brushed aside the possibility so quickly. Who knows—maybe if I had gone on to serve in the military someday I would have been similarly vexed by my father's unwillingness to consider Raymond Stoddard and Monty Burnham's war experiences as the early stimulus for Raymond's murderous deed.

Years later, however, it was my mother's behavior that I mentioned to my sister. The occasion was Christmas, and in the past she had always traveled to Bismarck for the holiday. Our mother, however, had died months earlier, and since my unmarried sister had no other family, she spent the holiday with my wife, daughters, and me in Montana.

It was late on Christmas Eve, and she and I were the only ones awake in the house. We were sitting in the living room, in front of a fire's dying embers, and we each had a glass of calvados, her Christmas gift to me, purchased on a summer trip to Normandy. We were reminiscing, as brothers and sisters do, but unlike other siblings, we were working from a script. No one who lived in 1961 within the radius of that small circle that took in the capitol building on its eastern edge and Keogh Street on the western margin could talk about the past without eventually, inevitably, discussing the Stoddard-Burnham tragedy.

I had just expressed my long-ago puzzlement about why our mother had found the onetime relationship between Alma Stoddard and Monty Burnham to be of so little interest, and before I finished the thought, my sister began to laugh softly.

Didn't I know? Our mother was engaged to be married when

she was still a teenager, and not to the man who would be our father. All I could do was shake my head.

Our mother grew up in a small town in western Minnesota, not far from Fargo, North Dakota, and her boyfriend, a year older, lived on a farm. They dated throughout high school, and on the day of his graduation he asked her to marry him the following year when she received her diploma. Our mother certainly had opportunities aplenty to observe the harsh realities of farm life, but the notion of an isolated, rural existence held a kind of romantic, bucolic appeal for her. And she loved the young man.

"Well, what happened?" I asked. "What made us a lawyer's kids and not a farmer's?"

"He was helping out on someone's farm, and he was in an accident. A tractor flipped over on him. His legs were crushed, and he couldn't stand the thought of being a cripple, so he broke off the engagement. Or tried to. Mom, being Mom, said that his condition didn't matter to her, that they'd find some way to make a life together. She could keep her job at the drugstore where she'd been working since she was fourteen. She'd support them."

"Sounds like love, all right."

"On Mom's part. But he ended up marrying another girl, a girl who lived on that farm where he'd been working when he had his accident. So I guess their relationship was a variant of the farmer's daughter joke. And since she was pregnant, apparently he wasn't completely disabled. But Mom really took it hard. She said she wasn't sure how she'd be able to go on."

I'm sure my sister believes to this day that I set down my drink and walked from the room because I was upset by the news that our mother had once had a youthful romance that fractured her heart.

But that was not it, not at all.

Akira Kurosawa said that to be an artist means never to avert one's gaze, advice I've tried to take to heart as a writer and as someone who wants to understand the human mysteries. Even without knowing any specifics, I had readily acknowledged that my parents had lives before they became spouses and parents, and I never held them to any standard that lay beyond the obligations of those roles. Besides, I once lived on Keogh Street—where was there a better school to learn the lesson that the life of every man and woman was so much more than it appeared to be?

No, disclosures about my mother's and father's pasts weren't likely to distress me. The real reason I couldn't remain in my sister's company wasn't the story she told, but what in hearing it I learned about myself. How could I have been such a fool as to think that our mother dismissed the relationship between Alma Stoddard and Monty Burnham because it was a product of their teen years? She rushed past it *because* she knew how deep and durable a long-ago love could be.

The next day—Christmas day—I told my sister I was sorry I'd walked out on her, and I let her think that the subject had simply been more than I could handle.

She waved away my apology. "I knew you hadn't heard the story."

"Did Dad know about it?"

"He knew she once went with a boy she was serious about. He didn't know they were engaged."

I wanted to defend my father, to say that knowledge of his

wife's past wouldn't have made a damn bit of difference in his life, but I couldn't, not with complete confidence. The events of January 1961 kept me from that certainty as well. "So that was a secret best kept from the males in the family?"

My sister shrugged. Every sibling wants to believe that he or she is favored in some way, and what could confer that status better than to be taken into a parent's confidence? Maybe my sister held on to that story because our mother had asked her to tell it to no one. Or perhaps my sister hoarded it for a small measure of revenge because years before I had been included in some of our parents' conversations while she was excluded. Whatever the reason, I was willing to let my sister have her satisfaction. Moreover, though what I learned about my mother forced a revision of who I had always believed she was, it did nothing to any theory I held about why Raymond Stoddard did what he did.

I was worried about riding to school with Gene on that first day when he would be permitted to drive the family car, and my worry was quite specific. I feared that if people saw us getting out of the same car, it would only contribute to their confusion about us.

Because we grew up together on Keogh Street and were so often in each other's company and because we were similar in so many respects, Gene and I were frequently mistaken for the other. We were both brown-haired, slender, and slightly taller than average. For the second consecutive winter we dressed in identical dark green overcoats. We were both serious about our studies, reasonably well behaved, and responsible. We were both shy and comfortable with silence. We were among the youngest of our class, our birthdays one month apart to the day—his October 2 and mine November 2. Indeed, if the world were intent on telling us apart, it had little to go on. Eye color—his brown, mine blue and peering out from behind glasses. He played the clarinet; I ran on the cross-country team. He had a girlfriend; I did not. I had tonsils; he did not. I had a father; he did not.

As a teenager I was, like many adolescents, frustrated by my anonymity. I wanted, I thought, to be known, to have a reputation, an identity. I wasn't a hood, a rebel, a varsity athlete, a class officer; I wasn't popular with girls or watched by the police. I wasn't tough or talented. But suddenly I saw that fame—or notoriety—could attach itself to you and yet have nothing to do with you. Gene Stoddard had been, like me, simply one of the indistinguishable mass of nice guys until, overnight, he became Bismarck's most famous teenager. And he would have given anything to be obscure again. Or, put another way, to be mistaken for me. If I could have, I would have worn a sign around my neck: I AM NOT GENE STODDARD.

As it turned out, Gene didn't drive to school, not that morning. Overnight the temperature dropped to almost thirty below, cold even by North Dakota standards. The Stoddards, no doubt because they couldn't bring themselves to enter their garage, had left their Ford parked outside, and in the morning it wouldn't start. My father ended up taking Gene and me to school, and for some reason it seemed to me a sufficient differentiation of our identities that we climbed from a car belonging to our family.

After delivering us to school, my father returned to Keogh Street and used his jumper cables to get the Stoddards' car running again. Then he told Alma Stoddard that while he could understand why she might have difficulty going into the garage, if that was the case, then she should consider having a headbolt heater installed in the Ford and plugging it in on winter nights.

~

I'm not sure if it was precisely *during* Raymond Stoddard's funeral that I fell in love with Marie Ryan, but by the end of the day it was a fait accompli.

The process began when she telephoned me the night before. No, no, it started before that. It started with her looks. Marie Ryan was a beautiful girl, and if her beauty occasionally passed unnoticed, it was because she herself paid so little attention to it. She had large, almond-shaped green eyes with a slight oriental tilt, high cheekbones, a strong jaw, creamy skin, deep dimples, and perfectly formed lips. Without the aid of orthodontia, her teeth were flawlessly straight. Although she was only fifteen, she had a woman's lush body on her compact frame. To save her from classical beauty's boring predictability, she had a chicken pox scar on her forehead, and her nose was a little wide, causing a series of diagonal wrinkles to break out along the bridge when she laughed. Consistent with her lack of vanity, she dressed plainly, almost carelessly, and wore her long lustrous reddish-brown hair in the simplest of styles.

But no amount of physical description—at least none within my powers to offer—will do justice to what Marie Ryan was. Today the term is "hot." Then, she was a babe, a honey, sexy, stacked. In 1961 we may not have known about pheromones, but we still trailed helplessly after someone who secreted them.

As incomparable as Marie Ryan was in appearance, she was also unique in character. She was intelligent, outspoken, and unconventional. Indeed, it was this last quality that enabled her to pick up the telephone and dial my number. In 1961 teenage girls simply did not call boys. Furthermore, the reason for Marie Ryan's call was another example of her ungovernable nature. Her parents had forbidden her to attend Raymond Stoddard's funeral, and she wanted to know if she could go with me. Without hesitation I said yes, and as evidence of how pleased I was at the prospect of being in her company, I even allowed myself to think, fleetingly, pathetically, inappropriately, that it was almost as if she and I would be on a date.

On the day of the funeral my parents needed to arrive early at First Lutheran Church. My mother, with a few of the women who belonged to the same Women's League as Alma Stoddard, would be serving coffee, sandwiches, and cookies in the church basement after the funeral, so she had to begin preparations an hour before the service. My father wanted to get to the church early because Alma Stoddard had asked him to be a pallbearer, and he had agreed. I dropped my parents off at First Lutheran, so when it was time to go to the actual services, I had the car to myself, and, according to our arrangements, I picked Marie Ryan up on a street corner between the high school and the church.

When she climbed into the car, I asked her if she had been excused from school.

She shook her head. "I just left."

"So your afternoon classes—those will be unexcused absences?"

Marie shrugged. "I'll tell Mr. Fedder where I was. He'll understand." Vernon Fedder was the school's vice principal and in charge of attendance and discipline.

"What if they call your house?"

"They almost never call if you miss in the afternoon," she said, and then turned to look at me. "Don't you want me to go with you? Is that what this is all about? Because if you don't, you can let me out and I'll walk. But I'm going to that funeral. I told Gene I'd be there, and I will be." And she was loyal. How could I have forgotten to mention that? Loving and loyal.

"I just don't want you to get into trouble."

"Don't worry about it."

I couldn't figure out why she didn't share my concerns about the possible consequences of her attending the funeral, especially since in doing so she was defying her parents and breaking school rules. (No one could be excused from school without a written note from a parent, and few parents, and certainly not Marie's, wanted their children at a service for a murderer.) Once we arrived at the church, however, I understood.

Together Marie and I walked up the steps and entered the church, but then she left my side and hurried up the aisle to where Gene sat with his mother and his sister. Marie slid into the pew right behind the Stoddards, leaned forward, and rested her hand on Gene's shoulder.

I trailed after Marie and seated myself next to her. My mother, coming up from the basement, soon appeared at the side door at the front of the church, and she also entered our pew. Before my mother sat down next to Marie, she bent over Alma

Stoddard, whispered something to her and, through the net of Alma's veil, kissed the new widow on the cheek. My father sat a few rows back with the other pallbearers.

The service was sparsely attended. I could count the mourners—no more than twenty—and most of them I could identify as well from our neighborhood. Mrs. Holan and Mrs. Gustafson (but without their husbands); Mr. and Mrs. Hendricks from the newer brick house on Divide Avenue across from us; Judy Neville, Marcia Stoddard's best friend in junior high and high school. There was also a tall balding man with a bulbous nose whom I took to be Raymond Stoddard's coworker or perhaps even his boss; Earl Shumate, Alma's brother, and her sister. Raymond Stoddard also had a brother and a sister but neither was present. Among the few faces I wasn't sure of were two men I believed had been at our house on the evening of the day of the murder. One I thought was a newspaper reporter, the other a police officer or sheriff's deputy, and unless they were both going to act as pallbearers, it looked as though Raymond Stoddard would come up short of the traditional six.

The police or the press couldn't have been present for any reason but to satisfy their own curiosity. There was no crime that required further investigation, and the media had quickly run out of things to write and say after the facts had been reported and Monty Burnham's life had been celebrated.

Indeed, the assassination seemed especially troublesome to journalists. They wanted to continue to write and report on the incident—interest remained high, people couldn't stop talking about it, and, best or worst of all, depending on your point of view, the murder had brought attention to Bismarck and North

Dakota. But what were the media supposed to *say*? They had chronicled Burnham's life, emphasizing the small-town-boy-rises-to-prominence story line; offered testimonials from friends, colleagues, and constituents; and played over and over the film clip (or displayed an accompanying still photograph) of Senator Burnham heartily welcoming presidential hopeful Richard Nixon to the state in the campaign summer of 1960. Burnham personally placed a Sioux headdress on Nixon's head and handed the candidate a bag of dried buffalo chips "so he'd have something to fling at the Democrats when they started throwing their bull . . . manure his way." Nixon was a good sport, but you could tell he wanted to shed the headdress at the earliest opportunity. Another media favorite was a photograph of Monty Burnham in midair. As a high school senior he took first place in the broad jump in the state track meet, and the picture caught him during one of his prize-winning leaps, arms and legs akimbo, and his mouth wide open as if he were shouting the commentary to accompany his own feat.

What seemed to frustrate the media was that they could not close off Monty Burnham's life with a theme. If only they could have written or said that Monty Burnham had died for a cause, but that plainly wasn't so, and it wasn't possible to make someone a martyr to senselessness or enigmatic violence. (In their efforts to make Monty Burnham one of North Dakota's distinctive citizens, they might have pointed out how rare he truly was: In 1960 there had been only six murder victims out of the state's population of 640,000. I looked up that statistic quite recently.) Journalists were no different from the people for whom they printed their newspapers and magazines, or broadcast their reports and features. What else was to be done about an event obviously momentous but to which the response ultimately seemed to be little more than a throwing up of hands?

Raymond Stoddard's life and behavior might have presented a potentially greater problem, but since he wasn't famous, it was much easier to summarize him with relatively few words. In this regard, Pastor Lundgren had the advantage. He could follow the standard funeral service, take refuge in the platitudes of religion and scripture, and never refer to Raymond Stoddard in any but the most general outlines. And I don't mean to mock what the minister said. Alma, Marcia, and Gene Stoddard and most of those in attendance probably took comfort in his words. I know I did. It would be a few years before I lost my religion, and I was relieved to hear that Raymond Stoddard, no matter that he had committed murder, was not disqualified from entry into heaven.

Yet it was as a murderer that I kept trying to think of him. Since we were confined to those hard pews for an hour, and assigned, so to speak, to reflect on Raymond Stoddard's life, I scavenged my memories for anything that, with the benefit of hindsight, I could now point to and say, yes, there it was, murder's earliest sign. Raymond Stoddard was a murderer for only an hour of his time on earth, but that deed's stain immediately seeped backward throughout his existence. He would be defined forever after as a murderer, but that identity must have shown up before his final day.

Yet for the life of me, I couldn't see him as anything but one of the standard fathers of my boyhood, less outgoing than some, more generous than others, a father who took his turn giving us rides to the movies or picking us up after the basketball games; who gave his son money to buy ice cream at the Dairy-O or a hamburger at Jack Lyon's; who taught Gene how to throw a spiral or oil his baseball glove; who borrowed money to send his daughter to college; who mowed his grass in summer, shoveled his walk in winter, put up his storm windows in autumn, and turned over his garden's soil in spring. I couldn't think of a single example of behavior tinged with cruelty, much less evil, or any instance of a violently insane act.

The best I could come up with was an incident that occurred a couple years earlier. For much of August, Mrs. Stoddard had been out of town, gone to Fargo to help an elderly aunt recovering from surgery. In her absence Mr. Stoddard was in charge of preparing the meals for himself and Gene, and for Marcia on the few occasions when she was home. One evening Gene invited me to join them for supper, and I accepted.

On the menu were tomatoes and corn on the cob, both products of the Stoddard garden, pork and beans, and fish—walleye caught in a Canadian lake and given to Mr. Stoddard by a coworker. If the fare wasn't particularly notable, the method of preparation was.

At the edge of their lawn, Mr. Stoddard dug a shallow pit and bordered it with stones. From the garage he brought out scrap wood, a small stack of lath, and blocks of two-by-four. He arranged those in the pit with some newspaper for kindling and squirted on a little lighter fluid. He lit the pile, and over the blaze placed a wire rack. The Stoddards, like everyone else in the neighborhood, had a conventional charcoal grill for cooking outdoors, but Mr. Stoddard insisted on this open fire. It was, he said, exactly how his father used to fry freshly caught fish when the family spent their summers in a cabin on the bank of Lake Liana.

Mr. Stoddard seemed uncharacteristically lighthearted as he built the fire and fixed the meal, his mood perhaps attributable to what was in the glass he sipped from as he worked. He made a special effort to show us the steps of preparing the fish. He dipped the long white filets in egg and milk, and then dredged them with a mixture of crushed soda crackers, corn flakes, and bread crumbs. He had placed an iron skillet with a half inch of oil on the rack over the fire, and when the oil was heated to bubbling, he dropped in the slabs of walleye. While he cooked and moved back and forth from the kitchen to the makeshift grill, he kept up an almost steady stream of talk, behavior as unusual as his mood. He chattered about how his father used to time himself—with his railroad watch—to see how quickly he could have the freshly caught fish transferred from the lake to the frying pan, and how the entire Stoddard family would get in on the game—calling out the time when their father pulled his boat up to the dock and then continuing to shout out the elapsed minutes.

Next door to the Stoddards lived Bill and Mary McCutcheon and their three children, a family fairly new to Keogh Street. While we were watching the fish fry, Mr. McCutcheon walked over from his yard to the Stoddards'.

"Your grill rust through or something?" Bill McCutcheon asked. "I would've loaned you ours."

From the way he glowered at the fire and hesitated before answering, it was apparent Mr. Stoddard didn't welcome the question or the offer. "Just thought I'd try an open fire," he said.

"Using a frying pan isn't exactly the same, is it?"

Mr. Stoddard poked at the fish but said nothing. The smoke from the fire and the frying fish mingled in a blue-gray cloud, and when the wind blew it in Mr. McCutcheon's direction, he waved it away with an exaggerated motion.

"That fish come with some guarantee of freshness?" Mr. McCutcheon asked. "Because I have to tell you, you can smell it up and down the block, and it sure as hell ain't doing anything for my appetite."

At this remark, Mr. Stoddard rose from his crouch next to the cooking fire and walked away without saying anything about where he was going or why. He soon came back with the spade he had used to dig the fire pit.

Still without explanation, he scooped up a shovelful of the loose dark loam from the pile next to the fire, and he dumped the dirt on fish, pan, grill, and fire. The oil ceased its spattering with a final choking hiss, and the smoke plumed out to the sides. Raymond Stoddard kept shoveling dirt onto the fire until it was extinguished and only the frying pan's handle stuck up from the tiny burial mound.

"Jesus Christ, Ray," Bill McCutcheon said, but I'm not sure Mr. Stoddard heard. When he finished shoveling, he flung the spade into the garden and marched toward the house. Gene and I followed him, and once we were all in the kitchen, Mr. Stoddard, his usual dark and doleful demeanor returned, announced that he would boil wieners for our supper.

To his son's stricken face, Mr. Stoddard said, "Don't worry. They're the skinless kind you like."

This was the episode I thought back to while Pastor Lund-

gren intoned his vague and uncertain eulogy. It was, however, exceedingly difficult for me to dwell on Raymond Stoddard's soul
when the body of Marie Ryan was so solidly beside me.

She was sitting close enough—the cotton sleeve of her white
blouse brushed the wool sleeve of my suit coat—that I could feel
her heat and smell her hair spray and hear her sniffling attempts
not to cry too loudly. Ah, but not a single sensual detail—or a
page full of them—can adequately convey what it felt like to have
her near me! I could only hope that if anyone noticed how I kept
trying to take in great gulps of air, they would merely think that
I was trying to compose myself. Like the speaker of Robert
Frost's great poem "To Earthward," when I was young it didn't
take much to stimulate me, and for the span of Raymond Stoddard's funeral, it seemed as though I too "lived on air / That
crossed me from sweet things . . ." That day I would have said
that to breathe in the warm essence of Marie Ryan was enough.
Forever. That's what I would have said that day. But read the
poem for yourself.

In the car on the way to the cemetery we replicated the seating
arrangement from the church. I drove, Marie sat next to me, and
my mother sat by the door. My father rode in the hearse, two vehicles ahead of us in our abbreviated procession through the city.

During the ride, my mother asked how Gene was holding up.
Although her question may have been meant for both of us,
Marie and I shared the assumption that Marie was the one who
should answer.

"He hardly talks at all," Marie said. "He just goes around with this look like he's not really there."

"Pastor Lundgren asked me if I thought he should call Gene in for a talk."

"I don't think that would do much."

"A psychologist? I wonder if it might not be better if Gene visited someone like that."

Marie shook her head so vigorously that I could feel the movement.

"I *know* he wouldn't like that," Marie said. "Mr. Wallich"— he was a guidance counselor at our high school—"suggested Gene come see him, and Gene got mad. He said, 'I'm not the crazy one in the family. That was my dad, not me.' "

I wondered if Gene had said that only to Marie or to Mr. Wallich as well.

"Is that what he believes," my mother asked, "that his father was insane?"

Marie turned toward my mother and asked, a note of incredulity in her voice, "Doesn't *everyone* think that?"

Out of the small group of mourners at the church, fewer still made the trip to the cemetery. North Dakotans will sometimes say that "it's too cold to snow," but the day that Raymond Stoddard was buried provided one more example of the falsity of that belief. The sky had been clear that morning but soon turned leaden, and while we stood clenched and shivering around the grave, a light snow began to fall. The flakes were so dry they hardly had weight to find their way to the ground, but a few caught in Marie's hair and remained there until the end of the ceremony.

Hardly had Pastor Lundgren finished his final words regarding the certainty of resurrection when Marie fairly ran to Gene and threw her arms around him. When she tilted her head back to look up into his red-rimmed eyes, those same snowflakes that I had watched gather tumbled from her hair.

Just as quickly as she had raced into the embrace, Marie broke free and walked away from the small gathering.

I had never been to a graveside service before, and its sudden conclusion—as well as Marie's departure—caught me off guard. I was still dwelling on other matters of weight and weightlessness—weren't we going to witness Raymond Stoddard's coffin lowered into the earth?

But I soon collected myself and ran after Marie.

"Where are you off to? Aren't you coming back to the church?"

She shook her head and swiped the tears from her cheeks. "I have to get home."

"I'll give you a ride."

"I don't mind walking."

"It's a long way. Just wait a minute. I'll tell my mother, and she can ride with someone else."

"I *want* to walk." Her jaw was set determinedly. "Thanks for bringing me today." And with that she was off.

It didn't take me long to decide what to do. I ran back to my mother, gave her the keys to our car, and told her I was going to walk Marie Ryan home. "Wait," she said. "How far is it? You're not dressed warm enough. . . ."

But I was already on the move and making my own heat, sprinting after Marie.

I caught up to her as she was exiting the cemetery gates, and she seemed unsurprised to see me. When I paused to catch my breath, she didn't stop but only slowed and, walking backward, said, as if we had been discussing this matter all along, "Did you know Mrs. Stoddard had to pay extra to have the ground thawed?"

My puzzlement must have shown.

"To bury him," Marie said. "When the ground's frozen, it has to be thawed. Otherwise they store the body until spring. So of course people will pay. No one likes to think of their loved one stuck in a freezer."

"Is that what it is—a freezer?"

"I assume. I mean, it has to be someplace cold."

"You'd think it would be storage you'd pay extra for."

"Maybe you do. They probably charge you more no matter what. They're such crooks. Anything to get their money . . ." Marie was walking so quickly I had to lengthen my stride to keep up. "Did Gene tell you about the coffin they ended up buying?"

"No."

"He was excited about it because it's almost the same color as their Ford. My God, if I hear another word about that car, I swear I'll scream. Gene keeps talking about how he's sure he'll get the car anytime he wants now."

"Yeah. He said the same thing to me."

"Did he? I mean, I know he's having a hard time, and he's just trying to find something good in all this, but if he says that around the wrong people, they're liable to misunderstand and think he's happy his dad died."

Her remark pleased me because she apparently thought she and I belonged in the same category—people who understood, and although I knew it was concern for Gene that was truly supposed to unite us, I didn't care. I would welcome anything—a funeral, a friend—that brought Marie Ryan and me closer.

My mother was right. I wasn't dressed warmly enough, and Marie's house was miles away. I could hardly complain, however, since Marie's winter coat was thinner than mine, and under it she had only a cotton blouse, while I had the additional layer of a suit coat.

We walked mostly in silence, and not only because I was tongue-tied in Marie's presence or because funerals push everyone deeper into their own thoughts. Theories abound on the reasons for Midwestern taciturnity, but anyone who has spent time outdoors on a sub-zero day knows that at some point speech becomes physically difficult. The hinges of the jaw stiffen, the nose becomes clotted with mucus, and real effort is required to form words and propel them toward another person. Even then every utterance comes out cloaked in its little cloud of steam, a visual reminder of how difficult clear communication can be.

Nevertheless, some signal must have been transmitted between us because when Marie and I came within a block of her home, we both began to run.

We entered through a garage door and then into the house, but I didn't get far. A short flight of stairs led up to the kitchen, but Marie stopped on the first step, turned, and in a whisper thanked me again. It was all so abrupt that I knew I was not being invited to stay, something I certainly wanted, not only because it would have given me more time with Marie but also because it would have afforded me a chance to warm up before the walk home, still another mile.

"Anytime," I said breezily. "Feel free to call whenever there's a funeral you don't want to miss."

She scowled and put a finger to her lips. I had forgotten that her parents had forbidden her to attend the funeral.

I turned to go, but Marie put her hand on my shoulder to stay me for a moment. "Don't ask Gene what he saw when he went into their garage. Don't ever ask him. Trust me—you don't want to know." She didn't say so, but her warning made it clear: Gene had told her what he saw.

She released me, and I left the darkened entryway for the dim garage and then the barely brighter day.

I walked a long way before the sensation of being cold replaced the tingling in my shoulder where Marie had touched me. She had touched Gene's shoulder in the church . . . and when she stood on the step above me, she had been standing, I knew, right where Gene often kissed her good night. He was willing to tell me about every increment in the physicality of their relationship—kisses, their variance in number and kind, where and when he touched her and for how long—and he had said that Marie especially favored kissing just inside her door, where that step made them nearly equal in height. . . . I didn't want to be Gene Stoddard, I didn't—no matter that she had put her hand on his shoul-

der and mine, had stood on that step. . . . But I wore glasses and
he did not; I had tonsils and he did not; while he stood at his father's grave, I was walking at his girlfriend's side. His girlfriend.
His.

In time, I would be invited inside Marie's home, and I would
learn that the reason she was reluctant to allow me—to allow
anyone—inside was that her mother was an alcoholic. When
Marie entered the house on the day of the funeral, she immediately recognized the signs—no lamps burning on an overcast day,
dolorous piano music coming from the living room—and knew
her mother was drunk.

And eventually I would see for myself the process by which
the earth was thawed for winter interment. When I, like so many
other Americans, took up jogging, one of my preferred routes
was through a cemetery in the city I lived in at the time. Oak
Lawn Memorial Gardens had flat paved paths, little or no traffic,
and enough shade to be slightly cooler in summer than the surrounding city streets. And when I ran there in winter, I occasionally saw placed on the ground a fire-blackened metal hood,
shaped like a large coffin lid, and inside a hole on one end of the
dome, something like a large blowtorch was inserted, its flame
heating the ground until the backhoe could dig it to grave depth.
Later still I had a friend who dug wells for a living, and he informed me that in some snowless winters the frost line can go so
deep that every burial must wait for spring—ice's triumph over
fire.

Both my parents asked to be cremated, and I often wondered if their decisions originated on that January day when the earth had to be heated to receive Raymond Stoddard.

As I walked home from Marie's, I passed the Stoddards' and saw their Ford, lightly sprinkled with snow, in the driveway. Were the day's rituals now complete, and all the Stoddards returned to Keogh Street? Or had Gene or Marcia left early and returned home? I didn't speculate for long on why the car was there, because its color commanded my attention. Yes, I supposed its dark blue, a shade just short of black, was the same color as the coffin. And without question, Raymond Stoddard had loved that vehicle. How often I had seen him in the driveway, carefully washing, drying, and waxing the car, jobs that other fathers often entrusted to sons and daughters. You probably remember as well as I the media reports of a man who was buried in his beloved car. Raymond Stoddard was ahead of his time. I never rode in that Ford again without thinking, *I'm climbing into the coffinmobile.*

Then I crossed the street and soon was in front of my own home with its warmth and normalcy. Yet in spite of the fact that I was so cold I could barely feel my toes, and my shoulders were hunched so tightly to my neck they felt as though they might never come down, I would have turned around gladly and walked back to Marie's and, risking frostbite, circled her block endlessly if I had thought there was a chance she might see me and ask me in. It's tempting to say that that's what it is to live in love—the willingness to sacrifice even physical comfort just to be near the object of one's love—but I was probably experiencing an even more accurate definition: Love is the willingness to turn away from one's home.

~

Monty Burnham's funeral was held the next day, and according to my uncle, it was an event as grand as any in Wembley's history.

The town's florist could not handle all the orders that came in, and the hotel and two motels didn't have enough rooms for all those who traveled to Wembley to pay their last respects. Schools and businesses were closed on the afternoon of the funeral, and Good Shepherd Methodist Church was literally filled to over-flowing. Once there was no longer any place to sit in the pews or even to stand in the back or along the side, folding chairs were set up in the church basement, and the service was piped down there over loudspeakers.

Among the congregants were three members of the United States House of Representatives, a U.S. senator, the under secretary of agriculture, and two former governors of North Dakota. Roger Maris, a Fargo native and the New York Yankee who would break Babe Ruth's single-season home-run record before the year was out, sent condolences, a brief message that the minister read during the service along with the announcement that a Wembley grade school would be renamed. Washington Elementary School would become Monty Burnham Elementary. A scholarship would be established in his name for a student majoring in political science at one of the state's universities, and if the funding came through for a new gym for the high school, it was agreed it would bear Monty Burnham's name.

If the dead could be embarrassed by excessive displays of veneration and grief, Uncle Burt said, almost any corpse would have blushed over how Wembley turned itself inside out over Monty Burnham. Then again, Monty might have been the only man who, could he have witnessed his own funeral, would have thought the whole affair fell a little short of what he deserved. Uncle Burt also advanced the theory that if Raymond Stoddard had not disrupted the natural course of things, Monty Burnham might have eventually revealed his true self, got caught in some political scandal, and died in disgrace. And Wembley children could have kept walking through the doors of Washington Elementary School.

All of this my father reported again to my mother and me after the nightly phone call with his brother, and I guess I had been brought in on enough of those conversations that I finally felt I could ask a question of my own.

"Did you dislike Senator Burnham as much as Uncle Burt did?"

My father seemed willing to repeat all his brother's remarks, no matter how tasteless or mordant, but now that he had been asked to offer his own view, his characteristic caution returned. "I had very few dealings with the man. Not back in Wembley and not in the years since."

"But did you *hate* him?"

"He wasn't our kind of people, let me just say that."

Our? Did that pronoun refer to him and his brother? Were my mother and I included? Could it have meant my father's and Raymond Stoddard's?

"Why not? What kind was he?" I have often thought that I would have gotten much further had I asked, *whose* kind was he?

As I recall, my father once again subjected me to a long gaze of assessment. He was uncertain about my ability to understand, yes, but I believe he was also unsure about whether he could truly articulate his thoughts and feelings about Monty Burnham.

"He was dishonest."

"You mean like a crook?" It didn't take long for my imagination to fashion a fantasy—yes, yes, Monty Burnham was a crooked politician; he was stealing money that should have gone to schools or hospitals or to the poor. Raymond Stoddard somehow discovered what Burnham was doing, yet he couldn't get the authorities to believe him, and the only way to stop the senator was to—

"A crook?" My father shook his head. "I don't believe Monty Burnham was a crook. The man had all the money he needed and then some. He had no reason to steal. Besides, money wasn't what mattered to him. Fame—that's what he was out for. No, that's not the sort of dishonesty I'm talking about. I mean, he was the kind of man who had no regard for the world as it is. He had his way of seeing the world, and he had no doubt about the rightness of his view. Monty Burnham, like most politicians, wasn't burdened with doubt. So he went right ahead and said, in so many words, 'This is the way things are.' "

"So he was a phony?" If there is anything teenagers understand, it's hypocrisy, and no failing is greater.

"A phony?" My father ran his fingers through his hair in frustration. "Not exactly. I mean, maybe that's part of it. But only a small part of it. Men like Monty Burnham—if they have their way, we'll never get at the truth of things in this world. And they won't mind one damn bit."

By now I thought I understood what my father was talking about. "He was a liar?"

But that remark only brought home to my father how wide the gulf was between what he said and what his son comprehended. He shook his head and winced. It was a characteristic expression for him—my father felt frustration as pain—and I've seen that same look—you have too—on Humphrey Bogart's face in movies, and just as with my father, it was usually accompanied by a death-deep drag on a cigarette.

"I'm not explaining this very well. He wasn't necessarily lying. He just didn't give a damn that what he said might not be true. He probably believed that as long as his heart was in the right place, it would be okay."

"And his heart—"

By this time my mother took pity on both of us, but her interruption was also in the interest of keeping the record straight. "We might not have cared for Monty Burnham's type, dear, but that doesn't mean we wished him ill. Besides"—now she addressed my father—"if you still lived in Wembley, you probably would have voted for him, wouldn't you?"

My father might have disapproved of Monty Burnham's character, but that didn't mean he could bring himself to vote for a Democrat. "Probably," he said, and walked from the room.

⌒

Marie didn't warn me not to ask my father about what *he* saw when he opened the door to the Stoddards' garage, but she didn't have to. I loved my father and he loved me, but nothing in our relationship furnished the kind of intimacy that would have to exist before I could ask, What did Raymond Stoddard look like when he was hanging from the crossbeam? I don't doubt that there are sons in the world who could pose such a question and fathers who could answer, but we weren't of that breed.

Nevertheless, my father did eventually volunteer information about Raymond Stoddard's appearance in death, though strictly speaking, my father told us—my mother and me—about something he *didn't* see.

People who hang themselves usually die slowly—they choke to death—and they have time to reconsider their action and attempt to undo it. Almost always their hands exhibit the signs of their self-doubt, the palms and fingers raw with friction burns from grasping at the rope, cord, string, line, or wire that is cutting off their oxygen supply. Raymond Stoddard's hands were unmarked, evidence of a mind undeterred from its purpose and able to overpower the self-preserving impulses of the body.

My father came into possession of this arcanum of the self-destructive through his friendship with the Bismarck police detective who had been at the funeral (my guess had been right) and at our house the night of the murder-suicide. Soon, in fact, this new friend, Lee Mauer, was a regular visitor in our home, and even without knowing that some men were our kind while others were not, I knew that Mr. Mauer was not. He was a big, beefy, barrel-chested man, vulgar, loud, and profane and about as unlike my father as another man could be. They had curiosity in common, however, and each believed the other might possess some information that could solve the mystery of Raymond Stoddard's motive.

Initially, Lee Mauer came to our house mostly by invitation.

My parents felt sorry for him because he lived alone—he was divorced and his wife and two children lived in Casper, Wyoming—and my mother believed that what was most lacking in his life was home cooking. He came often for Sunday dinner, our most formal, elaborate meal of the week, and he ate so heartily my mother had to increase significantly the size of portions to accommodate Mr. Mauer's appetite. Furthermore, she had to counsel her children to overlook Mr. Mauer's poor table manners and his inappropriate talk. Her warnings were futile; almost everything Lee Mauer said—and how he said it—I found fascinating.

He had difficulty getting through a sentence without a profanity, something he was aware of, because he told my sister and me that we should be careful that we didn't develop the "bad speech habits" that he couldn't rid himself of. Worse, in my mother's view, was his willingness to bring up topics unfit for the dinner table or for children. For that matter, some subjects were probably matters of police confidentiality and shouldn't have been discussed in anyone's presence.

He said, for example, that he suspected a Bismarck politician of driving down to South Dakota in order to visit prostitutes, and although he didn't give the man's name, Lee Mauer implied that he was hoarding the man's identity for possible future use. A name he *was* willing to mention was a local doctor's, a man Lee Mauer said was nothing better than a drug pusher. Lee Mauer's ex-wife and her friends had become virtual drug addicts, hooked on the sedatives and painkillers that the doctor prescribed. Lee Mauer told us that the police were keeping their eye on a well-known local athlete, a recent graduate of Bismarck High School, because they suspected him of stealing cars. Before any of my friends knew that the son of a sheriff's deputy had been arrested for selling liquor to minors, I acquired that information courtesy of Lee Mauer.

His gossip favored the lurid, the gruesome, the dangerous, and the scandalous, and all those qualities were enhanced by his side-of-the-mouth confidential style. One could easily imagine him passing on a bit of intelligence about the hands of a hanged man. In fact, if there were ever any doubt about his willingness to discuss any disaster in detail, it was dispelled completely when he told about the death of two young people in a motorcycle accident the previous summer. It happened in Bismarck's Riverside Park, and Lee Mauer happened to be in the park that evening and so hurried to the crash scene to see if he could be of help. "Split in two that young fellow was," Lee Mauer said, "from crotch to neck. Like he was a goddamn wishbone for a couple of giants. I've never seen anything like it."

Tales like that, coupled with Mr. Mauer's general crudeness, finally alienated my mother completely, and she stopped inviting him for meals.

But he kept coming, usually in the late evening. No doubt he came out of loneliness, but since he couldn't admit that, he always had an excuse for stopping by. He was investigating the report of a break-in nearby or he had to check out a suspicious vehicle parked on a neighborhood street. Even when he said he had been driving past, saw a light, and decided to stop, he made it sound as though that too was official business. Because he had learned that we didn't have much in the way of liquor in the house, he often brought with him a six-pack of Grain Belt Premium beer or a pint of schnapps or blackberry brandy. My father would occasionally drink a beer, but he seldom indulged in anything stronger, and certainly none of Lee Mauer's sweet liquors.

Through Lee Mauer I first learned the lesson—the one I had to learn and relearn over the years and which I still haven't mastered—that even (or perhaps especially) the motives of others are often understood by reference back to the self.

Lee Mauer grumbled constantly about politicians, "those greedy sonsabitches," with their unconcern for everything but their own advancement. "They don't give a good goddamn who they step on." And Lee Mauer could voice those sentiments over and over and each time act as though the emotions were newly minted. His voice would rise to a brassy pitch that rang with anger. His features would bunch and his face would redden. He'd pound the table with his big square fist. There, one couldn't keep from thinking, was the kind of rage that would drive a man to murder.

Furthermore, Lee Mauer fixed his political anger on an issue, and there, he believed, his emotions and Raymond Stoddard's coincided. The 1961 North Dakota legislature, as one of its first orders of business, voted itself both a raise and a cost of living increase, yet a 4 percent wage increase proposed for the state's classified and unclassified employees was voted down. This inequity was worsened, in some people's view, by public statements by legislators, such as Monty Burnham, who cheerfully professed not to have known that their salary hike had been attached to a particular bill. Lee Mauer had no trouble imagining that a disgruntled state worker—like Raymond Stoddard—could take out his anger and resentment on a legislator—like Monty Burnham— who had enriched himself while denying the clerks, secretaries,

bureaucrats, and administrators their share of the state's re-
sources.

My father didn't argue with Lee Mauer, but he didn't buy the
policeman's theory and instead saw it stemming from Lee
Mauer's own job dissatisfaction. Lee Mauer held the rank of lieutenant with the Bismarck police department, yet he felt continually slighted in the workplace and complained constantly of the
"ass-kissers and brownnosers" who surpassed him in rank,
salary, or privilege. My father knew all this, but merely shook his
head and to my mother and me said, "Lee just doesn't get it. It's
exactly his griping that makes trouble for him. The police department is like any organization. They want the good team players,
not someone who's poisoning the well."

This judgment my father expressed with more than a touch of
disapproval. In his view men and women were supposed to work
hard and keep their complaints to themselves. It's worth noting,
however, that he always practiced law alone, in spite of offers to
work for various firms, companies, and institutions. He must
have known his nature well enough to realize that he would be a
saner, if poorer, man if he kept to a minimum the number of people with power and authority over him. My father's son, I earn
my living as a novelist, an occupation as solitary as any.

But you must decide for yourself. Have you had experiences
that would lead you to believe a man's perceptions of injustice in
the workplace could move him to murder? In 1961 the term
"going postal" wasn't part of our cultural vocabulary, but language often lags behind deeds.

When I recall my father and Lee Mauer sitting in our darkened kitchen nightly, their white shirts the only brightness in the

room, a brimming ashtray between them, each man's hand curled lightly around a can of beer, it seems as if they turned the room into their private enclave, taking up almost all the space in the room and forcing anyone who wanted to enter to wedge themselves in and then slide along the walls. Perhaps I have that impression because my mother assiduously avoided the kitchen when the men were in there, or perhaps it comes from Lee Mauer sometimes obviously and deliberately falling silent when someone came in. But I hung around the edges as often as I could, and on one of those occasions I overheard a Lee Mauer remark that was so unsettling it haunted me for years. I finally exorcised its effect with a narrative of my own.

In December 1942, when she was nineteen years old, Alma Stoddard had a series of experiences that made her feel as though she were living in a world turned upside down. She left Wembley, North Dakota, her little town near the top of the country, for a visit to a city on the bottom—Killeen, Texas—and when she left North Dakota in December the weather was uncharacteristically mild. Temperatures were in the fifties, and there was no snow. Texas, she expected, would be hot. After all, the letters she received from her husband were often filled with complaints about the heat, yet when she stepped off the bus in Killeen, a good three inches of wet snow covered the ground, and a cold northwest wind blew so hard that tears sprang to her eyes. As it turned out, the weather was the least puzzling feature of her visit.

She had traveled to Texas to see her husband, Raymond,

who was stationed at Camp Hood. He would soon be sent overseas, and since they were both realistic people who were not automatically given to optimistic assumptions about the future, they knew they might not have another chance to be together again for a long time, perhaps ever again. As it was, they had already scaled back on their plans. For a while they had discussed the possibility of Alma moving to Texas but had finally decided that would be impractical. By the time she found a place to live and work, Raymond might be relocated, and then Alma would have given up her job at Hudson's Pharmacy back in Wembley and her rent-free home with her mother.

There had been other compromises. For a time it seemed possible that Raymond would be able to come home to North Dakota for an extended leave. But then all furloughs in his unit were canceled, and the best the Stoddards could arrange was a three-day weekend in a Texas hotel whose lobby was decorated with a dried-out pine tree sparsely decorated with a few glass bulbs.

Alma was sitting on an overstuffed chair near that tree when she saw something more surprising—and more unsettling—than Texas snow. She was waiting for Raymond to meet her, but the first man in uniform to walk through the glass door was not her husband but Monty Burnham, a young man she had dated in high school.

Then, as if to demonstrate that human relationships had been turned as upside down as the country's climate, Monty Burnham greeted her with the words "Alma! There's my girl!" And he said this within earshot of the man who came through the revolving door right behind him—her husband.

She had known, from Raymond's letters, that Monty Burnham was also stationed at Camp Hood, but she didn't think the men spent much time in each other's company. Her husband hadn't said anything more than that he "saw Monty and Dusty Boyd, and a few other guys from back home, around the camp."

The men took turns hugging her, and because she had spent more time in Monty Burnham's arms over the years than in Raymond's, both embraces felt familiar. Alma had been Monty's steady girlfriend from the age of fifteen to the age of seventeen. She and Raymond had been together—dating, engagement, and marriage combined—for only a little more than a year. Both men smelled of tobacco, damp wool, and hair tonic, but she gasped when she felt how thin and bony Raymond seemed. She hoped that he would think her response came only from emotion. And perhaps her shock was merely a consequence, now as in the past, of having first had her arms around Monty's more substantial girth.

Even though Monty Burnham was standing right there, Alma asked her husband, "Do you want to see the room?" In one of their late-night telephone conversations Raymond had been unashamedly, even shockingly, specific about what they would do when they were together once again.

Now, however, Raymond said, "Later's fine." Then he asked, "Did you have to show your marriage license?"

Raymond had repeatedly told her to bring it with her, that she might need it to check into the hotel, but she had still forgotten it at home. Fortunately, she had not been asked for it. She shook her head.

"Because you look so respectable," Monty said. She couldn't tell if there was any irony in his remark. "No one would ever expect anything untoward of a woman who looks like you."

Raymond said, "Monty's going to join us tonight. He knows his way around town, and he can keep us moving in the right direction." He said this without enthusiasm, and for the first time Alma considered the possibility that Monty Burnham had somehow forced his company upon Raymond. She knew little about Army rank, its designations and privileges, but the differences between Monty's uniform and Raymond's were obvious. Perhaps Monty was there as the result of a military command that Raymond had to obey. Her husband's sullen remoteness could certainly be explained as the behavior of a man who had been forced into his circumstances. Alma wondered if she should say she wasn't feeling well enough to go out; perhaps that would send Monty on his way and allow her and Raymond to be alone. She kept quiet, however, because she felt there was a chance that Raymond might then choose to spend the evening out on the town with his comrade.

"Monty's got a girl who's going to meet us later."

To Alma, Monty explained, "She's working now."

Alma brightened at this news. "Oh, where does she work?"

"At a laundry. She's off at five, but she has to clean up and change clothes. She works up such a sweat she has to sit under a cold shower for damn near an hour to cool off."

She wanted to encourage Monty to talk about his girl. "Does this young woman have a name?"

"Dinah. And she's older than us."

"That's a pretty name. Do I see signs you might be serious about Dinah?"

Monty laughed. "Not likely! She's what soldiers call a diversion."

Whatever term soldiers had for a woman like Dinah, she knew it wasn't "diversion." For that matter, she was surprised that the word was part of Monty Burnham's vocabulary. Perhaps Raymond would tell her later what Dinah was more likely to be called.

"Anyway, you'll meet her later," Monty said. "But don't get your hopes up."

"Monty Burnham! What kind of thing is that to say?"

He merely shrugged.

Alma turned to Raymond for support, but he was busy looking his wife up and down, an examination Alma thought more appropriate for a stranger—and a rude one at that—to be conducting than a husband. She knew he hadn't seen the dress before; it was a royal-blue cotton print, and she'd bought it at Whitestone's right after Thanksgiving, when it had been on sale because it belonged to a different season. Perfect for Texas in December, Alma had thought, and had justified the purchase on that basis. It clung to her in a way that she thought was just this side of immodest.

To cover her discomfort under his stare she stepped back and tried to make a joke. "Well, soldier, do I pass inspection?"

"I just wondered if you were ready to go, or if you wanted to change."

"Isn't this appropriate for . . . where we're going?"

Apparently Monty took it upon himself to answer because

he would be their guide for the evening. "You look great. But bring your coat."

And then they were off, leaning into the cold Texas wind, threading their way carefully down sidewalks clotted with soldiers and shopgirls. Alma was glad to be in the company of Raymond and Monty. She had never seen so many men publicly intoxicated and behaving so badly. Even a woman walking arm-in-arm with a man was likely to be subjected to crude remarks and propositions.

Their first stop was a restaurant large enough to be a dining hall, and it too was crowded with soldiers. Casa Robles was unlike any eatery Alma had ever been in. Its walls were painted the color of mustard, brown-skinned waiters scurried about carrying enormous serving trays, and the general din made conversation next to impossible. Alma wanted to suggest they find a quieter place to eat, but before they were even seated at a table, Raymond and Monty ordered beers. Alma rarely drank beer, and they were served a brand she had never heard of. She said she'd prefer Coke.

Monty shook his head. "Not with Mexican food. Coke won't put the fire out."

Raymond agreed. "Pretty spicy."

Alma couldn't eat more than a few bites of her meal, but the heat wasn't the problem. She had told the men that she didn't like spicy food, so they had studied the menu carefully, trying to find something mild for her. But the food's textures were all wrong—mealy and soft—and the restaurant made no effort to separate one item from another on her plate. Neither of the men noticed how little she ate.

Raymond didn't finish his food either. He pushed aside his half-eaten tamales and lit another cigarette. Alma still could not get used to the sight of him smoking. He had taken up the practice when he'd joined the service because, he said in a letter, smokers were given extra breaks. He wrote about his "new habit" in a joking way, but there was nothing lighthearted in the grim, resolute way he pulled smoke deep into his lungs.

They had entered Casa Robles in the full sunlight of afternoon, but when they exited, the streetlamps had all come on. This too shocked Alma. So many miles separated Texas from North Dakota—yet December dark came as early to one place as another.

Monty announced their next destination, and its name sounded more exotic and interesting than it turned out to be. The Alhambra was nothing but a bar, small, smoky, and dimly lit to hide its dirt and disrepair. After a couple of drinks they walked to another bar, Vic's Place, but since it was so similar to the one they'd just left, Alma wondered why they had bothered to move. She supposed it might have been to meet Monty's girlfriend, yet he had made no effort to survey either establishment for her presence. He didn't even bother turning to look when the door rattled open with new customers and a breath of cold wind.

After their second round of drinks was served—the men had switched from beer to rum and Coke—Alma asked, "What does this girlfriend of yours look like, Monty?"

"A Mexican. But she's not. And I told you, she's not my girlfriend."

"Your date, then. Dinah."

"Why do you ask?"

"That girl over there is up on her tiptoes looking around, and I wondered if she could be Dinah."

Monty shook his head.

With his index finger Raymond nudged Alma's drink, a Schenley's and Seven, closer to her. "You're not drinking," he said. "You want something else?"

"It's fine." She was disappointed that he didn't seem to re-member how little taste she had for either liquor or its effects.

"You got to drink up, Alma," Monty said. His ruddy cheeks, part of his soft, youthful good looks, became even more flushed as he drank. Even in the bar's gloom she could see his ears glowing bright red. "This is a celebration!"

"What are we celebrating?"

"Why, that you made the trip! Welcome to Texas!"

Alma glanced at Raymond to see if Monty spoke for both of them.

But Monty wasn't finished. "And I never had a chance to drink to your marriage." He raised his glass again.

"We didn't have any alcohol at the reception," Alma said.

Raymond raised his own glass but only inches off the table, and he addressed Alma's earlier question. "Because we haven't shipped out yet," he said. "Because we can still breathe the open air, and we're not trapped in a tank somewhere waiting to get blown all to hell. Not yet."

"Jesus Christ, Ray," Monty said.

Alma put a comforting hand on her husband's wrist, but he misunderstood her gesture. He obviously thought she was trying to keep him from bringing his drink to his lips, and he twisted away from her touch.

"I'm just saying what we're all thinking."

"That doesn't mean you have to say it. It's going to happen or it isn't. No point in dwelling on it."

Monty's view on this matter was Alma's, too. She dreaded the possibility of spending these days with Raymond and having him fill the hours with talk of all the horrible things that could happen to men in war. She'd prefer they spend every moment together in complete silence rather than have to listen to her husband's hideous, hopeless thoughts. Did that make her a bad wife? She didn't care if it did.

"Can we go back to the hotel?" Alma asked apologetically. "I couldn't sleep much on the bus."

She directed her request to Raymond, but Monty rose as well. He, in fact, reached into the pocket of his khakis and brought out a money clip with a tight packet of folded bills. He tugged loose a dollar and dropped it carelessly onto the table. Alma had never seen a man keep his currency in anything but a billfold, exactly where Monty had kept his during their time together. What strange practices men adopted when they left their homes.

They did not walk directly to the hotel. Monty Burnham insisted on stopping at a liquor store, and Alma and Raymond remained outside on the sidewalk. Alma hoped the frigid air would help sober her husband, who had slipped into a slow-blinking, slack-jawed silence. He looked as though he could fall asleep leaning against the liquor store's brick wall.

She tugged on the sleeve of his uniform. Without her gloves she could feel how rough was the wool of his jacket. "Ray. Have you ever met this Dinah?"

"I dunno. Maybe."

"Well, have you or haven't you? She was supposed to meet us, but there's no sign of her. I'm beginning to wonder if she's just one of Monty's stories."

Either her question or his effort to answer her seemed to sober him momentarily. "You know him better'n I do. He seem like the sort who needs to make up a woman?"

There was no right way for Alma to respond. She stepped away from her husband and looked up the street as if she were the one expecting to meet someone. On a wire above the street hung two slices of tin cut in the shape of Christmas bells. In the wind the tin bells had slid out of place on the wire and were rattling against each other. Why, Alma wondered, had the town not had to donate those tin decorations to the war effort? Back in Wembley the townspeople had already collected enough tin cans to build a tower as tall as a house. She turned back to Raymond, thinking she might put him in an improved humor with this observation about their hometown, but he had already drifted back into his drunken trance.

Then Monty burst out of the liquor store, his smile wide, his cheeks as red as his ears had been earlier. "Let's go," he said. "Let's show these folks how North Dakotans celebrate!"

But his remark made no sense, since they proceeded directly back to the hotel and to Raymond and Alma Stoddard's room, where, once the door was closed behind them, no one would know whether the people inside were raising their glasses in celebration or hanging their heads in despair.

Monty pulled the cork on the newly purchased bottle of rum, and using a bottle opener screwed into the wall next to the bathroom sink, he levered open a bottle of Coke. The room had only two glasses, so after mixing drinks for Ray and Alma, he poured rum into the Coke bottle for his own drink. "I didn't make yours quite so strong," he said to Alma. "As I recall, you'd just as soon not taste the liquor."

She didn't want another drink at all, but she accepted it without comment or complaint. The day had been so filled with the unexpected that she hadn't even been surprised when Monty followed them to the room and walked right in behind them.

"To the newlyweds!" Monty said.

"Hardly," Raymond said, and sat down heavily on the edge of the bed, which gave out a stiff-springed rusty groan.

Alma didn't raise her glass either, but Monty was undeterred. "I can't imagine a couple better than the two of you!"

In order not to hear the demurral that she feared Raymond might make, Alma excused herself, went into the bathroom, and closed the door behind her.

Alma took out her cosmetics from her overnight case and lined them up on the back of the sink. Some of the makeup was newly purchased, never opened, and she had brought them from North Dakota with a specific plan in mind. In Wembley she would never dare venture out in public wearing much more makeup than a little rouge and lipstick. "You're pretty enough all on your own," her mother used to tell her. "You don't need that gunk." Alma had never doubted that she was pretty, but what she had in mind wasn't simply to make herself more attractive. She wanted to transform herself into a woman who would be regarded as—she didn't even know what term men used. Not "pretty." Not "a diversion." Some word or phrase that had more than appreciation in it, that expressed not just a woman's looks but a man's desire. All she could think of were the words from movie magazines. "Glamorous." "Stunning." "Alluring." Not the language that a man would use when a woman with a certain look passed, and he'd nudge his friend and say— Well. Even if Alma couldn't put a word to it, she knew what the look was. And she set about giving it to herself.

With her rouge she made her cheeks look as if they were flushed with passion. With lipstick she not only darkened her lips, she swelled their outline as well. With her eyelash curler and eyebrow pencil she gave her eyes what she considered a cruel, dramatic look. She believed that no one but Raymond would see her this way. Soon Monty would leave, and then she would walk out of the bathroom, startling her husband with her new glamorous look. She and Raymond would spend most of the remainder of her visit in their hotel room—alone *in their hotel room*—and if he wanted her to use her makeup to recreate this movie star mien, she would happily do so. Or if he preferred her scrubbed as clean as the morning of their wedding day, that would be fine, too.

Alma put her ear to the bathroom door. She couldn't hear any drunken voices or clinking glasses or matches being struck. She supposed it was possible that Monty had left when she was running water in the sink and therefore she hadn't heard the door open and close, but then why wouldn't Ray call out to her and tell her they were alone? Deciding that she'd simply wait a little longer, she sat down on the edge of the bathtub.

During this visit Alma had hoped to discuss with Ray a matter that had been weighing heavily on her. She was living in her mother's house, and since Alma was married to a serviceman, she thought it was perfectly legitimate to affix a gold star to her mother's window. Then, just last week, when Raymond's parents learned that Alma would be traveling to Texas, they invited her over for supper and to give her a small package to carry to Ray. As Alma stepped onto the Stoddards' front porch, she saw a gold star shining in the corner of their living room window. Was this all right, Alma wanted to ask Ray, two homes and two stars yet only one serviceman? But somehow, in the miles between North Dakota and Texas, the dilemma had lost its importance. In fact, if she were to tell Ray about it now, she was certain he would laugh at the foolishness of her concerns.

At the bathroom door came two soft knocks and Alma jumped up to answer. When she opened the door, however, it was Monty Burnham's face that peered into the room.

"Well, I got him tucked in," Monty said. "And he's on his stomach just in case—don't want him gagging on his supper. I put that wastebasket beside the bed, too."

Monty announced all this as if it had been done according to some plan worked out with Alma in advance of the evening. She didn't know what to say but thank you.

Because Monty was wearing his officer's cap, Alma assumed he was about to leave, but he tilted the cap back on his head, stepped into the bathroom, and reached for a cigarette. He *leaned back against the door until it shut softly. The room was tiny, and Alma backed up until her legs touched the cool porcelain of the bathtub.*

Monty blew a cloud of smoke toward the ceiling, and in a voice barely more than a whisper said, "Old Ray. He's holding on but barely."

If this was to be a conversation about her husband's state of being, Alma would welcome it. "I believe he's lost weight."

"That ain't the half of it." He cocked his head as if the bathroom's bright light allowed him to see Alma in a new way. "But you—you're looking prettier than ever, Alma. And that's saying something."

"Pretty," he had said, but she realized that her face was made up in that other way, and she stepped quickly to the sink with the intention of washing immediately.

Monty must have misunderstood her movement. He came up behind her and put a hand on her shoulder. "Alma? You okay?"

She nodded but turned on the faucet and began to splash water on her face.

"Thought you were gonna be sick or something."

"I'm fine."

Monty didn't move away but started to rub Alma's back, his hand caressing a small circle high between her shoulder blades and on her neck up under her hairline.

"When I saw you today . . . ," he said, "well, it just started up all over again. I mean, not that they ever went away, my feelings for you. But Jesus Christ, I was a fool to let you go."

Let me go? Alma believed she had been the one to walk

away from their relationship, fed up with the number of times he'd stood her up because he preferred hunting or fishing with his friends or drinking beer and shaking dice at Sugar's Bar to being with her. But there was no point arguing with him. He obviously had his own version of their breakup.

"What makes me so damn mad," Monty continued, "is that I'm a better man now. Stronger, more sure of myself. Now I could put up a helluva fight for you, Alma. A helluva fight."

He was fairly murmuring these words in her ear, bent over her back, his hands braced on the sink on either side of her.

"If I could make Ray straighten up and treat you right, I'd cut the orders tomorrow."

This remark she might have disputed, but by now Monty's hand was at the front of her throat, softly stroking its length as if he were trying to help her swallow his words.

It would not have been accurate or honest for Alma to pretend that what happened in that hotel bathroom was completely without her acquiescence. But neither would it have been far from the truth.

She may have been mistaken in thinking that what was happening was happening in discrete stages, that the process that had been set in motion could easily be halted or altered at anytime, one moment easily snipped away from the moment that preceded or followed it. But Monty's seduction was, like so many events in life, composed of units of action and time linked inextricably to one another.

And then, of course, what was occurring was not entirely unfamiliar to Alma. During their time together Monty had often

*touched her here and here, like this and like this, and he had
tried to touch her there and there. What was different now was
that it was now . . . and Monty was soon doing what Alma
didn't know could be done.*

*But a woman doesn't allow herself to be fucked standing up
and holding on to a bathroom fixture just to satisfy her curiosity or dispel her disbelief. She must have been willing. . . . She
must have been. . . .*

*Because she certainly could have stopped it with a scream or
a violent twist of her hips, or she could have grabbed his hand
and wiped it across her face so he could feel her tears or maybe
it would have been enough to lift her head so he could see her
reflection in the mirror. . . . As his thrusts increased in force and
frequency, the sink's plug, a black rubber stopper hanging from
a little chain looped over the spigot, began to move back and
forth. Alma watched it closely, and as it swung from side to
side, she imagined it was swinging between the poles of her
life—North Dakota, Texas, Texas, North Dakota, Raymond,
Monty, Monty, Raymond. . . . Even after Monty gasped and
staggered back from her, she kept her focus on the chain and the
plug. Soon it was motionless again, hanging above a drain circled with a rusty stain from a faucet that must have dripped for
years with no one bothering to fix it.*

*The following morning, as the first light of a cold Texas dawn
found its way into the room, Alma stared up at a blotch on the
ceiling. It was about the size of a pumpkin, and its irregular
shape was outlined in the same rust-orange color as the stain in
the bathroom sink. Only moments before, Raymond had finally*

roused from his rum-steeped stupor, and now, as she lay under his weight, it was all Alma could do not to interrupt her husband's grunting efforts to ask him if he thought water was leaking in the room above them.

In the original version of this story, the characters were named Donald and Lois Culpepper and Nick Anschutz. Otherwise the story is exactly as it appears, under the title "A Mild Winter," in my MFA thesis and later in *The Bozeman Review,* a now discontinued literary magazine once published at Montana State University. I have never included it in any collection.

Readers sometimes ask me where I get my ideas, and I'm seldom able to provide a satisfactory answer, so vague and various are the sites where most of my fiction is born. But if I were asked about "A Mild Winter," I could provide a number of answers, all true and all inadequate, as explanations of creative work so often are.

On one of the few occasions when Gene, Marie, and I were together in the Stoddard house (after his father's death, Gene seldom invited anyone into his home), we looked through the Stoddard family photo albums. One black-and-white photograph, blown up to an eight-by-ten, depicted a small gathering of casually arranged laughing soldiers standing in fresh snow, and Raymond Stoddard, with his lopsided smile and eyes squinting against the sun, stood in the back of the group. The back of the photo carried the penciled caption "761st Tank Battalion, Camp Hood, Texas, December '42." If Monty Burnham was in the picture, I didn't recognize him.

In addition to what the photo provided, I had, in the writing of "A Mild Winter," my parents' recollections of life during the war (as I recall I cut a passage of dialogue between "Donald" and "Lois" about ration cards), a little research (also eliminated was a brief mention of mixing egg yolks with margarine to give it the color of butter), and of course the date and year of Marcia Stoddard's birth. And, more than anything, I had the stimulus—or the irritant—of that Lee Mauer remark I alluded to earlier.

On a warm summer evening I was sitting on our front porch watching for a group of friends to drive up and take me to an American Legion baseball game. My father and Lee Mauer were in the kitchen and, though they kept their voices low and the window screen sifted out parts of their conversation, I heard enough to know they were talking about, as usual, the why of Raymond Stoddard's last day on earth. Months had passed, and the event had exceeded most people's attention spans but not my father's and Lee Mauer's. Their interest was undiminished, and a new season simply brought new theories, as when Mr. Mauer said, "That Miss Stoddard—am I the only one who sees a helluva resemblance between her and a certain state senator?"

Jay Garner's Plymouth pulled up to the curb, so I didn't hear my father's response, but I had eavesdropped on the two men often enough to know what pattern their talk would follow. Soon one or both of them would be speculating on what might have happened if it were determined that Marcia Stoddard was Monty Burnham's child.

And suppose Ray found out?

But how could he? After all this time?

Same as I did. He looks at the girl one day, and god damn—
he knows. He just knows.

*A man makes a discovery like that—he's sure as hell going to
get himself a gun.*

Sure as hell.

I never saw the likeness that seemed so obvious to Mr. Mauer,
nor do I know if my father did. At one point, years after his remark, I went so far as to lay open two high school yearbooks,
one with Monty Burnham's senior picture and the other with
Marcia Stoddard's. I couldn't see any resemblance besides youth
and the unlined optimism that so often attends it.

Writing "A Mild Winter" didn't purge me completely of the
idea that Monty Burnham was Marcia's father, but at least I was
finally able to do something useful with one of the many notions
that kept bubbling to the surface of my thoughts over the years.
Far more plentiful are the false starts, the abortive attempts, the
unrealized fragments that have accumulated in my notebooks
and journals, fading and yellowing in filing cabinets and manila
folders.

My father not only had a need to know what had happened with
and to Raymond Stoddard, he also felt an obligation to Raymond's family. Perhaps that began when Gene discovered his father's body and decided my father was the person to call for help.
From that day forward, he was ready to provide any support the
Stoddards might need, whether it was jump-starting a car, providing legal advice (adding to the bureaucratic complications that
can accompany a death was the fact that Raymond didn't leave a

will), helping with lawn care or household repairs, or offering sympathy. My mother certainly helped Alma Stoddard too, but her aid was perhaps less obvious since it was consistent with the kind of comfort that women generally provide for each other. Lee Mauer was a handier man than my father, and eventually— I think it began with an electrical wiring problem—my father recruited Lee Mauer to join him on those missions to make Alma Stoddard's life easier. By the time summer came around—and Marcia Stoddard returned to Bismarck—the two men were as likely to be doing chores at the house down the block as they were to be sitting in our kitchen drinking beer.

The amount of time my father—and Mr. Mauer—spent at the Stoddards' finally led to a quarrel between my parents.

My father and mother had been to a hardware store and had returned with samples to help them decide what color to paint the house. They walked from back to front, holding those little rectangles of color against a sunlit wall and then a shaded one, but they were talking about much more than tints of blue.

They had obviously been arguing for a time when I heard them, their voices raised near my bedroom window.

"Are you jealous?" my father asked. "For Christ's sake, are you *jealous* of Alma Stoddard? After what she's been through?"

"Don't be ridiculous. Although I am curious to see whose storm windows get taken down first, mine or Alma Stoddard's. No, you know what's bothering me: Your reason for being down there. If I could be sure you wanted nothing more than to help someone whose life has turned into hell on earth, I'd say fine, wonderful. But if you're just down there to spy on that poor woman—that I can't forgive."

"Spy . . . ?"

"Oh, don't pretend. Please. You know what I'm talking about. You and your newfound friend would like nothing better than to discover some kind of secret down there. Playing detective. . . ."

I heard a faint scraping sound, as though one of them were flicking the siding with the cardboard paint sample.

"*Playing?* Is that what you think we're doing? Jesus. . . ."

"What I call it or what you call it isn't the issue. Alma Stoddard deserves some peace in her life. And the two of you intend to use her for your own—"

My mother stopped then, but if I could finish her sentence, my father certainly could as well. *Pleasure.* My father and Lee Mauer wanted to use Alma Stoddard for their own pleasure.

As it has been tiresomely noted, the early 1960s were a sexually repressed era, at least as far as public expressions were concerned. The teenage males of that time—I include myself—were starved not only for sexual experience but for sexual knowledge, but since so much was denied us, almost any phrase that had—or could be twisted into having—a sexual connotation was titillating. To get inside. To enter. To penetrate. And we had somehow learned that "to know" had the archaic meaning of "to have sexual intercourse," so that verb too was an occasion for sly smiles or outright ribald laughter.

Yet when I overheard my mother scold my father, the denotative and connotative meanings of words suddenly collapsed onto themselves, tangled, and could not be teased apart.

I knew, on an imaginative if not an experiential level, what it meant to use a woman for one's own pleasure—it certainly involved *know*ing her—but my mother accused my father and Lee Mauer of using Alma Stoddard for knowledge of the epistemological rather than the sexual sort. They wanted to get inside, to enter, to penetrate the Stoddard house, the Stoddard psyche, in order to know.

Moments after my mother's sentence fragment, the front screen door slammed. I peered out of my bedroom and saw that it was my father alone who had walked away from their argument and back into the house.

And whether it was the result of my mother chastising him I couldn't be sure, but in the house was where my father was soon more often to be found. His fellow spy, however, the real detective, began to log more hours at the Stoddards'. In fact, instead of parking in front of our house and sauntering up our walk with a six-pack under his arm, Lee Mauer was now more likely to pull up to the Stoddards' curb, and while his presence there was often visible—edging the sidewalk, sealing cracks in the driveway, cleaning the window wells—on as many days and nights he couldn't be seen. But his car was there. Explanations that he was working out of sight in the backyard or in the basement or garage could last only so long, and with my new awareness of sex and secrets conflated, I soon concluded that Mr. Mauer was there for reasons other than being a Good Samaritan.

It wasn't quite the same as when I looked out the window on that January day and wondered why my father's car was parked at the Stoddards', but I was still curious about why Lee Mauer was so often there. And since my interest was prurient, I was reluctant to ask my parents or Gene Stoddard, the people who would best be able to satisfy my curiosity.

I decided I'd ask Marie Ryan, and of course what I was really doing was using my concern as an excuse to call her.

When I telephoned and told her that I wanted to talk about the Stoddard family, I tried to imply that the matter was serious enough that we shouldn't discuss it over the telephone. My strategy worked. She invited me to meet her at Elks Swimming Pool during the evening hours set aside for family swimming. She would be there with the two children she was babysitting that summer. Gene had a job with his uncle's construction crew, and when the weather was good he worked late.

Here is how memory can deceive: I know perfectly well that in North Dakota the summer sun sets late, and for much of the season, darkness doesn't descend until close to ten o'clock. I showed up at the swimming pool at around six—an hour when sunlight was unabated. Yet it seems to me that when I stepped out of the locker room and saw the lovely, voluptuous Miss Marie Ryan sitting on the concrete at the edge of the pool, she was washed in the golden light of the setting sun. Perhaps I misremember reality because of the way her tanned skin replied to the sun's glow—and still more radiance caught in her hair, turned amber in that light. At the sight of her I must have gasped just as I had seconds earlier when I'd walked through the cold shower on my way out to the pool. So let's allow this trick of memory to stand—it creates something truer than the inexpressive, unalterable fact of the hour and minute when the sun sinks below the horizon, and reminds us that we see with more than our eyes.

Marie's swimsuit was the color of lime sherbet, and it didn't have straps but a loop that circled her neck and left her sweet shoulders bare and unmarked. She was toweling the blond hair of a chunky sunburned little girl who was shouting an accusation of some sort at her brother, who was still in the water. The flesh of Marie's back was as smooth and unblemished as the little girl's. Marie didn't see me approach, for which I was grateful. I wouldn't have wanted her to scrutinize my gawky, sharp-shinned, long-boned pale body the way I examined hers.

As I squatted down next to her, I felt as though I were there merely to present a contrast in geometry—my abrupt angles alongside her luxuriant curves. I also noticed that though Marie was sitting at the pool's shallow end, not all the footprints around her were child-size. Men and boys must have made up any excuse they could in order to walk out of the water near where she sat.

We couldn't make anything but small talk with the little girl on her towel between us, but when the child fussed to go back into the water, I was only too glad to lead her by the hand and help her wade out to where her brother was trying to keep a beach ball submerged. Again and again it exploded back to the surface, and he acted shocked every time. His sister lent her weight to his, and while they worked on sinking the ball for good, I told Marie about what was on my mind.

"Has Gene said anything about that police detective hanging around all the time? His car is there almost every evening."

She kept her eyes on her charges in the water, so I couldn't glean much from her expression as she spoke.

"He thinks something is going on, all right. A few nights ago he came into the house through the side door, and his mother and Lee Mauer were sitting at the kitchen table. But side by side. And close. Gene thought maybe his mother rearranged her blouse when he walked in."

I didn't have to feign shock. "She's fooling around with Lee Mauer? Her husband hasn't been dead a year!"

"Gene doesn't know that for sure. But he said that ever since then Mr. Mauer has been real buddy-buddy to him. He even asked Gene if he wanted to drive his police car."

"Mrs. Stoddard and Lee Mauer? I can't believe it!"

Marie obviously didn't find it so hard to believe. She merely shrugged.

Our talk had turned frank enough that I could share with Marie my theory that Lee Mauer was trying to get close to Mrs. Stoddard because he thought that she, and perhaps the Stoddard house itself, was holding back a secret that would explain why Raymond had behaved as he had.

This line of speculation didn't particularly impress her either. She said matter-of-factly, "Men are always trying to see what they can get." The knowing smile that Marie turned on me said that she knew this generalization could apply to me as well. I was flattered and chagrined to be one of her specimens, but she had me so neatly pinned I couldn't do anything but sit and squirm.

When I finally found my tongue, I asked, "What does Gene think about all this?"

"He acts like he doesn't care. His mother has her life, and he has his. That's what he says, anyway. But he doesn't like it. The house feels strange enough without having a stranger in it."

I nodded eagerly. "That's sort of what I thought. I'm hardly ever around the house anymore, though."

Marie held me in her gaze. "Whose idea is that?"

When I didn't answer, she released me. "He sure as hell doesn't care about driving a police car."

To cover my discomfort I stood and stepped into the pool, pretending as though the children's play needed correction. Someone needed to show them what to do with a beach ball.

With my instruction and encouragement the kids eventually took to batting the ball back and forth rather than trying to drown it.

When I splashed out of the water, I found Marie was not alone. Standing over her, blocking her sun and probably trying to look down her swimsuit, was a lifeguard. I knew him, or at least knew his reputation. Tim Townley had just graduated from Bismarck High School and in the fall would be heading to St. Olaf to major in music and to compete on the college swim team. Slender, tanned, sun-bleached blond, and handsome, he had, so gossip had it, been successfully seducing the city's girls for years. He usually targeted females a few years younger than himself, no doubt believing that they would be especially susceptible to the attentions of an older boy.

That was probably his strategy with Marie, but when I came closer, I heard her sternly say, "I'm going with someone."

Tim Townley turned in the direction of my wet feet slapping on the concrete. When he saw I was coming toward Marie, he looked questioningly at her. She said nothing to correct his impression, and Tim Townley shook his head and walked away. A profound gratitude instantly augmented my already considerable love for Marie Ryan.

She signaled the kids to come out of the pool and began to

gather up their towels. I asked her if I could give them a ride home, but she told me that Mrs. Linstrom would be picking them up.

Before we parted, she said, "You know, you could have asked Gene about all this yourself."

Her remark sounded like a mild reproach, and I took it in that spirit. But I had never received a scolding that came accompanied with a smile like the one Marie Ryan shone on me.

If the purpose of Marie's observation had been to suggest that I could be a better friend to Gene, it was right on the mark. I know it now, and I knew it then, yet I couldn't seem to find the actions that corresponded to that knowledge. I knew how not to hurt but not how to help.

I can think of only one occasion when I did something that, in a small way, might have aided Gene during that difficult time.

He and I were at a party at Jay Garner's house, and though Jay's parents were out of town, the gathering wasn't a large or wild one—just six or seven of us, all males. The month was April, but in North Dakota that's often nothing but a calendar page. While the temperature had been in the seventies the week before, that night a wet snow was falling, fat heavy flakes filling up the window well right outside the basement rec room where we sat drinking beer, our empty cans carefully stacked atop Jay's father's bar. Just below the ceiling's acoustical tiles blue smoke pooled from our cigarettes and cigars (someone had stolen a box of White Owls). Most of our conversation I can't recall, but I'm still certain of what we talked about: athletic skills and how they could be improved; cars and how they could be altered to run faster; and girls and how they could be induced to put out. As predictably as the belches that accompanied our beer drinking, those subjects came up whenever our group gathered. On other occasions we might also have talked about why Raymond Stoddard had killed Monty Burnham, but since Gene was present that night, the topic had to be avoided, even if the sight of Gene was enough to bring the question to mind all over again.

On that evening, however, the taboo was violated, and while I was there to witness the occurrence, I'm still not quite sure how it came to pass. We were at Jay Garner's house, and perhaps he believed that privileged him. Or maybe he was too drunk to observe the usual restrictions. Whatever the cause, at some point in the evening, Jay asked Gene if he had a theory about why his father had done what he'd done. Jay asked the question politely enough, and he seemed motivated, at least initially, by nothing but curiosity. For his part, Gene simply tried to deflect the question. "Sorry, I don't."

We were all relieved when Gene's shrugged apology seemed to close off the subject, and we quickly returned to our discussion of carburetors.

But Jay got drunker, and as he did, he resumed his interrogation. At least an hour had passed since his impertinent question, but Jay picked up right where he had left off. "That's fucking hard to believe," Jay said to Gene. "That you don't have a clue about why he did it. I mean, he was your dad, for Christ's sake."

"Hard to believe or not," Gene said, "it's true. Sorry."

"I'm not saying you know for sure. I'm asking for a fucking

hunch. A goddamn guess. A hypothesis. You sure as shit have one. Everybody does."

"But I don't."

Jay turned to the rest of the group, most of whom were staring uncomfortably into their beer cans. "You know what we ought to do? We should torture him until he tells us what he knows. What do you say?"

Someone, it might have been Bill Forston, said, "Why don't you give it a rest."

But something—or someone, and maybe it was Gene's passivity—had opened a vein of meanness in Jay Garner. And, typical of a drunk, he was now taken with his own sadistic idea. He scraped the ash from his cigar, then blew on the tip until it glowed red-orange. "If someone'll hold him down, I'll administer the pain."

No one moved, but Bill Forston said, "I know you're just trying to be funny, but you're not. You're not fucking funny."

Jay continued to contemplate his cigar.

I looked over at Gene, expecting him to tell Jay where he could stick his cigar, but Gene said nothing and didn't move. It seemed to me, however, and here perhaps I gave myself more credit than I deserved, that his eyes were taking on the first glisten that would eventually lead to tears.

"I have a better idea," I said. I stood and walked over behind Jay. "How about Chinese water torture?" And with that I poured beer on his cigar.

The cigar hissed, Jay yelped and jumped back from the beer streaming down on him, everyone laughed, and the moment's tension, along with all talk of torture and truth-telling, was extinguished.

As I was returning to my chair, Gene rose and walked silently past me.

I couldn't give myself too much credit for bailing out my friend. After all, I hadn't directly confronted Jay on his stupidly cruel comments; instead I had tried to use a joke of my own to defuse the situation. And had it been compassion for Gene that finally prompted me to act, or a wish to save him, me, all of us, from the embarrassment that would have followed if he had begun to cry? This for a young man who should have been understood and forgiven if he broke down in tears every single day.

Time passed and it became apparent Gene had not merely gone to the bathroom or to get another beer, so I drained the remainder of my beer, conspicuously shook the can to demonstrate that it was empty, and then left the room.

I couldn't find him anywhere, not in the bathroom, not in the laundry room, where the beers chilled in a cooler, and not in any of the upstairs rooms, generally understood to be off-limits to us. I would have assumed he'd left the party altogether, but his coat was still draped over a kitchen chair.

As I turned to go back downstairs, I glanced out the back door and saw him.

Gene was standing on the small porch, unsheltered, the adhesive spring snow cloaking and capping him.

I opened the door and stepped out, and he didn't even turn to see who had joined him. Maybe he assumed all along that I'd come after him.

"Hey, Garner's an asshole," I said. "Everybody knows that."

Gene nodded. If I was looking for an expression of gratitude, it was not to come.

"I thought maybe you'd take that cigar and put it out on his forehead."

We both knew how out of character that would have been, and he didn't bother responding to my suggestion. Instead, he turned to me and through the veil of the falling snow said, "I don't know anything. I *don't*." The tears that I believed I saw forming in his dark eyes earlier were now in his voice. "If he doesn't stop, I'll . . . I'll . . ."

If there was a threat behind his words it wasn't intended for Jay Garner but for Gene Stoddard himself.

"Okay," I said, putting my hand on his shoulder and then bringing it back cold and wet with snow. "Okay. I'll say something. Now let's go back inside. I'm freezing my ass."

We both went back into the house, but Gene didn't follow me down the stairs. Behind me I heard the door open and close again. Gene was not driving that night, but I felt certain that if I checked on the direction of his footsteps in the snow, they wouldn't track north, toward his home and mine, but south, toward Marie Ryan's, only three blocks away and where he'd find comfort that he couldn't in the company of his oldest friend.

As a way of honoring my promise to Gene, I said to Jay, upon rejoining the party with a fresh beer, "Lay off Gene, why don't you." I might have added but didn't—Besides, what makes you think you can conceive of a torture more painful than his daily life?

- 99 -

This happened, as I said, in April, months before Marie delivered her mild reprimand at the swimming pool, and though I didn't bother trying to defend myself to her, I might have pointed out that the distance between Gene and me had been increasing for some time. He soon had an entirely new set of friends, and between those companions and Marie, he probably didn't have much room left in his life for me.

Adolescents have always been adept at categorizing (even as they resent it being done to them), and nowhere are systems of classification as rigorously imposed as upon high school populations. Over the years there have been jocks, preps, greasers, and hoods, nerds, brains, foxes, and studs, gearheads, metalheads, losers, and geeks—and that's without even venturing into the innumerable sub-genres. Yet Gene Stoddard's new friends were a kind of featureless mix that defied designation.

Today they might be characterized as slackers, but back then we had no term for them. They were heavy drinkers, and if drugs had been available then, I'm sure they would have been among the first users. They were poor students yet did enough to get by. None was on an athletic team or belonged to an extracurricular organization. They lacked the dark-hearted malice of the hoods, yet they were in and out of trouble mostly because they were inattentive or not clever enough not to get caught. Most of them worked, but only so they'd have money for gas, booze, or cigarettes. They lived in their cars but did nothing to customize or personalize them. Their usual gathering spot was the gravel lot behind a Mobil station on the east end of the city, and from there they drove endless circuits of Main Avenue. A few girls, plain and anonymous, hung out with them, but I think Gene was the only one who had a steady girlfriend. Gene's cousin, Del Shumate, provided the entrée to the group, and a similar family connection, Del's father and Gene's uncle, arranged for Gene's summer job with Harbring Construction.

From my perspective they seemed an apathetic bunch, but perhaps that was precisely what made them attractive to Gene. Your father was a murderer?—We don't care. You found him hanging in the garage?—Who gives a damn. You caught your mother with another man's hands on her?—It doesn't matter. Your past looms so hugely and darkly over your life that even the light of the future can't find its way in?—Shut up and have another beer!

I had never shunned my friend, but I'd be a liar if I didn't say that a certain relief flowed in to fill the widening gap between Gene and me. There'd be no further possibility of confusion between us, and no more uncomfortable questions that assumed I had some insider's knowledge of the Stoddard family.

But while the diminution of a friendship didn't concern me greatly, something else did. Without Gene I'd have fewer opportunities to get close to Marie Ryan. No more double dates (there had been only a few), no more tagging along with them to a school function or sporting event, and no more hanging out with them at a party. After my swimming pool meeting with Marie— ostensibly about my unease over Lee Mauer—I couldn't manufacture another reason to call. Gene, however, just as he had on the occasion of his father's funeral, unwittingly provided a means by which I could have access to Marie Ryan.

It was close to eleven o'clock on a hot summer evening when the telephone rang. My mother and I were the only ones up—we were watching *Lost Horizon*—and after she answered the phone, she handed it to me with a disapproving twist of her eyebrows.

It was Marie, and her first words were, "Is he with you?"

"Who?"

"Who else? Gene."

"He's not here. I haven't seen him today." Or this week and maybe not even this month, I might have added. I'm not sure why I couldn't admit that I seldom saw him. Hadn't Gene told Marie that our friendship had dwindled to almost nothing?

"That figures. I should have known. He told me that you two were doing something together and then he'd be here before ten. Well, guess what. He missed."

"I'm sorry."

"He didn't even bother talking to you first so you'd cover for him? Stupid bastard. Stupid, stupid, *stupid*."

"You called his house?"

"Twice. Even though his mother gets pissed off when I do. Your mom probably isn't too happy I called either."

"No, it's okay." From the kitchen I could see into the living room, where my mother sat on the couch. Anyone else might have believed that all her attention was focused on *The Channel Twelve Late Show,* but I could see signs that indicated otherwise. She exhaled cigarette smoke with a little more force than usual, and one tanned leg bounced impatiently. "Look, do you want me to go down to his house and see if he's there? Maybe he went in the side door, and his mom doesn't even know he came home."

"Don't bother. I know where he is. Out drinking with those low-life friends of his."

"Sorry."

"That's the second time you've said that. It's not your fault. Don't apologize for him."

"There must have been some kind of mix-up. . . ."

Her laughter came through the telephone line as if it traveled on its own impulse of energy. "He doesn't *have to* set up anything with you beforehand," Marie said. "You make excuses for him all on your own."

When I returned to the living room and Ronald Colman's dilemma, my mother said, "Rather late for telephone conversations, isn't it?"

"Sorry. That was Marie Ryan. Gene stood her up, and she wondered if he was here."

"Is she worried?"

"Just hurt, I think. And mad."

"Are those two serious about each other?"

"I think it's mostly one way." And then I added, as if clarification were necessary, "Marie for Gene."

So much time passed before my mother spoke again that I thought she was entirely engrossed in the movie. Then she leaned forward to stub out her cigarette, and said, "Plenty of that going around."

The next day Marie apologized for having called so late, but over the coming weeks we had a few more similar conversations about Gene's whereabouts, though they were usually held after the fact. If she saw me on a Saturday morning, for example, she might ask if Gene had been with me the night before. I couldn't lie to her, yet I still felt some residual loyalty to my friend. Or maybe the loyalty wasn't to Gene but to my gender, an allegiance still strong in adolescence. "Was he supposed to be?" I had learned to ask.

She would return my smile. "You just answered me."

But on a night in August this matter took a turn that neither of us could joke about.

I was sound asleep when I heard my name being called, but rather than wake me, the sound insinuated itself into my dream, and in that dream I strained to hear who was summoning me. It seemed as though the voice were faint because it had to travel over a distance not of space but of time, as though someone far in the past or in the future were trying to gain my attention. The voice's persistence finally cracked my slumber, and I woke with the realization that someone was outside my bedroom window.

It was Marie, hissing my name and scratching the screen.

I slept in nothing but my briefs, so I dragged the sheet with me as I got out of bed and crouched down by my window.

More than her presence at that place and time, her somber expression and tear-spangled eyes told me that something was seriously wrong.

"What is it? What's happened?"

"Gene . . ."

"Is he—? What happened?"

She shook her head violently. "I don't know. I don't know. He's . . . I don't know where he is!"

Behind her, every window in every house was curtain-drawn and dark, and the street down which police cars had once careered was empty and quiet. The night was hot and still, and Marie's urgency and distress seemed one with the steamy air.

I glanced back at the clock. It was almost two o'clock. "Can you tell me what happened?"

We both leaned forward, and as she began to whisper to me, her lips were barely more than an inch from mine, but of course the screen was between us.

Gene and Marie had gone out that evening, one of their first dates in weeks, first to a movie and then to Teen Canteen, where they danced until the lights were turned up and the club closed. Her father and mother believed Marie was sleeping at Donna Petracca's house that night, and since Donna's parents wouldn't notice or care when—or if—Marie came in, she and Gene could stay out as late as they liked.

They drove around for a while and then parked behind the museum on the capitol grounds. She didn't tell me what they were doing there, but she didn't have to. I no longer had reports from Gene on how far he was getting with Marie, but I had no reason to think his sexual progress had slowed or halted. She was wearing a sleeveless white blouse that fastened up the back.

She shrugged her shoulders forward, the blouse fell onto the floor of the car, and Gene tossed it into the backseat. He reached behind her and unclasped her brassiere with a deftness that surprised her. Usually he groped clumsily for so long that they both had to make a joke—Mr. Fumble Fingers!—before Marie went ahead and did the job for him. Was it possible that being drunk made him more dexterous rather than less?

So she was naked to the waist as she lay back across the front seat, and that was often enough for him, but this time his hands dove almost immediately for the waistband of her shorts, and rather than try to squeeze his hand inside, he tried to tug them down. She decided to allow it, though when she felt her panties slipping off with her shorts, she reached down to grab them and keep them on.

"Those too," Gene said, his voice so husky the words almost seemed croaked.

In the future when Marie Ryan thought or felt or said she was ready for sex, she would almost always mean nothing more than physiologically ready, and in the front seat of that Ford her body was certainly as ready as it would ever be—her own panting breaths came echoing back to her from the little cavern under the dashboard, and she was moist everywhere with her own heat and the night's. But at sixteen she was not simply a body.

Was it the smell of bourbon on his breath, distressingly similar to her mother's when she would bend over Marie's bed, ostensibly to wish her good night but really to scold Marie once more for that day's minor misdeed? Was it that Gene, in this moment of sexual exigency, had stopped kissing her and his caresses had become unimaginatively monotonous, as if he were counting repetitions before moving on to another part of her body? Was it that her sweating skin was sticking to the upholstery and made a vulgar sucking sound whenever she shifted positions? Was there some symbolism in the location where they were parked that made it impossible for her to relax into the experience? They were secluded behind the museum, yet nearby was the state capitol, at seventeen stories the tallest building for hundreds and hundreds of miles, its rectangular height insistently phallic, its rows of windows inscrutably watchful, and when Marie lifted her hips to let Gene pull her shorts off, she

*tilted her head back and saw—or imagined she saw—the build-
ing and knew that what was happening was within its energy
field. Or did the building cause her to make connections that
could override even the oblivion-inducing ardor of sex? In that
structure a man was murdered. I am practically naked in the
murderer's car. The murderer's son's hand is between my legs—*

Whatever the cause, Marie pushed Gene away—

They had a quarrel, about what, Marie didn't say, but just before Gene walked away, he said, "Maybe my dad had the right
idea."

"Jesus," I said. "Had he been drinking?"

Marie nodded.

"Didn't you go after him?"

"I couldn't. Not right away. When I did, I couldn't find him."

"Maybe he went home."

"I checked. I looked in his window. He's not there. I know
it."

"Did you look"—I swallowed hard before asking this—"in
the garage?"

She nodded again.

"And he walked away from his car?"

"I didn't know if I should drive it or leave it there. Then I decided that where I was going to look for him I couldn't drive. If
he'd walked off into the trees on the capitol grounds, I'd have to
be on foot to find him."

"The trees? Why would he—" Suddenly I realized what she
was telling me: Gene had threatened to hang himself, and the first
opportunity that would present itself would be from the branch
of a tree on the capitol grounds.

Usually no matter how much Gene Stoddard drank, he could keep the world in focus, but as he looked down at the nearly naked Marie Ryan, her outline kept blurring.

My next question was a coldly practical one: "Was he wearing a belt?"

He had the most difficulty with the borders on her body where her tanned flesh gave way to the pallor her swimsuit had created. But sometimes she had the straps down, or they shifted, or she wore longer shorts, or she borrowed a swimsuit from a friend and that allowed the sun to shine where before it had been forbidden, and the lines weren't as sharp as they used to be. And the front seat of the car was dark, and Marie was moving sinuously under his touch and sight, and all that made it still harder to know where something left off and something else began. He could eliminate the problem by closing his eyes, but then even the darkness would shift and sway and he was liable to get sick. Besides, he couldn't get enough of the sight of her— the sudden flash of white as her eyelids fluttered briefly open, the dark circles of her nipples, the faint shadows as her belly sank below her ribs, the brighter swell of her thighs. . . . He had to stare, yet the harder he stared the more unfocused everything became. It reminded him of being in first grade, when he was trying to learn how to read. He knew being able to read would come only from looking at those letters, yet he looked and looked and they would not yield what he needed from them.

It occurred to him then that his difficulty might be arising not from bourbon but from desire, swirling in him like those powerful currents that were said to rule the Missouri just below its murky surface. He unbuckled his belt.

Marie nodded, and with her index finger began to rub her lower lip, a gesture that meant—as I would have ample opportunity to learn in the future—that she was trying not to cry.

"Just a minute. I'll get dressed and come right out."

In my youth I was as modest as they come, yet at that moment I heedlessly dropped the sheet that covered me and reached for the clothes I had thrown onto a chair.

They had done this often enough that Marie knew what he wanted—or thought she did—and reached inside the waistband of his briefs.

"Huh-uh," Gene said. "Not tonight. More. I want more."
He knew that wasn't the way he should say it—it wasn't the way he wanted to say it—yet when he tried to improve it, he only made it worse. "Not with your hand."

She propped herself up on her elbows. "What?"

He pushed her back down. "You know."

And when her eyes closed again and her head lolled to the side, and when she lifted her hips off the seat and let him pull down her shorts, Gene believed he would have what he had to have. But then she grabbed the waistband of her panties to keep them from slipping off with her shorts.

"Those too," he said in a voice that he barely recognized as his own, but before she could answer or act, he lay down on top of her, hoping that his volume, his entire being, pressed down upon her would convey to her the urgency and import that his words couldn't carry.

She lay unmoving under him for so long that Gene wondered if she had fallen asleep. Then it occurred to him that perhaps her stillness was a kind of permission. But he hadn't done anything more than move his hand a few scant inches down her side when she spoke, and she obviously had no trouble locating the language or voice she needed.

"No," Marie Ryan said.

Maybe, he told himself, she was talking out of a dream, and he kept her pinned under his weight.

But another single word issued from her—"Off!"—and this time action accompanied it. Somehow she got her hands between her chest and his and thrust him upward. He had been working on a construction crew that summer, and his own strength had increased significantly. Furthermore, he knew what the repetition of each task—lifting plywood sheets, carrying bricks and buckets of mortar, hoisting lengths of lumber—had done to harden each group of muscles, yet Marie's strength astonished him, and Gene wondered what she had done over and over again in her life to give her the power to push him off her with what seemed to be such ease.

But Gene wasn't about to give up. He knew, however, that if he was going to get what he desired, it would have to be with language. Up until that night Marie had let him have what he wanted, and all he had had to do was reach for it. But now what was he supposed to say? I want to fuck you, screw you, sink my cock into you? That was the vocabulary of his friends, of the men he worked with, and of his own mind, yet he knew that those words would get him nowhere.

Then Gene glanced out the window, and when he did, a better idea occurred to him. A short distance away was the capitol, its height hovering over them as if it were a spaceship slowly landing in that area. He usually tried not to look at the building—next to impossible since it loomed over the city and could be seen from every direction—because he couldn't stop thinking of it as the place where his father's life ended. Gene knew that wasn't literally true—his father died in the garage— but if it weren't for what had happened in the capitol . . .

He opened the car door and stepped out, then bent down and leaned back in. He would have thought she'd cover herself, but she sat up unashamed of her nakedness. Boys in the locker room were more self-conscious about their bodies than Marie Ryan.

"Maybe," he said, "just maybe my dad had the right idea."

He turned then and began to walk away, knowing that she'd call him back, knowing that by the time he climbed back into the car, she'd be lying back down, her panties off, her legs spread as wide as the front seat would allow—

I stayed close to the wall as I crept past my parents' and sister's bedrooms, knowing that the floor could creak and give me away if I walked down the middle. The screen door opened noiselessly, and then I was free, ready to join Marie in her search.

For the first few blocks as we walked, we watched for motion—Gene's form under the light of a streetlamp or his silhouette against a house's white wall or his shadow stretching toward us as he was backlit by the headlights of the occasional car—but once we entered the dark aisles of trees on the capitol grounds, we were on the alert for stillness—his lifeless body hanging from a low branch.

It was Marie's idea that we search separately so we could cover a larger area in less time, and while I didn't argue with her, I wasn't convinced that was the best strategy. I didn't want to be alone when I found him, and I didn't want her to be either. We agreed that we'd shout out for the other if we saw Gene, no matter what his state.

Anyone walking through the North Dakota capitol grounds and its paved arboretum trail today would find the trees widely spaced and clearly labeled. Plaques set into the earth at the base of every bush or tree identify the Russian olive or the ponderosa pine or the Chinese or American elms or the green ash or the cottonwood. But on the night I hunted for my friend, the trees were more thickly planted, and they were simply trees—black vertical shapes whose trunks could be mistaken time and again for the hanging figure of a young man. Although the summer had been dry, the earth was soft and loamy underfoot, and I stumbled more than once because it was impossible to see where I was stepping. I was further slowed by having to walk hunched over, the only posture that allowed me to look upward and distinguish dark forms by examining them against the lighter darkness of the night sky. Had I had any foresight at all, I would have brought a flashlight, but then someone driving past or gazing out a window across the street might have seen a beam of light moving through the trees and called the police. More than once I wondered if that was exactly what we should have done.

Occasionally I could hear Marie, just a corridor or two away from me, and I could tell she was moving much faster than I, but then being in love equips us well for moving blindly through the dark.

Those of you who have been with me for these many pages must possess by now a sense of the man behind these words and of the boy behind that man. It should come as no shock or surprise to learn that I was ambivalent about my friend's possible fate. I can't say that I hoped to find him dead—to contemplate that prospect was not just horrifying and sorrowful but grisly—but I certainly calculated the advantages that might accrue to me if Gene were no longer alive. Marie would require solace, and I would be there to provide it. Furthermore, Gene would no longer block my path to Marie. But I also knew that loss can preserve love forever in a present state—seal it, as it were, in amber—and turn the loved one into a timeless ideal with whom no living human can compete.

After searching for close to two hours and not finding Gene, Marie and I finally gave up. But in a curious application of faith—belief in things unseen, as it is defined in the Old Testament—having not found him, we became convinced that he was dead. If not in the small night forest where we were searching, then hanging from another branch, beam, or rafter for someone else to find. We debated whether we should take his car back to his house, but decided that it would be too upsetting—to say nothing of mysterious—for Mrs. Stoddard to see the Ford parked in the driveway yet with her son nowhere to be found.

Marie wanted to check his house one more time, so we walked together away from the capitol and toward Keogh Street. As we stepped out of the trees and into the light, I dared put my hand on her shoulder, a gesture that I hoped she would read as intended only to comfort.

"God, your hand's sweaty," she said, and I took it away.

We were crossing Keogh, still a couple blocks from Gene's house and mine, when a car approached. I've often wondered, since Marie and I turned toward the car simultaneously, what she saw and heard that caused her to begin running immediately toward its headlights. However, I too must have soon perceived the truth of the situation, because I never called out or ran after her, even when the car kept coming at her.

It was Gene, and by the time the car pulled alongside me, Marie was already inside. I looked in the open passenger window and saw that she was practically curled into his lap, and Gene had one hand on the steering wheel and the other arm casually draped around her. Marie's face was turned from me, but I guessed tears of joy and relief were staining his shirt.

"Hey, man," Gene said. "You want a ride?" It was difficult to imagine that anyone so cheerful might have been considered capable of suicide.

I shook my head and waved them on their way. They didn't try to argue with me but sped off. I stood and watched the Ford's taillights until they disappeared around the dip and curve that Keogh Street makes where it intersects with Cooke Avenue. Then I walked home, but when I got there I didn't go inside.

Instead I sat on our front porch step. From there I could see when Gene returned home, no matter which direction he came from, yet it was unlikely he would notice me keeping my vigil. Time passed slowly, and every hour Gene didn't appear made the next hour longer.

Dawn finally came, light suffusing the block so subtly and gradually that even the most attentive observer would have found it impossible to name the instant when darkness gave in to day. One moment the numbers on the house across the street couldn't be read, and the next moment there they were. Preceding any visible glow was the chirp and twitter of birds, but they were soon in full-throated song, gloating or sighing that they had made it through another night. Gene had still not driven past, and that fact alone provided me with all the information I needed. I gave up and returned to my bed.

⌒

I tried many times to write a story about that night, but every effort frustrated me. Because there was so much backstory—the film term that my writing students invariably use when referring to almost anything in the past—I finally decided to limit the narrative by concentrating on what happened in the car between the two lovers, to write, in other words, a seduction story. Neither the male nor the female quite worked as the focus of narration, so I alternated points of view. Still the story wasn't what I hoped it would be. Perhaps, as so often happens in life, the present has too little meaning when it's not attached to the past, the past with its power to clarify and distill. And perhaps that story was simply not meant to be because it was willed into existence—over and over again—not by a desire to make something artful and true but by a compulsion to lacerate myself with my own imagination.

⌒

But while the Ford's absence that night and early morning took on such importance in my psyche, the car's actual appearance had, for another viewer, significance of quite a different sort. A friend of my father's believed it explained Monty Burnham's murder.

As law students at the University of North Dakota, Ross

Wilk and my father roomed together, and while both eventually found themselves practicing law in Bismarck, Ross Wilk was a more financially successful attorney than my father. Mr. Wilk did a great deal of work for the oil companies that swarmed over the state in the 1950s, and though the boom didn't last long, by the time it was over, Ross Wilk was a wealthy man and a partner in one of the city's top law firms. He would gladly have brought my father into the practice, but my father always refused, citing as reason not his stubborn independence but that he didn't "look good in a cowboy hat." The remark made sense only to those familiar with Ross Wilk's appearance and then only barely. Ross Wilk wore expensive, hand-tooled boots and wide-brimmed Stetsons, attire that wasn't—and isn't—especially unusual in Bismarck. (In his *Travels with Charley,* John Steinbeck said that the West began at the Missouri River, and Bismarck was built on the river's eastern bank.) Ross Wilk, however, had no Western roots or cowboy experiences in his past. He came from a small town in northwestern Minnesota where his father had been a dentist. But he knew, in a way my father never did, how a persona could be shaped and projected for one's personal gain. An insider in state and local politics, Ross Wilk had considerable influence in both circles (largely through the Republican party). My father generally trusted his friend's take on issues, believing they were arrived at by Mr. Wilk's keen intellect and by his access to information that most citizens didn't have.

Once or twice a year my parents had the Wilks over for dinner, and that was the occasion that brought Ross Wilk to our living room on a warm October day in 1961, nine months after Monty Burnham's murder. Mr. Wilk looked down the street and saw the Stoddards' Ford outside their house, and at the sight of the car, Ross Wilk tapped his index finger against our window. Along with his hat and boots, Ross Wilk affected a kind of Gary Cooper laconism, and he turned to my father (the wives were in the kitchen) and simply said, "There's your answer."

The men had not been talking about Raymond Stoddard or Monty Burnham, and Ross Wilk's comment was made without preamble, but in Bismarck during that period—and nowhere was this more true than on Keogh Street—that subject was close enough to the surface of every conversation that it needed no introduction. Neither did Ross Wilk need any encouragement to give voice to his theory.

"For some reason when I learned that Raymond Stoddard had recently purchased a new Ford, I kept thinking that had to be important. I just didn't know how. And then when I had a talk with the governor, who was mad as hell about the prices Bob Borglund was charging to make repairs on state vehicles, it all started to make sense."

Robert Borglund owned a very successful Ford-Mercury dealership in Bismarck, and for years he had the contract for providing—and servicing—vehicles to the state. The arrangement seemed to work to everyone's satisfaction until North Dakota elected a Democrat as governor. Then George Bartell, the new governor, found out that Borglund Ford-Mercury was charging the state exorbitant rates for routine repairs to its vehicles. When the governor began to look into that irregularity, he discovered an even greater one: The state was not receiving a particularly favorable price when it purchased its new cars.

Now what state agency, Ross Wilk wondered, would be able

to find out what the bill was for a new car? Why, Accounts and Purchases, of course, the department that employed Raymond Stoddard. And who would notice that what the state paid for a new Ford was out of line? An employee who had recently bought a car for himself, that's who. And that employee might then point out this discrepancy to his superior, who in turn would report it to the governor.

Furthermore, the governor learned that the connection between the state's purchase of new Fords and state politicians was even tighter than first suspected. Robert Borglund was not only a heavy contributor to the Republican party, he was often mentioned as a future candidate for political office, perhaps the governorship. He was ambitious and wealthy; he was comfortable in front of the cameras (he appeared in all his own television commercials for Borglund Ford-Mercury); and he came across as confident, cheerful, honest, and direct. He was, in other words, a man cut from the same cloth as Monty Burnham.

According to Ross Wilk, the men were more than similar personality types. They shared a political philosophy built on thrift, self-reliance, patriotism, and tough attitudes toward criminals and foreign governments. In practical terms most of these lofty values translated into little more than attempts to keep taxes low, to balance budgets, and to reject social programs. Both Monty Burnham and Bob Borglund liked to pretend—or perhaps they believed—that they had risen to stature and success on nothing more than strength of character and hard work. In truth, both men stepped into prosperous, established family businesses, and the businesses were the same—selling cars, specifically Fords.

Ross Wilk believed that Monty Burnham had somehow influ-

enced the system that awarded the contract for state vehicles—
sales and service—to Borglund Ford-Mercury. Bob Borglund returned the favor by donating generously to Burnham's campaigns
and by sharing a portion of the state contract with Burnham Mo-
tors (also a Ford dealership), all on an unofficial basis, of course.
And once again, Ross Wilk pointed out, a man with a new car
(purchased at Borglund Ford-Mercury), a man who worked in
the state's Accounts and Purchases department, would be the one
likely to discover and then unravel these strands of corruption.

But if this man had his own connection to Senator Burnham—as Raymond Stoddard had—then he could perhaps be
brought in on the plot. So instead of an employee who informed
his superior of the corruption, there's someone who, by virtue of
his position in Accounts and Purchases, was able to contribute
to the scheme. He could hide or alter documents, manipulate
figures—he'd be a perfect partner. And maybe it was no recent
discovery. Maybe it had gone on for years, an operation successful because many people benefited—maybe Raymond Stoddard's
new Ford was a payment for his participation—and so few people were harmed. Who would have thought this new governor
would get so worked up over something as minor as what the
state was being charged for an oil change? One discovery leads to
another, and before long you have a man taking his own life to
avoid the humiliation of being uncovered as a crook. And, Ross
Wilk concluded, he takes down with him the fellow who talked
him into being a part of the plot. Or maybe he wants to put a bullet in the good senator because he knows that the senator will sell
him out to save his own hide.

"I'm not convinced," my father said.

"Because the man was your friend, and you don't want to believe it of him. But people don't commit murder for noble reasons. And they kill themselves out of desperation. Shame. Even embarrassment. You know that."

"It just doesn't feel right."

"Feel? What do feelings have to do with anything? What would old Professor Saint Clair say if he heard you talking like that? Evidence. Logic. Reasoning. That's how guilt and innocence are determined. If you like, I can keep digging. I have no doubt the evidence is out there."

"Not necessary," my father said, waving his hands at his old friend as if in surrender. "Not necessary."

Later that evening, after our guests had gone home, my father summoned my mother and me to the living room. My mother was in the midst of putting away the good china she had used for that day's meal, and ordinarily she would have preferred to finish that task, but something in my father's voice must have told her this matter couldn't wait.

He sat back in his overstuffed chair while my mother and I perched on the edge of the sofa's cushions. He related Ross Wilk's theory about the plot to overcharge the state, and with Raymond featured as a willing accomplice it was a convincing presentation. Nevertheless, as my father finished talking, he wore the same distressed look as when he had begun.

My mother, on the other hand, received this latest hypothesis with a mixture of exuberance and relief. "Well, that's as plausible as anything I've heard," she said.

"I suppose."

"What's wrong? You act as if you're disappointed. Why—because you didn't crack the case? You and your detective friend?"

Her remark struck me as cruel, yet my father didn't flinch or attempt to defend himself.

In the absence of any further comment from my father, my mother turned to me and volunteered her own explanation of where we had now arrived. "This is exactly why your father gets in trouble with some of his cases. He identifies too much with his client, and then when the verdict doesn't come out the way they'd hoped, he takes it personally."

She rose and walked over to sit on the arm of my father's chair, leaning her weight seductively against him and running her fingers through his hair. He stared straight ahead. "You probably thought," my mother continued, "that your dad was only interested in finding out the truth of that awful day. What you didn't know, what none of us knew, was that he had taken on Raymond Stoddard as a client. An unwilling client, of course. Since Raymond was dead, he was in no position to retain counsel. But in your father Raymond had a devoted advocate, an attorney working pro bono. Not only without pay but without even being asked. And an attorney who wouldn't be satisfied with any verdict except one that found his client innocent."

Without saying another word, my father pushed himself to his feet and stalked out of the room.

For another moment my mother remained balanced on the arm of the chair, and the fingers that had been combing my father's thinning hair now scratched at the chair's nubby upholstery. "I guess I got a little too close," she said, and I knew she wasn't talking about physical proximity. Then she rose too and left the living room, but while my father had gone down the hall toward the bedrooms, she went back to her kitchen.

If I hadn't known it before, that scene between my parents tried to teach me the lesson: Lies can unsettle us and send us angrily from the room, but the truth can do the same.

⁓

Because time seems to have speeded up—and if it seems so, isn't it so?—you feel as though you must act swiftly. Were you not so pressed for time, perhaps you would evaluate your options carefully, and with that care you might be more realistic. Instead, once you happen upon a workable strategy, you must commit to it unequivocally.

For that reason you decide early on that it will be necessary to take your own life. You contemplated life in prison only for a moment, and perhaps not even for that long. You recalled a Sunday drive in the country, a mild March day when uncharacteristic warmth bumped against the cold of unmelted snow and a fog rose that made mid-afternoon as dusky as, well, dusk. The car swept around a curve and there it was—the state penitentiary, its walls burning their way blackly through the vapor, its stone towers too solid for a mist to cover. That was enough. Though on that day guilt had not yet encumbered your life, you stored away a realization unrealized until now—you could never handle life in prison. Not for a year and certainly not for ten.

Besides, it might be that your suicide will be regarded not as an admission of guilt, an attempt to escape the inescapable, but as an expression of frustration and exhaustion—because he couldn't convince the world of his innocence, he took the only way out available to him.

But you are not innocent. Oh, no. Even in those moments when you treat yourself most gently, when you interpret your actions as generously as possible, even in the depth of self-pity or at the height of indignation and self-justification, you still must admit: You are guilty.

When your brother-in-law/old friend/former classmate came to you with the scheme to fix prices/misappropriate funds/embezzle/steal/conspire, you knew what was being asked of you. Yes, yes; he talked you into it. Nothing was your idea, not initially. Only when you became necessary to a successful outcome, only then did you contribute what only you could contribute. But right from the start you knew. You knew and you assented. No matter that you were a minor (but essential) functionary in the plan; that role only adds pathos to your guilt; it does nothing to absolve you.

Odd, how familiar it all is. Until recently, you've led a fairly respectable life, you've committed no previous criminal acts, yet this feeling of being ensnared, guilty, caught, trapped, culpable, is one you know. You took fifty cents from your mother's purse. You stole a pack of your father's cigarettes. You lied and told your girlfriend you wouldn't be there, but then you were and so was she. The teacher compared your answers and your friend's and found them the same. You denied, you dissembled, you cheated, you pilfered, you pretended. . . . And you were caught. The scale so different, the potatoes so small, yet the feeling the same, as if now you are fulfilling your entire life's promise, fi-

nally enacting what you have rehearsed so long. Though now it may be the police/congressional committee/investigative journalist/government agent closing in on you, it feels no different from trudging home from grade school when you knew the phone call from the principal would arrive before you. It seemed then, as now, that the world was about to end.

Now you know of course that it will be over only for you. Or . . . ?

It's the only question that remains. Should you take your brother-in-law/old friend/former classmate/colleague out with you? To do so would be murder, an act of rage, retribution, revenge, or, less grandly, of petulance, but murder without question. Yet it would also contain an element of justice. It's quite possible that your death will end the investigation, close the case, stop the proceedings. Once, after all, a guilty party is identified and found, no one feels quite the same need to uncover another. So, who, if not you, can guarantee punishment to the blameworthy? In this you may well have a mission, a meaning, a reason for being that you never had when your life was innocently your own. . . .

That story, if it can be called that, was published in *Epiphanies,* another now-defunct publication. It was one of the longest pieces ever to appear in the avant-garde magazine; many of the "discoveries and revelations," as the editors said they featured in their pages, were no more than a paragraph. The story's McInerney-fashionable (at the time) second-person point of view probably gave it special appeal to the *Epiphanies* staff, but its source, of course, was that conversation between Ross Wilk and my father when Mr. Wilk speculated that in the corruption of the workplace Raymond Stoddard's murderous intention was born.

⌒

It would not be accurate to say that I was able to observe an actual lightening of my mother's spirit after the Wilks' visit, but I think it's fair to say that Mr. Wilk's rendition of the murder-suicide and what led to it satisfied my mother. I never again heard her express any curiosity about those awful circumstances, and if she didn't broadcast the Wilk theory to others, it was only because she didn't believe it was hers to share.

My father, on the other hand, resisted his friend's interpretation and, to some extent, actively lobbied against it. I know because I was one of those he tried to dissuade from believing that Raymond Stoddard murdered Monty Burnham and then killed himself because he was involved in a political scandal.

Every Halloween my father tried to organize his family for an evening of jack-o'-lantern decorating, an activity for which only he had any aptitude or enthusiasm. That year, however, I, unlike my mother and sister, was unable to come up with an excuse in time and so found myself sitting at the kitchen table alongside my father, both of us up to our elbows in pumpkin innards.

He introduced the subject of Ross Wilk as abruptly as Mr. Wilk had begun talking about Raymond Stoddard just a few weeks earlier.

"Ross Wilk is a helluva bright man," my father said, "but he's making the mistake a lot of people make. Just because something happens in a particular location doesn't necessarily mean the location has anything to do with it. They see Monty Burnham being murdered in the capitol as important, and since the capitol is a government building, they think the murder must have to do with politics. But for legislators and state employees it's the place they work, simple as that. Raymond knew Senator Burnham was in the building. Nothing more to it, as far as I'm concerned. If you want an explanation of why, you can't allow yourself to be distracted with where."

My father was not being disingenuous; he believed that. But another set of beliefs was also at work in him and leading him away from Ross Wilk's account. My father didn't want place to figure at all in what Raymond Stoddard had done because my father wanted to dissociate his city and state from the crime.

Although he didn't belong to any service organizations—no membership in the Kiwanis Club or the Rotary Club—and though he found embarrassingly superficial and hollow the Babbittry of many of the community's and state's boosters, my father took second place to no one in his love for North Dakota. He cherished its homesteading heritage of hard work and stoicism, its paradoxical high-plains ethic of both self-reliance and neighborliness, its lack of pretense, and its unspoken credo of honesty and forthright plain speech. He was neither hunter nor fisherman, but he loved the state's empty, almost featureless spaces, its shadowed valleys and sunlit prairies. Even North Dakota's fabled extremes of weather were for my father nothing but the tests that made us all stronger for having passed them. He couldn't stand the thought that people might see a connection between the state he loved and its most famous crime. It was bad enough that he and Raymond Stoddard and Monty Burnham shared a hometown—tainted forever by the murder—but he hoped that attempts to determine cause would concentrate on the murderer's psyche and not the place where he pulled the trigger.

I sympathized with my father's position, but I couldn't agree with it. I feebly believed at the time—and time has only firmed my belief—that what happens can't be pulled apart from where.

If we had been carving our pumpkins fifteen years in the future, my father's jack-o'-lantern might have been characterized as wearing a Jimmy Carter grin. As it was, I couldn't help but look at that horizontal, symmetrical smile and think of a Ford's small-toothed grille.

~

Every year the lawyer's wife suggested that he draw the face on the pumpkin before he began to carve, but he always disregarded her advice. Instead he proceeded freestyle, cutting into the hollowed-out pumpkin with one of his tools of choice, a fish fileting knife or an old paring knife, both of which could be sharpened to a razor's edge. Once the jack-o'-lantern's first features took shape—a wolfish smile, an astonished eye, a flared nostril—he invented from that beginning, sometimes letting an accidental slice dictate the entire design. It was as close as he came to improvisation, to art, or perhaps even to spontaneity. Certainly nothing in his professional life—his specialty was advising oil companies on how to deal with western states' land use policies and regulations—allowed him to act without a well-defined sense of outcome and consequence.

The telephone rang, and though it was only a few feet from where he sat at the kitchen table, he called out to his wife to an-

*swer it. In explanation he held up his hands, still wet and slip-
pery from scooping out the pumpkin's stringy pulp.*

She had been engrossed in an episode of Ben Casey, *but she
rose from her chair in the living room and soon held out the
phone to him, mouthing the words, "It's Lee."*

*It was not a call the lawyer wanted to take, but he felt he
had no choice. While he washed his hands, his wife patiently
dangled the phone from its cord as if it were an object she didn't
want to bring near her mouth or ear. Just before he took it from
her, she whispered, "He wants to ask for a favor." Then she left
the kitchen and returned to her television program.*

"Lee. What can I do for you?"

*"I hate to take you out of your house on a night like this"—
the day had not been only cold, but once the sun had set, the
wind occasionally tore loose a shower of fine-grained snow—
"but I could sure use a hand. Can I get you down here?"*

*The lawyer sighed, hoping the sound traveled through the
wire. He knew he would say yes to the request, but he wanted
Lee Mauer to hear his reluctance. "Can you give me a clue,
Lee?"*

"It's not something I'm eager to discuss over the phone."

*The lawyer might have been puzzled, even worried, if some-
one else had made that statement, but Lee Mauer, a former police lieutenant, never missed an opportunity to dramatize or add
intrigue to almost any situation. "I'll be there in a few minutes."*

"Just come in the back door. I'm in the basement."

*Since he was only crossing the street and walking a few
houses down the block, the lawyer didn't bother with a jacket.*

And he was familiar with the home he was visiting. His friend Raymond Stoddard had lived there until he had taken his own life the previous January, but it was still home to Raymond's wife and son. Lee Mauer originally began visiting the house, in the lawyer's company, to help the widow with yard work and light household repairs, but the lawyer's wife believed that a romantic—and sexual—relationship had now developed between Mrs. Stoddard and the former police officer. The lawyer, however, seldom committed himself to belief without substantial evidence.

Although he was uncomfortable walking into the house without knocking or ringing the bell, the lawyer did as Lee Mauer requested. Just inside the door, however, the lawyer called out, "Hello?"

From the darkened stairway came a feeble "Down here."

The Stoddard basement was only partially finished. The laundry and storage rooms, separated by only a wall of widely spaced two-by-fours, had concrete walls and floors and exposed ceiling joists. Before his death, however, Raymond Stoddard had made progress on a recreation room. He had installed ceiling acoustical tiles and recessed lights, and he had laid flooring with the markings for a shuffleboard court. On one paneled wall was a gun rack, though Raymond Stoddard owned no guns himself. Protruding from another wall were the pipes that were supposed to connect to the fixtures of a future wet bar.

In spite of Raymond's plans for the room, it had, as basements inevitably do, gone over to storage. The lawyer was sure that the cardboard boxes, the mildew-spotted suitcases, the dresser missing a few drawer pulls, and the cedar chest were all *full. Similar items in his own basement certainly were. Positioned almost in the center of the room was a space heater, its bars glowing orange and giving off the odor of hot dust. The appliance must have been running for hours. The basement was so warm that the lawyer felt immediately the onset of sweat prickling at his hairline.*

And in a darkened corner, lying flat on his back on a rollaway bed's bare mattress, was Lee Mauer. Mauer was wearing nothing but briefs, yellowed with age, and above the waistband rose the great mound of his belly, a shape like an overturned bowl. His stomach, chest, and shoulders were thickly covered with dark hair, and the pink nipples peeking through the thatch were an incongruous sight, looking as though they belonged on the body of a woman in an oil painting from another century. His round face was moist and flushed, and though he smiled at the lawyer, pain lined his forehead.

"Thanks for coming."

"What can I do for you, Lee?"

"My back's gone out." He twisted his lips as though the words themselves hurt.

"I'm sorry to hear that."

Mauer weakly waved away the lawyer's sympathy. "It's happened to me for years. There's a doctor who thinks he can fix it, but that'd mean surgery. You know me—no knives."

In fact, the lawyer didn't know Mauer well at all, and the revelations about both the man's back problems and his dread of surgery came as news to the lawyer.

"Usually," Mauer continued, "if I just take it easy for a couple days, the pain eases and then I'm okay until the next time it

happens. Not that I have any choice in the matter. I can't do much more than lie flat."

"Okay." The lawyer was not a fastidious man—he had, after all, recently had his hands covered with pumpkin slime— but he guessed that Lee Mauer was going to ask for his help in getting dressed and moving, perhaps up the stairs, and the lawyer wasn't eager to put his arms around the fat man's sweaty body.

"So there's some things I just can't do for myself when I'm in this condition. Goddamnit."

All right, here it comes, thought the lawyer.

"If you'd drive my car, I'd sure appreciate it."

The lawyer wasn't prepared for that request, but then he was thrown further off balance by something that hadn't oc-curred to him earlier. If Lee Mauer couldn't get up, how had he made the telephone call that brought the lawyer to where he now stood?

"Your car, Lee?"

"It's in the driveway."

"I saw it. . . ." But the lawyer would have to use his own car to take Mauer home, wouldn't he? Unless Lee wanted the lawyer to keep Mauer's car until he was up and around. And while the lawyer was trying to puzzle through this matter, the answer to an earlier question was provided. Just under the roll-away was the black shape of a telephone, and from under the foot of the bed snaked the telephone cord. The long cord ran to a wall where it was plugged into a phone jack, not secured but hanging from the outlet by its wires. Raymond, Raymond, to leave with so much undone . . .

Mauer said, "I wouldn't want the neighbors to see the car here all night."

Would the neighbors be likely to conclude something if they saw the car parked there at seven A.M. that they didn't conclude now when they saw it late at night? The lawyer supposed they would. After all, he had withheld his own judgment until, as he put it, all the evidence was in.

Just at that moment, as if she had read his thoughts on matters of proof, Alma Stoddard walked into the room. She was wearing an old flannel bathrobe, and from the way her breasts moved beneath the worn fabric, the lawyer guessed that she was naked under the robe. He also surmised that she had been in the room recently, and that its warmth was what had caused tendrils of her hair to stick to her perspiring forehead.

"His back . . . ," Alma said. She crossed her arms and held her elbows. "If you could just . . ."

The lawyer held up his hands. "It's not a problem."

She smiled gratefully and then, to save them both further embarrassment, hurried from the room. Perhaps she had made an appearance as a way of confessing to the nature of her relationship with Lee Mauer. Your life is your own, the lawyer would have said to her; you live it as you see fit. You don't owe me any explanations.

As soon as she was gone, Lee Mauer said, "I was thinking you could just park the car a couple blocks away. In the lot over at First Presbyterian, maybe. Then if I'm up and around tomorrow, I'll go get it. You wouldn't even have to come back here. You could just leave the keys on top of the right rear passenger tire. An old cop trick . . ."

The lawyer wondered what kind of trick that was supposed to be, but he didn't ask. Just as he didn't ask why Alma couldn't drive the car.

"Where are your keys, Lee?" The lawyer preferred to get on with the mission and return to his home. He planned to describe this scene to his wife and allow her the satisfaction of having her suspicions confirmed.

"Pants pocket." He pointed to the clothing draped over a rocking chair with a torn cane seat.

The lawyer picked up the trousers and carried them to Lee Mauer.

Before he turned the car keys over to the lawyer, Lee Mauer separated them from the rest of the keys on the chain. Holding out the keys, he said, "Park it under the light, if you can."

The lawyer was able to leave the car just where he had been instructed to park it, but before he reached inside the wheel well to put the keys on top of the tire, he surveyed the area. Most of the nearby houses were dark, and where there was a lighted window, he saw no human form looking out. When he was as certain as he could possibly be that he was not observed, he left the keys and walked away. Snow was falling continuously now, and though the flakes were still widely spaced and airy, by morning the car would be veiled in white.

There were two routes he could take back to his home and his waiting pumpkins. He could walk north and then east, staying on sidewalks all the way, until he came to his own block, or he could plot a diagonal course, which would allow him to come up through the Stoddards' backyard. That was the most tempting because it would allow him to peer into the basement where Lee Mauer lay and where, perhaps, he and Alma had resumed their sexual frolic. After all, for what other reason would Lee insist that the lawyer not bring the car keys back to the house?

But the lawyer had not traveled far in that direction when a number of thoughts stopped him. And it was not just his twined senses of pride and propriety that held him back. Enough snow had fallen that his footsteps across the lawn would be revealed, and he couldn't do anything to cover or conceal his tracks. Besides, Lee Mauer's injury, Alma Stoddard's sweaty forehead— whatever the act they had been engaged in, they were doubtless finished by now. And if not, Lee's back would prevent them from resuming.

So the lawyer took the longer route, staying on the sidewalks that still held enough of the day's heat that the snow couldn't accumulate on the concrete. He wished now that he had worn a coat. The web of dark hair covering Lee Mauer's torso probably would have done as much to keep out the cold as the lawyer's white shirt did.

Besides, even if the lawyer had indulged in that brief voyeuristic impulse, even if he had looked in that window and seen Lee and Alma naked again on that narrow bed, the sight wouldn't have satisfied his real curiosity about those two. He may not have been particularly knowledgeable or sophisticated when it came to sexual practices, but neither was he naïve; he was aware of a range of carnal activities that men and women could engage in, some more likely than others to cause a man's back to go out. But the question that most tormented the lawyer couldn't be answered by peeking through a window.

*What truly perplexed him had to do with the fully clothed Lee
Mauer and Alma Stoddard. How could a fat, bald cop, a loud,
vulgar man with two chins and no charm persuade an attractive
woman—a woman less than a year into her grief—to disrobe
and . . . and . . . what? To love him?*

*Once the lawyer's house came into view, he picked up his
pace to hurry toward its warmth. On his block, from front
porches and kitchen windows, his neighbors' jack-o'-lanterns
grinned, leered, or stared in cross-eyed disbelief at him as he
passed. His own pumpkins were of course still without expression. He had gotten no further than cutting open their skulls
and scooping out the tangled mess inside.*

~

That story eventually appeared in *The North Coast Fiction Review.* My father is, of course, the model for the lawyer protagonist, and Lee Mauer (Ken Crowder in the fiction) did injure his
back and call on my father for assistance. That incident occurred
not on Halloween but in the week before Christmas, and beyond
the fact that my father returned home shaken, I never knew what
happened when he went to Lee Mauer's aid. If he told my mother,
she never told me.

~

A little more than a year after I sat in an almost empty First
Lutheran Church for Raymond Stoddard's funeral, I attended another ceremony in the same building. Once again, few were present, and again, a Stoddard was the reason we were gathered. This
time, however, the sparse turnout was predictable. Alma Stod-

dard had not invited many people to witness her marriage to Lee Mauer. Furthermore she must have decided that since it wouldn't be possible to keep her dead husband out of people's thoughts, she might as well go ahead and recite her vows in front of the same altar where his coffin had been so recently stationed.

And those of us there . . . I have no doubt we all spent our time in the pews in the same manner—by trying to determine what had been in Alma Stoddard's heart and mind in the days, weeks, and months leading up to the wedding. What, we wondered, moved her to say yes to Lee Mauer's proposal? Among the countless varieties of human love was there one that explained what the widow of a murderer and a suicide might have felt for a fat policeman?

For her part, my mother didn't believe affection of any kind was involved. When she learned of the impending marriage, she had a simple explanation.

"She needs protection," my mother had said.

My father scoffed. "In Bismarck? On Keogh Street? Protection from what? From whom?"

"You're a man," my mother answered. "I wouldn't expect you to understand."

"Enlighten me."

"If you're lying in bed alone at night, and you hear something, it's no help to tell yourself there's nothing to be afraid of. You feel what you feel. And perhaps for Alma, having Lee Mauer beside her is preferable to having that feeling."

As he had in his conversation with Ross Wilk, my father rejected someone's theory of human motivation. And again, he had no formulation of his own to put in its place, for when my mother pressed him—"All right, then. You tell me. What's behind this? Has your friend taken you into his confidence? You seem awfully incurious about the upcoming nuptials."

My father answered with a question of his own. "Is that what you've felt, when I've been out of town? Afraid?"

"I'm not Alma Stoddard," my mother said, thereby ending both lines of inquiry.

I wasn't sure why my parents insisted that I attend the wedding. Perhaps it was a desperate attempt to swell the congregation. Perhaps they wanted to bring home to me, through the unmistakable parallelism of the two Stoddard rites, a lesson about the cycles of human life. If that was the case, it was wasted on me. I did observe that after the funeral and the wedding, similar fare—ham sandwiches and date bars—was served in the church basement, but I had no insight into the nature of the rituals that attended grief and joy.

After only a few minutes of milling around at the reception, Gene nudged me and asked, "Want to grab a smoke?"

I seldom smoked, and Gene and I had reached the point where we rarely said more to each other than a passing hello in the halls at school, but I followed him out of the fellowship room. How could I refuse him on the day when his mother had married a substitute for his father?

It was too cold to go outside, so we made our way over to another section of the church basement, the darkened wing where we had both once attended Sunday school classes.

Inside the boys' lavatory, with its undersize porcelain fixtures for its undersize patrons, Gene offered me a Camel. We lit up and before I had taken my first timid drag, he asked his question.

"Would you be my best man?"

Since my father had just served as Lee Mauer's best man, I assumed that Gene was asking me a hypothetical question, that the occasion had revived in him some of the affections of our once-close friendship, but I hadn't even formed a response on that basis when Gene added, "Marie's late."

I thought Gene meant that Marie was supposed to attend the wedding—I had wondered about her absence—but that her tardiness had caused her to miss the ceremony.

"And she's never late."

Struck suddenly by the full force of what Gene was telling me, it was all I could do to stop myself from saying what a naïve, self-deceiving, heartbroken parent might say—*how could this happen?*—as if the only consolation left was in learning that it was the result of a single, mindless, aberrant moment.

But Gene addressed the matter without my question, not that his response offered any satisfaction. "I don't even know how the hell it happened. . . ."

"Oh, come on."

"Really. We hardly even—Oh, what the hell." As long as I had known him, Gene had had a nervous little habit of tugging at a lock of his hair right at the hairline. When he did that now with the same hand that held the cigarette, I expected to hear the sizzle of burning hair. But, deftly, he managed the maneuver by pinching his hair with his thumb and little finger. "If that's the way it is," he said, in a phrase I had never heard him use before, "that's the way it is."

I knew I was supposed to commiserate with him and his predicament, but at that moment it was my own anguish I was concerned with. As coolly as I could, I said, "So, when's the wedding?"

Smoke tumbled out of his mouth with his sardonic laugh. "How about as soon as I get out of the hospital? Because that's probably where I'll end up if her old man finds out I knocked up his daughter. Unless he has a heart attack before he can kick my ass."

"Jesus, I don't envy you." In truth, I would have traded places with him in an instant. Even if a beating were a part of the exchange.

"Yeah, and then good old Lieutenant Mauer would probably want to get his licks in because I'd have upset his precious new bride."

Gene backed up and wedged himself into the space between the sink and the towel dispenser, a position that was doubtless a physical analogue for how cornered he felt in his life.

"How far along is she?" It may have seemed the most natural thing to ask, but I was still desperate to hear something that would make this news easier to bear—*I know exactly how pregnant she is because I got her drunk and raped her on*—

"Fuck if I know. She's supposed to keep shit like that figured out."

"You don't sound like you're ready to be a daddy."

"Ready? I haven't even . . . Yeah. Raymond Stoddard's kid has a kid. . . . What a fucking joke."

"And this is for sure? You're getting married for sure?"

He scraped the ashes from his cigarette on the edge of the sink. "If she told me she wanted to go to the Florence Crittendon Home, I sure as hell wouldn't argue. Or if she'd go live with her sister in Minneapolis and have the kid there. Or if she'd just . . . Hell, I don't know."

That did it. When Gene spoke of his wish to escape from a predicament I would have given anything to be in—I became enraged.

Anger, however, almost always renders me inarticulate, and I couldn't come up with anything more to say than, "Find another goddamn best man." A part of me must have sensed how inadequate that line was, because I accompanied it with a gesture, and for once action and intention matched. I flicked my cigarette at Gene, and the butt struck his lapel, spraying sparks down the front of his suit.

Maybe, I thought, as I walked out of the lavatory, the next time he puts on his suit—on his and Marie's wedding day, perhaps—he'll see a burn mark or two and remember this occasion.

But as I was walking home from the church in the glittering January sunlight, after having told my parents that I was leaving, I realized that Gene probably didn't have any idea why I was angry. Why would he? I'd certainly never told him how I felt about Marie, and nothing in our shared history would lead him to believe that I was the sort to become furious over his unchivalrous attitude. Then again, he was Raymond Stoddard's son, and no training in the world could have better prepared him for the irrational behavior of others.

⌒

Lee Mauer not only married Raymond Stoddard's wife and moved into Raymond's house, like Raymond he brought the sound of sirens to Keogh Street.

This happened a few years after I moved from my parents' home, but my sister remembered the incident vividly. Late on a Saturday night she was in the bathroom, scrubbing off her makeup and trying to stop singing to herself the songs from *Brigadoon,* the fall musical put on by Bismarck High School and in which she had performed.

The water was running, and that may have prevented her from hearing the siren earlier, but once she did, she knew it was coming toward Keogh Street. I didn't disbelieve her account, but my sister sometimes tries to wring more drama from a moment than it actually holds. She is also prone to claiming powers of prescience that are nothing more than a storyteller's hindsight.

But whether my sister's premonition at the time was fictional or authentic, the siren was real and fast approaching. And just as it had years before, the ambulance pulled up to the Stoddard house. But this time, my sister noted, when it sped away, its siren was wailing as loudly as when it had arrived.

Lee Mauer had had a heart attack, and as so often happens, there had been clues that such an event could occur and they had been ignored. For weeks he had been experiencing bouts of nausea, excessive sweating, and pain in his chest, in his neck, and between his shoulder blades. Like many men, however, he rejected the seriousness of his symptoms and treated himself with Bromo-Seltzer. But that night his heart clenched for good, and Lee Mauer was dead by the time the ambulance arrived at the hospital.

Alma Stoddard Mauer would once again sleep alone, but she was not the only woman on Keogh Street who had her bed to herself. When the siren came for Lee Mauer, the sound did not disturb my father's rest. He was sleeping 140 miles away in Wembley in the house that had once belonged to his parents and where he was then living with his brother.

My parents first separated, or so they both told it, when my father began traveling frequently to Wembley to assist his brother with a project that required a lawyer's skills. Uncle Burt had decided that the land that was his parents' homestead when they first came to North Dakota should be restored to the family. With my father's assistance, my uncle determined where the original house and acreage had been, and he negotiated to buy the property from its present owners. Before long, the brothers were working to remodel the dilapidated farmhouse where their parents had briefly lived before they'd moved into town.

Gradually more and more of my father's life was spent in the town he grew up in. Along with the small farm, he and his brother owned the house in Wembley, and after a time they were both living in the rooms that had been theirs as boys. Through that small real estate venture with the homestead, my father found other work in and around Wembley, and soon his services were more in demand there than in Bismarck. (I should add here that just as I was no longer living on Keogh Street when Lee Mauer died, neither did I make my home there when my father's relocation became permanent. His business trips to Wembley started when I was in college, and we never again dwelt under the same roof.) But had the advantages of my father relocating to his hometown been only financial, my parents would have found a different solution. My mother and sister would have moved to Wembley, if not immediately, then upon my sister's graduation from high school. Or my father would have said his Bismarck income was sufficient. No, something else kept him in Wembley and apart from his wife of twenty-plus years.

But neither of my parents ever talked much about the dissolution of their marriage, and when they did, it was only in the most general way. Their silence on the subject added more mystery to the way life was once lived on Keogh Street, that stretch of houses that had—pre–Raymond Stoddard—seemed emblematic of ordinary, predictable human existence.

And if I believe that Raymond Stoddard's fate played a role in the breakup of my parents' marriage, then I must also believe that their marriage began to crack very soon after that January day when the police cars skidded down Keogh Street. That meant I was there to observe the breakup in its first if not final stages.

Adolescents, however, are notoriously limited in their ability to see anything that lies outside their immediate concerns, and in that regard I was not merely a typical representative of my age group, I was probably worse. As an adult, I realize how frequently my self-involvement impaired my vision. For example, during part of the period when my parents' marriage was no doubt diminishing, all my powers of observation were instead keen for signs of growth. Specifically, I was watching for evidence of Marie Ryan's pregnancy, and I finally saw what I was looking for on a Friday night in late March.

Julie Benske's parents were out of town, and in their absence Julie decided to hold a party. She tried to keep the numbers down, but to no avail. By the time my friends and I arrived, cars practically circled the block, and the house pulsed with the sounds of a hi-fi turned to full volume and with the shouts of teenagers who were either drunk already or intent on getting there. The neighbors must have been very tolerant, or else they believed Dr. and Mrs. Benske had sanctioned the party.

I hadn't been there long when I saw Marie. And I heard her before I saw her. As soon as I entered the kitchen, I caught her laughter. She was with a group standing around a makeshift bar, and her gaiety traveled across the room as easily as her laugh. Why, I wondered, would she be as happy as she seemed to be, given her circumstances? Perhaps she and Gene had settled on what they'd do about their predicament, and what I saw as happiness was merely relief, even if for Marie Ryan a solution meant taking on the name more notorious than any other in the state. The crowd made it impossible to get closer to her, and I wasn't sure that I dared to anyway. I hadn't spoken to her since Gene had told me she was pregnant, and who knew how he had represented my boys' room behavior to her? I couldn't see Gene anywhere at the party, and I wasn't eager to.

While the hard liquor was upstairs in the kitchen, the beer was in the basement, and that was where my friends were headed. Without taking off my coat, I followed them.

Gene wasn't downstairs either, and then it was my turn to feel relieved. Which may be the reason I drank as much as I did. Or maybe it was because I was at the same party as Marie, though she might have dwelt in a different universe for all the good it did me.

So I huddled on the rec room floor and guzzled beer after beer, rising only when my bladder was full.

And I was on my way back up to the first floor—the downstairs bathroom was occupied—when I again caught sight of Marie.

In Bismarck in 1962 the markers signifying the status of the community's wealthier members were few and subtle. Even the city's doctors, lawyers, and business owners lived in modest houses that didn't stand apart much from the homes of their less prosperous neighbors. But there were differences, and I was standing on one of them.

The Benskes' home was plushly carpeted, even the stairs, and just as I was ascending them, Marie Ryan was coming down, and I stopped a few steps below her. The softness underfoot was such an uncustomary sensation that I felt for a moment as though I might keep sinking until I dropped from view, something I might have hoped for, so flustered was I by our meeting.

She laughed and, spreading her arms and legs wide to block my passage, said, "You can't get past unless you say the secret word."

I've never been quick-witted, and, then as now, drink only increases my tongue's sluggishness. No reply, clever or otherwise, came to mind.

But perhaps my being tongue-tied had another cause. With the three steps between us, Marie's waist and abdomen were right at my eye level. I did some mental arithmetic, difficult in my condition and further complicated by my ignorance of some matters of reproduction and anatomy. Gene had asked me to be his best man in January, and Marie was what—two or three months pregnant then? It was March now, which meant she could be at least four months along. . . . But she was wearing a white blouse tucked into a snug skirt, and if a pregnancy had swelled her tummy in the least, wouldn't it have been visible by now? Even clothed, however, wrapped tight in a girdle's spandex, a skirt's tight wool, a brassiere's hooks and straps, and a blouse's buttoned-up cotton, it was apparent that her body's sensual configuration was exactly what it had been the previous summer in a bathing suit.

Suddenly I had a new theory for her high spirits. She wasn't pregnant—she couldn't be, not looking like that—and perhaps she had only recently learned of her true condition. She wasn't celebrating her upcoming marriage—she was jubilant because it wasn't necessary.

Elated as I was to make this discovery, I kept my happiness tamped down. Not difficult, since in the essential way, her circumstances hadn't changed. "If you're looking for Gene," I said, "he's not down there."

She relaxed her stance, leaning against the stair railing. The pose was seductive, although I'm sure that was not how she intended it. "I know where he is. And isn't. He chose not to come tonight."

"Not his kind of party?" The question was legitimate. None of Gene's newer acquaintances was likely to be at a gathering at the Benskes', no matter how much alcohol was present.

"He's at home."

"Is he sick?"

"He's fine. But considering the occasion, he didn't feel like going to a party."

"The occasion?"

She tilted her head and gave me a sidelong flirtatious look, or so I perceived the gesture. She probably wasn't sending that message, but she couldn't help how I received it.

"Think about it," Marie said. "It's Gene's dad's birthday."

"Oh, yeah. I forgot."

The date had never had any purchase on my memory, even though on one awkward occasion I was a part of Raymond Stoddard's birthday celebration.

Maybe there were Bismarckers of that era who dined out often, but that certainly wasn't true of my parents—we could count on fewer than four or five such experiences each year, and those always occurred spontaneously, when my mother decided at the last minute that she didn't care to prepare the family's meal—and it was even less true of the Stoddards. But five years earlier, Gene had asked me if I'd like to come along with him and his family for a birthday supper at the Wagon Wheel, a restaurant on the city's east side.

The Wagon Wheel was not a supper club or steak house. It was a small diner, more likely to be patronized by truck drivers than Bismarck families. I wasn't sure why we went there, but it seemed to have something to do with Mr. Stoddard's preferences, some belief he held that the Wagon Wheel's chili or fried chicken was superior to any other restaurant's.

Yet his unhappiness at being there became obvious almost as soon as we slid into our booth. A cold rain had begun to fall, and Mr. Stoddard worried that it might freeze on the streets, making even the short drive back to Keogh Street treacherous. The food was not to his liking—"grease, nothing but grease," he complained—and the waitress failed to bring the full order.

Mrs. Stoddard tried to cheer him up. "Birthday boy," she

persisted in calling him. "Let's see a smile from the birthday boy." His mood only darkened, and before the meal was finished, he fell into a trancelike silence. Seated next to the window, he stared out at the puddles gathering in the parking lot's gravel. At one point he pressed the heel of his fist to the glass and rubbed small hard circles, as if the window were frosted or fogged and needed to be cleared. It did not, but we soon looked away, certain that we couldn't see what Raymond Stoddard saw, no matter how transparent the surface.

"But I just decided," Marie said, "no matter what day it is— I'm going out. I'm going out and I'm going to have a good time. Just because March thirtieth is a bad day for him doesn't mean everyone else has to suffer along with him."

"That's right. Your name isn't Stoddard." It was as close as I dared come. Now, if she wished, she could say, But soon it will be.

"Exactly."

"Did you say all this to Gene?"

"More or less."

"How did he take it?"

Something in her shrug told me they had probably quarreled over the matter.

"So," I said, "you're taking the day off."

She smiled, apparently pleased with the notion. "Sort of."

"How's your vacation going so far?"

"Very well."

Who knows what went into the mix that caused me to consider what I was about to say? Was it her good spirits? Our staircase rapport? Her disenchantment—even if only for the night—with Gene? The beers I'd drunk certainly contributed. But no matter what the reason, I decided I'd tell her about Gene's crude remarks about her condition—at least what they thought her condition was at the time.

Before I could frame the words, however, Doug Bauer appeared suddenly at the top of the stairs. "Cops!" he said. "In the driveway!"

I froze, but Marie acted instantly. She hurried down the stairs, sweeping me along with her.

The Benskes had a walk-out basement, and we scurried toward that door. Somehow, even without an explicit warning, everyone downstairs knew that the party was being raided, and there was much scrambling to get out. Together Marie and I pushed our way through the door and out into the backyard. People scattered in every direction, and if they were like us, they had no real destination in mind. We just knew we had to get as far from the Benske home as we could and in so doing stay away from the streets and streetlights.

Marie had to be cold—she had left her coat behind—and her low heels kept slipping on and breaking through the crusted snow we had to run across, but I heard only laughter from her and not complaint.

Eventually we decided that it would be safe to return to the sidewalks, so we cut through a yard, traveled down an alley, and came out on a street blocks from the Benskes'. At a stop sign just ahead we saw Rick Withers's car, jammed with fugitives from the party, and we ran to join them.

They made room for us, which meant that I was squeezed against the back door. As tight as the fit was, I didn't mind because Marie was forced to sit on my lap. I felt her shivering subside as the car's heater and all the bodies—there must have been nine or ten people in the car—generated their warmth. I smelled the sweet musk of her perfume and the slightly medicinal scent of vodka on her breath. When she turned her head, strands of her hair brushed across my face. I would have gladly remained in the back of that old Chevrolet forever!

But Rick Withers wasn't interested in driving around. Like almost everyone else who had been at the party, he was still shaken over his close call. He wanted to know where he should drop off his passengers, and sadly, Marie's house was nearby.

He pulled into her driveway, and she jumped out immediately. "Thanks for the ride," she said to Rick. And to the rest of the car, she added softly, "I'll bet we wouldn't have been as tightly packed in jail!"

"Wait!" I said. "I'll walk you."

I was still a little drunk, but fear and cold had sobered me somewhat. Fear . . . I *had* been afraid. If I had been arrested that night, my parents would have been angry and disappointed, and they certainly would have decreed a penalty of some kind. But it would have been relatively mild. They were not nearly as strict or severe as, for example, Marie's parents were. Yet throughout our getaway and flight, she had displayed no fear. In the car she hadn't gone on, as some of the partygoers had, about how narrow their escape had been or about how awful their punishment would be if they were caught.

Was Marie Ryan brave because she had once stood loyally beside a Stoddard as that family went through their terrible ordeal, and in the process had she acquired a courage that would serve her forever after, no matter what the situation? Or had she always possessed the kind of bravery that allowed her to step forward and stay when almost anyone else would have hung back? But even if the source of Marie's courage might have been unknowable, the fact of it was without dispute.

And perhaps I took a cue from her character and elevated my own courage that night, for I attempted something that was for me uncharacteristically bold.

Once again we were in her garage, darker now than it had been on the day I had walked her home from Raymond Stoddard's funeral, and once again she stood on the step above me just where she'd be when she'd kiss Gene good night.

"Do you mind if I kiss you?" I asked.

At least I asked, though I leaned forward with the hope I'd get the answer I wanted.

She didn't say no. Neither did she laugh at me or slap me or turn away in disgust. She had too much grace for any of those actions. Instead, she gently said, "Do you think that's a good idea? I'm still going with Gene."

What could I say to that—let me make my betrayal complete? She was offering me the opportunity to be better than I was.

Without saying another word I hurried from the garage. The night's cold couldn't touch me, burning as I was with my own shame.

❧

Monty Burnham considered making his confession on the day when the Sherman tank he commanded was mired in black volcanic ash, and Japanese artillery fire was shrieking all around.

He believed then that it was only a matter of time before one of the armor-piercing 150-millimeter shells found its target and he and his crew of five were incinerated in their vehicle. For good reason the tanks had been nicknamed "Ronsons." And with death imminent wouldn't it have made sense to blurt out a soul-cleansing statement right at that time, especially since the man whose wife Burnham had fucked was right there in the tank with him? And if the confession weighed down one soldier at the same time that it unburdened another, so what? They were all doomed anyway.

He tapped his friend, Corporal Raymond Stoddard, the tank's loader, on the shoulder with the full intention of owning up to what had happened between him and Raymond's wife, Alma. Yet when Stoddard turned toward him, Burnham couldn't speak. He and Stoddard had attended the same high school in Wembley, North Dakota, and they had played football together, and at that moment his former classmate, his features almost erased by grease and dirt, looked, in his leather tank hel-met, just the way he had looked on the playing field. Monty Burnham shook his head and waved away Raymond's inquiring glance. He could have confessed to a fellow soldier, a subordi-nate, but not a former teammate.

Two weeks later, at their island camp, Monty and Raymond Stoddard were sitting outside on planks placed on top of stumps, watching The Affairs of Susan *with a hundred other men. For the hour before the movie began, Monty and Ray-mond Stoddard had been drinking, passing back and forth a pint of Four Roses with two other members of the tank crew. So* maybe it was the whiskey. Maybe it was something Joan Fontaine said to George Brent up on the screen. Whatever the cause, the impulse to confess returned, and Monty Burnham nudged Raymond Stoddard. As casually as he might comment on something happening in the movie, he said softly, "Hey. I fucked your wife, you know. Back in Texas."

The rain that had been falling steadily for days had subsided now to little more than a mist, just enough to keep the moviegoers wet but doing nothing to cool them. Monty and Raymond were sitting apart from everyone else, in a back row near the projector, and in its flickering beam the drizzle separated into individual droplets that looked like tiny bits of silver floating in the light.

Raymond Stoddard didn't acknowledge Monty's remark in any way, but when Monty leaned in to repeat his disclosure, Raymond said, "I ain't deaf. I heard you."

Someone else obviously heard as well, and not just Raymond's response. From one of the rows ahead a soldier said, "Christ. There's a buddy for you."

Immediately Monty wanted to seek that man out, to explain that he and Raymond's wife had a history, that they had dated throughout high school, and that she had all but acknowledged that marrying Raymond had been a mistake. First, however, he had to make Raymond understand.

"It's not like I planned it," Monty whispered.

"If you say so." Raymond kept his eyes focused on the screen. On a tropical night like this one, how you could tell whether the moisture on a man's face was rain, sweat, or tears, Monty had no idea.

"*It's not like it was even my idea. Not entirely.*"

"*Uh-huh.*"

"*It was just something we had to get out of our systems.
Both of us.*" Monty had now returned comfortably to the mental script he had prepared well in advance of this occasion.

Raymond Stoddard, however, didn't offer any of the lines that Monty had rehearsed on Raymond's behalf. Without saying another word, Raymond slid off the plank, as if it were one of Dennis O'Keefe's remarks that upset him rather than Monty's confession. Monty almost shouted out an order—*Soldier, get back here!*—before he realized that would not be the appropriate tone for the transaction he was trying to conduct with Raymond Stoddard.

From boyhood Monty Burnham had known that in his nature ran two parallel streams. One was the pleasure he took in inflicting pain. Oh, not serious pain—just teasing that sometimes went on a little too long, roughhousing that might cross a border but still didn't venture far into the territory of hurt, or joking that had a jagged edge. The other current running through him was the need to be liked and the need to overcome any prejudice, animosity, or grudge someone might hold against him. Occasionally these two streams could converge, and Monty Burnham would find that the person whose goodwill had to be restored was exactly the person he had insulted, injured, or grieved. When this occurred, when he had to persuade a girl he had stood up to let go of her anger or a soldier he had ridden too hard to give up his resentment, Monty would attempt to set things right with talk, with charming, candid talk. He would usually be able to accomplish this without explicitly *asking for forgiveness or apologizing, but he knew he always had those in reserve. And Monty Burnham could not be contented until approval was once again flowing his way.*

This was why Monty Burnham left the movie to find Raymond Stoddard. The theater, however, had been set up near a small forest whose trees had provided the stumps for movie viewing. If Raymond wandered into that dense, dark grove, Monty might never track him down.

He was standing at the entrance to the trees, trying to look down their lightless corridors, when he heard the clank of a Zippo lighter off to his left. There was Raymond Stoddard, lighting a cigarette and shielding it expertly to keep it burning in the rain.

"I had a few more things I wanted to say," Monty said.

"And you think I want to hear them." Raymond stood next to a knee-high pile of brass—anything above .50 caliber in size—that only days before the infantry had been forced to pick up from the battle lines. The rain brought a dull glint to the shell casings.

"I guess I figure you have a right to know."

"About you and Alma. I know all about it. She told me."

"What happened back in Killeen? She told you that?" Monty considered the possibility that Raymond now only pretended to know about what had gone on in that hotel bathroom, in order to save face. Monty decided to test him. "Everything? She told you everything?"

"Enough." The smoke Raymond Stoddard exhaled seemed to hang in the air as if it couldn't make its way through the drizzle. From the nearby forest came the hisses, chirps, scrapings,

whines, and pipings of strange insects and even stranger birds. If Monty stepped even a few feet into the jungle, some of those calls would cease immediately while others would become louder and more rapid.

"Then I suppose you know I had her like you never did." *The streams in Monty had diverged once again, and there was no doubt which current was running strongest now. He did find it odd that war hadn't satisfied that need to hurt. Then again, maybe it had only stirred the desire.*

Raymond Stoddard, however, was not outwardly perturbed. "You mean I never had her like that *before. I sure as hell did after.*"

"Glad I could show the way."

To that Raymond Stoddard said nothing. He simply raised his hand to his forehead in a parody of a salute. God damn, would nothing rile this man?

"I don't know," *Monty said,* "how a man can talk about his wife like that."

Again, Raymond said nothing, but this time he snorted softly, and the sound coincided almost exactly with a burst of laughter that came from the rows of soldiers staring up at the screen. Was Raymond even listening to him, Monty wondered, or was most of his attention focused on the movie?

Monty took a step back and straightened his shoulders. "Well. I just needed to get that off my chest. I can't imagine it was too easy to hear. You probably feel like taking a poke at me. Can't say I blame you. Officer or not, I'd probably slug a man who told me a tale like this one."

"Take a poke at you? Take a poke at you?" *This time Ray-*

mond's laugh came out as sharp as a dog's bark. He flicked away his cigarette and stepped so close to Monty that Monty could smell the rank, curdled odor of tobacco and whiskey on Raymond's breath. "I never climbed into a tank with you but that I thought this would be the time I pulled the pin on a grenade and blew the both of us to kingdom come."

"And every other soldier in there with us?"

In the summer of 1935 Monty Burnham was eleven years old and returning from a morning spent fishing in Ripley's Creek, just outside Wembley. He was less than a mile from his home when he came across an excavation site near an abandoned farm. Curious as to why a sizable hole had been dug out there in the country, Monty climbed to the top of the pile of dirt and sod in order to survey the entire scene.

He guessed someone was digging the foundation for a house, but the hole was crudely, unevenly dug, and Monty saw no sign that any work had been done recently. While he was wondering how he might have missed this alteration to the landscape on the other occasions when he'd walked out to Ripley's Creek, three boys approached. Monty didn't notice them until they were right behind him, and then they caught his attention by throwing a dirt clod that barely missed his head.

Monty turned quickly. The three had spread themselves out at the base of the mound as if they planned to attack him from different directions. From their similar high foreheads, close-set eyes, and dirty, ragged overalls Monty guessed they were brothers. The oldest was probably a year or two older than Monty, but he was so skinny Monty figured he could handle him. The other two might have been twins, and though they were smaller and younger than Monty, they had a determinedly nasty look that said they would have been trouble even in a fair fight. And three against one wouldn't be fair. . . .

"Hey," Monty said in a voice as friendly as any he owned, "you live around here?"

"Yeah," the oldest one said, "and you're trespassing."

Monty pretended to look over the surrounding countryside. "Nothing says this land is posted."

"Well, now you know."

One of the twins kicked at the fishing pole Monty had set down before he'd scrambled up the dirt pile. "And you ain't fishing the creek no more without our say-so."

"All this is our property now," the other twin added.

"Not the creek. Nobody can buy the creek." Monty gestured toward the water, and as he did, as if on cue, a red-winged blackbird whistled its three notes from that direction.

"Like hell," the oldest said, and when he reached down to pick up a dirt lump, it was plain he'd had enough of oral argument.

Monty tried once more to extricate himself from the moment with words. "So if I ask first from now on, you'll let me fish in your creek?"

The twins were silently sorting through the dirt at their feet. Their feet were bare. They were searching for rocks.

Because of the hole on the other side, Monty couldn't take flight down the hill away from the brothers, yet if he tried to run in any other direction, he'd only charge right at them. And maybe, he decided, that was exactly what he should do. Charge them, swinging wildly all the way, and hope that he could get past them onto the road and then outrun them. Even if he took a few punches in the process, that would be better than standing here and allowing himself to be a target for their rocks and dirt lumps.

Before he could put his plan into action, however, someone else appeared on the scene.

From out of a field of tall grass came a boy Monty's age. He too was carrying a fishing pole, and as he walked, grasshoppers leaped in arcs all around him. It was Monty's friend Raymond Stoddard, and he must have been fishing upstream from Monty, near the bend in the creek where the cottonwood trees shaded the water.

Raymond said, "Hey, Morris. What the hell are you and your snotnose brothers up to?"

Morris dropped his dirt clod, but the twins continued to gather stones.

"This fella's trespassing. . . ."

Raymond also positioned himself at the bottom of the dirt pile, but he stood apart from the other three. "You're the ones trespassing. Just because you moved into that old barn don't mean you own the place."

"We're gonna build here. My dad says—"

"Your folks are nothing more than squatters. That's what my old man said." He set his fishing pole down carefully. To Monty he said, "What do you say. You want to come down here and help me beat the shit out of these assholes? Maybe that'll send 'em back where they came from."

Monty, however, could not call up a desire for brutality on

such short notice. Furthermore, he could not abandon so quickly his earlier strategy, which was to escape through charm.

"Where are you boys from?" he asked his enemies.

Raymond answered for them. "Iowa. Lost their farm down there and now they're gonna mooch off their North Dakota relations." To Monty he explained, "Their mom and my mom are sort of cousins."

Monty believed that conversation would now ensue among the five of them, that goodwill would be the rule all around, and that if he ever needed the aid or service of the dull-witted Morris or the malicious twins, they would be available.

But Raymond had other ideas. He lurched threateningly toward Morris and the other two, stamping his shoe in the dirt as if they could be frightened off like animals. "Go on," he said. "Get the hell out of here. Crawl back in your holes and stop making trouble for folks."

And that was all it took. The three of them backed away slowly, gradually moving together like birds in flight resuming their formation. Side by side they walked back down through the field. Monty noticed, however, that the twins had never dropped the stones they'd collected. Sure enough, once they gained some distance, the twins turned and heaved them at Monty and Raymond. They were out of range, however, and the two older boys just laughed as the missiles did nothing but kick up dust at their feet.

The boy who saved Monty on that day had grown into the man who now made his own confession. Once Raymond Stoddard's laughter subsided, he said, "That's right. I didn't give a shit who I took with us."

"So what stopped you?"

Raymond shrugged. "Figured the Japs would do the job for me."

"You know, I could have you court-martialed for what you just said."

"But you won't."

"Don't be so sure, Soldier. Don't. Be. So. Sure."

The two men were still standing so close together that Raymond Stoddard had to raise his hand right in front of his own face in order to give Monty the finger.

Now Monty understood. Raymond wanted Monty to swing at him. A man who was willing to take the consequences that might come from leaving his wife alone with an old boyfriend would certainly be willing to take a punch just to get his superior officer in trouble.

"You know what, Ray? I feel sorry for you. I surely do."

Raymond Stoddard's only response was to dig into his pocket for another cigarette. As Monty walked away, he heard again the clink of Raymond's lighter. And was there a similarly distinctive sound, Monty wondered, when the pin was pulled from a grenade? And would he ever be able to stop listening for either sound, whether in war- or peacetime?

Of my many fictions, and fictional efforts, that had their origins in the Stoddard-Burnham saga, the preceding narrative ("Got a

Light?" as it was titled when it appeared in *Blue Parchment,* a Seattle magazine) was the only one that featured Monty Burnham (Tony Kroll in the published story) as a protagonist and point-of-view character. While there was never a point of personal contact—an observed gesture, an overheard remark—that allowed me to conjure that character's inner life (or to imagine an entire series of fictional episodes in which he played a prominent part), and while there's little reason to believe "my" Monty Burnham bore any resemblance to the actual one, I've always felt that my early attempts to imagine my way into the real Raymond Stoddard's mind (and only after the man's death) inevitably led me to try to enter others. And disposed me to create fictions more concerned with the motives behind actions than with the actions themselves.

During my senior year I signed up for Introduction to Psychology, a course that had never been offered before at Bismarck High School. Edith Ehrlich taught the class, and I suspect she was given the assignment as a reward for having taught for almost fifty years in the city's school system. Miss Ehrlich looked forward to the prospect of spending months with us exploring "the mysteries of our mental processes," but the semester had barely begun when her health forced her out of the classroom and out of the profession altogether. Miss Ehrlich had a stroke that deprived her of the power of speech, probably the only infirmity that could have kept her from taking her place in front of rows of students.

The school was in a quandary. No one else was willing to step forward and take over Miss Ehrlich's class, yet something had to be done with the students who were enrolled. We couldn't simply be given credit and sent on our way, and the semester was too far along to place us in other courses. The administration took the unusual step—for this they must have needed a special dispensation from the board of education—and hired an outsider, a non-teacher, to take over Introduction to Psychology.

That was how I came to know Frances Fenzer, Ph.D. Dr. Fenzer was a Bismarck psychologist, and someone on the school board apparently thought he would be a perfect substitute for Miss Ehrlich. And it worked out exactly as hoped. On a Wednesday, Miss Ehrlich was taken to the hospital. On the following Thursday and Friday, our Introduction to Psychology class was turned into a study hall, but when we showed up on Monday, we were met by a pink, plump, smiling man in a rumpled brown suit.

We were immediately pleased with the new development. Rather than stand behind a lectern, Dr. Fenzer sat on top of the desk. He straightened and twisted paper clips while he talked, and he freely admitted that this nervous behavior was caused by having to go an entire hour without a cigarette. Best of all, Dr. Fenzer didn't so much lecture as gossip. He refused to use the textbook that Miss Ehrlich had ordered, and instead structured the class around case histories—culled from his own experience. Furthermore, we knew that the patients—the neurotics, the compulsives, the depressives—were almost surely Bismarck residents. He never used real names, but hadn't his entire professional career been spent in North Dakota? From what other sources could he be lifting those examples? He even teased us occasionally with a remark like, "Now, this is behavior you've all had a chance to observe, especially if you've spent any time at all in a certain local establishment." Talk like that probably violated the standards of his profession, but we felt fortunate to be in his class and privileged to be taken into his confidence.

He favored us—a few of us—further by inviting us to his home, a small stucco house not far from the high school and surrounded by gardens unlike any other in Bismarck. "Flowers and imported cigarettes," Dr. Fenzer said, "my indulgences." Some of the students were invited to visit him after school; others in the evening.

I went, along with Mike LaPorte and Joe McDonald, on a rainy night in April. I remember the weather conditions so well because Dr. Fenzer unapologetically required us to remove our wet shoes before we stepped on any of his rugs.

The house was as elaborately furnished as any I had ever been in. I realize now how much time and money Dr. Fenzer put into his home—the walls were covered with paintings and prints, objets d'art were everywhere, a grand piano filled a sunporch, and every piece of furniture was covered with rich fabrics or made of heavy, polished woods—but to my adolescent sensibility it all seemed fussy, ostentatious, and uncomfortable.

Dr. Fenzer was a gracious host, providing us with soft drinks and potato chips and encouraging us to smoke if we were so inclined. I sank into the corner of a brocade couch and lit a cigarette, eager to hear what kinds of anecdotes the psychologist would tell outside the school's walls, since his narratives in the classroom could often be outrageous.

Somehow we began talking about suicide, a subject that any psychologist, even one practicing in a community as stolid and stoic as Bismarck, could hold forth on for hours. Dr. Fenzer told us that, contrary to the belief that attempted suicides were cries for help, many of these people were quite determined to die. What did he do when he had a patient with that resolve? he asked rhetorically. After a dramatic pause, he said, "I watch the obituaries." Then he moved to the case closest to all our hearts.

Dr. Fenzer said, "Take for example that fellow who murdered the legislator and then took his own life. . . . I've believed all along that the crime was puzzling to so many people because they couldn't figure out why he'd want to kill the good senator. But perhaps they couldn't come up with an answer because they'd asked the wrong question. They should have looked into why the fellow wanted to take his own life.

"Suicides are often motivated by a sense of worthlessness, of smallness, and more than one man has taken his own life thinking that at last he is doing something large, something dramatic. This chap may have felt as though he'd always been anonymous, overlooked, misunderstood. So he decided he'd do something that would finally cause people to notice him. He'd perform some act, commit some deed, that couldn't be disregarded. As a result, he'd become famous. The pathogenesis is really quite remarkable. These people feel so insignificant, yet they grow these monstrously large egos. . . ." Dr. Fenzer looked around at his rapt, slightly shocked audience. "Well? Have you any thoughts?"

After Dr. Fenzer's brief monologue, the conversation, which had been lively in its back and forth until then, fell silent. The doctor didn't know that Raymond Stoddard's son was our classmate, much less that I had a special connection to the family.

Mike and Joe looked to me in deference to my Keogh Street address. This was my moment to shine, to show off my insider status, and to impress Dr. Fenzer, all of which I thought I wanted.

Presented with the opportunity, however, I merely shrugged and said, "Makes sense, I guess."

Dr. Fenzer must have sensed something in my recalcitrance that I didn't wholly comprehend myself. He quickly changed the subject, and for the rest of the evening I had no responsibilities but to listen and keep my cigarette's ashes from drifting to the floor.

Two days later, however, at the end of the school day, Dr. Fenzer stopped me in the hall as I was on my way out of the building. "Do you mind if I walk with you?" he asked.

The day and its sudden changes were typical of spring—warm when the sun was shining, chilly when clouds obscured the sun. Dr. Fenzer lit a cigarette as soon as we stepped outside the school, but we didn't walk far. We stopped at a fairly new white Lincoln Continental, easily the grandest car in the faculty parking lot. "All right," he said, smiling sheepishly. "Flowers and cigarettes aren't my *only* indulgences."

"It's nice."

Small talk finished, he got down to business. "The other night at my house, I might have caused you some discomfort with my remarks, and I wanted to apologize. After you left, Joe mentioned that you were a close friend to the Stoddard boy and a neighbor to the family. I had no idea. I'm sorry."

"That's okay."

"That friendship must have weighed you down at times."

Even as a callow adolescent I knew that to accede to that

point would represent a failure of proportion. No matter how much I had come to dislike Gene, I had to admit that I could never own troubles that remotely rivaled his. "Not really."

Dr. Fenzer was a good six inches shorter than me, so he stood on his toes and leaned forward to force me to look him in the eye. "Perhaps your experiences are something you'd like to talk about. Sometimes we're so focused on someone else's pain that we lose sight of the fact that we're hurting too. We somehow think that we're not entitled."

I was not a tough kid, not physically or emotionally, but like most males of my era, I knew how to fake it in certain situations and with certain people. "It wasn't that big a deal."

With that, Dr. Fenzer gave up. He stepped back, bowed, and made a sweeping motion, a gesture that indicated both my dismissal and his defeat.

Dr. Fenzer invited me neither to his home nor to a private conversation with him again. In Introduction to Psychology I received a B, in spite of what I was sure was a poor performance on the final exam.

The night I graduated from high school was warm for May, and for weeks we had had no rain. As a result, my life took a turn that would not have been possible had the temperature been ten degrees cooler or the Missouri River six inches deeper.

The river's sandbars used to be (for that matter, perhaps they still are) a favored location for parties. We gathered there day and night, playing football or softball in the sand, swimming in pools and potholes, building bonfires, and drinking beer no matter what the hour. Depending on the river's height, we either drove out to one of those stretches of sand or trekked through a channel of icy, muddy, fast-flowing water. The Missouri was notorious for its treacherous currents and invisible drop-offs, and every summer it seemed to claim at least one drowning victim. Only someone very drunk or unfamiliar with the river and its reputation tried to swim through the main waterway. And the Missouri didn't care who it swallowed.

But the sandbars' remoteness and inaccessibility were exactly what made them so popular with the area's young people. Only the sheriff and his deputies had jurisdiction on the river (and the matter of jurisdiction was complicated by the fact that the river separated Burleigh and Morton counties), and even on the rare occasion when the law did try to patrol the area, we could usually spot them coming from a long way off.

So of course the river was a logical place for Bismarck High School's class of 1962 to hold its graduation party, and since the spring had been so dry, the river was low, which meant we could easily drive out to a sandbar southeast of the city for the night's festivities.

I'd had family obligations earlier in the evening that prevented me from appearing at the river until well after dark, and by that time, hundreds of cars were parked in a line the length of at least two football fields, and bonfires of various sizes burned along the water's edge. The stage for the party itself was the long, narrow strip of sand between the cars and the river. Kids were everywhere, saying hello and goodbye to their fellow graduates, offering one another a beer or a drink from a bottle of hard liquor, throwing chunks of driftwood onto one of the fires. Many people were already drunk by the time I arrived, and the jubilation and delirium that traditionally accompanied the occasion had been replaced in some cases by belligerence—rumor had it that kids from Mandan were among our number, and a group of wrestlers and football players were patrolling for party crashers—and lust: Couples had not only gone off into the backseats of cars, but were also making out in full view. Among this second group I saw Gene and Marie. They were leaning against his car, tightly, passionately, locked in each other's arms. Marie stood on a case of beer—whether the cans were empty or full, I couldn't tell—the additional height facilitating their deep kisses and allowing their bodies to mesh in a way no doubt special to them. It was probably a fair approximation of the difference in height provided by the step inside Marie's garage. I walked close to them, testing not only their oblivion (it was complete) but also my vulnerability.

To say I was unaffected by the sight of them would not be true, but neither was the pain as sharp as it might have been. The entire evening I had been feeling a bit above it all, and not just in a metaphoric sense. Before I joined the party, I drove around for a while, at one point crossing the river and returning over the Memorial Bridge, whose height allowed me to look down on the sandbar and my classmates, at the dark glimmer of their cars and the blaze of their fires.

High school was over, and I had only a few months left in the city. In the fall I would be attending the University of North Dakota in Grand Forks, where, as far as I knew, nothing would mark me as a Bismarcker. I had done a fair job of convincing myself that I would enjoy living in a place where I wouldn't have an identity that I'd have to share with anyone or anything Stoddard. Of course I had also often wondered how far the notoriety of the Stoddard name had spread and what subtle methods might be available to me to let others know that I had dwelt on Bismarck's Keogh Street during that stretch of pavement's most infamous hour.

Even though I was moving at thirty miles per hour, my position on the bridge looking down at my classmates below provided a fitting emblem for my character. Did he wish to join the party or stay above it? Did he wish to be involved or ignored?

Metaphors and symbols aside, any thought I might have entertained about living a lofty (in both senses of the word), solitary, or isolated existence no longer had to be merely theoretical. I now had my own car.

Earlier that day, at a private graduation party to which only family and neighbors were invited, my parents presented me with a 1947 Studebaker Commander Regal DeLuxe. It had a flat-head six and a balky manual transmission, and though its original color had been red, the finish had oxidized over the years until it was a dusty pink. My father bought the car (or more likely accepted it in lieu of a fee) from a client—a literal little old lady—who lived in Sterling, a small town east of Bismarck. It was, in short, a car so obviously uncool that I felt an instant, inexplicable affection for it.

I was certainly not embarrassed to be driving it, though when I finally decided to unite with my classmates down on the river, I didn't park on the sandbar but in a stand of cottonwoods farther up on the bank. The walk down gave me more time to consider what, if anything, I wanted from the night.

As I said, the party was in full progress when I arrived, and for the first hour I did nothing but stroll the sand and observe. As a result of some odd, unthought-through notion that self-denial could uplift my character, I opted not to drink that night, which meant I had to say no to any number of freely offered cups, cans, and bottles. I had to stay away from my friends, since a simple refusal would not have been enough for them. They would have insisted on an explanation for my abstinence, and I knew I couldn't make them understand what I couldn't understand myself.

Eventually I settled into a conversation with Bob Mullen and Diane Burgie, boyfriend and girlfriend and both planning to attend Carleton College in Minnesota in the fall. We stood near the biggest bonfire, which had in turn attracted the largest crowd to its fiery border. Nearby a smaller fire failed in its attempt to compete for people's attention. Someone had thrown an inner tube onto that fire, and as it burned it not only gave off the stink of scorched rubber, but its smoke rose black, even against the night sky. Bob and Diane weren't drinking either—in fact, I was surprised to see them at such a gathering; I don't think I had ever seen them at a party before that night—and the three of us made sad, ironic comments about our classmates' drunken behavior and what it portended for their future. Right in front of us, for example, a shirtless Mickey Lawson was lying flat on his back and trying, without anyone's help, to bury himself in the sand. He had barely covered his torso when he heard—we all heard—the persistent bleat of a car horn. That sound was accompanied by the roar of an engine. Everyone looked to the right, and Mickey did more than look—he scrambled to his feet, the dry sand showering from him while the wetter stuff fell in clumps. A car was coming right toward him, churning its way along the open strip between the water and the line of parked cars. It lurched and wallowed through the soft sand and finally stopped near the largest bonfire, very near the space where Mickey had lain only moments earlier.

Well before the driver came into view, I knew who he was. I had recognized those headlights and that grille coming out of the dark on another occasion. But before I looked to confirm that Gene was driving, I checked for passengers. He appeared to be alone.

Once the car stopped, the crowd that had pulled back, unsure of the car's direction and intent, surged forward, so when Gene opened the door and stepped out, he was surrounded by many of his fellow graduates. He tugged at his T-shirt, stuck to him with sweat—both his and Marie's, I couldn't help thinking—and combed his fingers through his dark hair. Smiling widely, he raised his arms over his head in that gesture that's supposed to quiet an assemblage but just as often serves to excite it. With everyone's attention focused on him, Gene stepped up onto his car's back bumper and proceeded to clamber from there onto the trunk and then to the roof of his car. I wondered what Gene's father would have said if he'd found the finish of his car scratched from Gene's shoes.

Backlit by the bonfire's flames, he raised his arms again and shouted, "Stew-Dents! Stew-Dents!" Just that word, pronounced with two distinct, equally accented syllables, was enough to bring laughter and applause from the crowd. One of Bismarck High School's most eccentric and unintentionally comic teachers was the large-bosomed, blue-haired Miss Bonner, and when she needed to restore order in her sophomore English classes, she waved her arms and cried out, "Stew-Dents!" The previous year we were afforded even more opportunities to hear her hail us in her singular way: She was promoted on an interim basis to vice principal, and she often delivered announcements over the PA system and settled the crowd at school assemblies. She always began with "Stew-Dents," though the volume at which she spoke the word varied.

Gene continued with his imitation. "I have an announcement to make . . ." It was not just this extravagant, attention-seeking public display that told me Gene was drunk; if I'd had no other evidence to go on but the toothy width of his smile, I would have reached the same conclusion.

". . . to all the wonderful, important, special, *special* members of the class of '62." Now his impression of Miss Bonner turned into an imitation of Mrs. Harway, a school counselor who used the same approach in trying to help every student who came into her office, no matter what his or her problem. Mrs. Harway praised them, fawned over them, and told them what wonderful, unique individuals they were and how, if they could just accept that about themselves, their troubles would soon fade away. Mrs. Harway was decades ahead of her time.

"And you know what makes you so special?" Gene cooed to us. Had he somewhere along the way spent enough time in Mrs. Harway's presence to work on this impression? Was it possible that he'd asked for Mrs. Harway's help when he was worried that Marie was pregnant? That possibility I rejected quickly. After all, he'd completely scorned the suggestion, right after his father's suicide, that he should see the school counselor, and if he wouldn't visit Mr. Wallich's office, he was not likely to seek Mrs. Harway's counsel. Then again, there had been so many ways that my friend had astonished me over the course of the previous year. Why couldn't a gift for mimicry simply be another surprise?

Gene was drunk, of that there was no question, but every-thing—his entrance, his impressions, his timing—spoke of some-one confidently at ease in front of that drunken throng, someone who knew he had everyone's attention and was now able to toy with it. Here was a Gene Stoddard I had never seen before.

He turned first in one direction and then quickly pivoted to face another, almost as if he were expecting an attack.

"Do you?" Gene asked again of the young people clustered around his car. "Do you know why you'll always be a special, special member of Bismarck High's class of '62?"

I attributed Gene's out-of-character behavior to his drunken-ness. If he weren't drunk, I reasoned in my sober state, he wouldn't have been able to act like that. And his drunkenness, I had concluded long before that night, was due to his being Ray-mond Stoddard's son. Father had bequeathed to son not only a penchant for alcohol but also a reason for drinking it. But as I watched Gene sway and balance on the roof of his car, another thought came to me. What if alcohol played no part in the alter-ation of his personality? What if the change in him occurred en-tirely because he lived inside the walls of a stucco house where a man had hanged himself? Surely that life-transforming event sent out ripples well beyond the walls of that home, ripples that rocked the neighborhood, the city, the state. . . . But if the lives closest to Raymond Stoddard were most affected, wasn't it logi-cal to suppose that those next closest were the next most changed? Could there be a way to calculate closeness other than physical proximity? Was there a method that would allow another Keogh Street resident to believe that he was who he was through the strength or weakness of his own will rather than the accident of his address? Was it the weight of realizations like those that Dr. Fenzer had wondered if I needed help carrying?

But though such thoughts were earth-unsettling enough to make the sand underfoot feel solid by comparison, I set them aside when I saw Marie running down the beach.

She appeared to have her bathing suit on, and over it she wore cutoff jeans and a man's shirt, which, unbuttoned, fluttered whitely about her as she ran. She pumped her arms strenuously and lifted her knees high to keep from bogging down in the sand, and by the time she reached Gene's car—her obvious destination—her chest was heaving for oxygen. But she was not about to let shortness of breath keep her from her mission. "No," she cried out. "Gene, *please*!"

Up until that moment, I had tried to appear as nonchalant as possible at the spectacle of my former friend on top of his car. I hung back from those crowding forward and, unlike them, did nothing to cheer him on. But Marie's presence always quickened my interest, and now I was torn. Did I take her side in wishing he'd stop whatever he was doing or did I want more than ever—because someone wanted him not to go on—to hear what he had to say? Was it possible that he intended to announce something about his father that had never before been revealed? With that thought I considered trying to pull Marie back from the car myself.

Her pleas did nothing to deter him, however. He drew himself up to his full, unsteady height, and answered the question he himself had posed. "Because of me, that's why. Me. Because you graduated in the same class as Gene Stoddard, son of Raymond and Alma Stoddard."

"Don't do this," Marie begged. "*Please,* Gene." She moved closer, and now she too was both shadowed and illuminated by the flames behind her. In their flickering light her reddish hair took on a coppery glow.

"I made you all famous," Gene said. "No matter where you go, you can always say, 'I went to high school with—' "

Her spoken appeal ineffectual, Marie took action. Following the same route that Gene had taken, she began to climb onto the car. She had barely stepped from the bumper to the trunk, however, when Gene turned to repel this encroachment on his territory.

"God *damn it*!" he said. "Let me do this—this is mine!"

Gene had stepped toward Marie, and she obviously believed he was coming to help her up to his post. She reached out to him, but rather than grab her open hand and pull her to him, Gene pushed her.

Her balance on the car was precarious, so not much force was necessary to send her reeling backward. She fell in two stages. First she groped behind her with one foot, trying to find a stable step, and for an instant it seemed as though she might regain her balance as she teetered on the bumper. But then she half-slid, half-fell from that perch, toppling sideways to the sand. If her arms had not been reaching in Gene's direction, she might have been able to break her fall. As it was, she struck the earth with a thud as audible as Gene's shouted curse.

But her tumble brought only laughter from the throng. They were glad she'd failed. They were enjoying Gene's performance and wanted it to continue.

Her fall—her fall and Gene's cruelty—must have knocked the breath from Marie, but she was soon on her feet and shoving her way through the crowd and away from her boyfriend's car.

Gene meanwhile barely missed a beat. "As I was saying . . ." Cheers now accompanied the laughter.

As fascinating as I found Gene's performance, I had to turn away to see where Marie was headed. As she wove her way through the rows of parked cars, I had a moment of panic when I lost sight of her, but her white shirt soon reappeared. She was obviously walking away from the party and by the most direct passage available.

"No matter where you go," Gene continued, "you can say, 'Remember that guy who shot the senator—' "

Ahead of Marie I could see glinting in the darkness a channel of the river that cut into the sandbar. If she walked right through the water, she'd have a head start that I'd have difficulty over-coming. As determined as she was, however, she still circled around, and I took that to be a sign. I pushed back from the crowd, and ran after Marie. Before Gene's voice faded completely from earshot, I clearly heard, ". . . the assassin's son!"

Up ahead, Marie had a steep grassy bank to negotiate, and for some reason I believed I had to get to her before she struggled to the top. That meant I had to go through the water, and as I approached the channel, I looked for the furrowed shadows of car tracks—their presence would mean that it was shallow enough to run through. I saw none, but by then I had made my commitment. I went in at a full run, and initially at least, the footing was firm.

My third stride, however, carried me to a point where the bottom dropped away sharply, and I splashed face-forward and went under so suddenly and completely it seemed for an instant as though the elements had become mixed up and it was the sky that had turned to river water and night that had closed over my head. To further the confusion the icy water tasted like dirt.

I must not have truly believed I would drown because I was able to appreciate the irony of the moment: You are going to drown chasing after a girl who belongs to someone else. . . . Within that inlet the river didn't seem to have sufficient power to do anything but steal my breath with its cold. No current tried to pull me down or push me out into the main channel, and I soon adjusted to my situation enough to probe for the bottom. It was near and firm enough that I could thrust back to the surface. When I came up I was soaked, sputtering for air, and missing my shoes, but half-paddling and half-running, I continued after Marie.

She had heard the splashing behind her and had stopped, no doubt hoping it was Gene pursuing her. From the top of the bank she gazed down at me, and it seemed as if she were about to say something, but in the dark it was hard to tell. Before I could climb to her height, she turned and disappeared.

Each step I took came with more difficulty since both sand and water weighted down my socks, but I kept on and my perseverance was rewarded. Up on level ground, not far from the cottonwoods where my car was parked, Marie had paused to empty sand from her tennis shoes.

"What's the matter," I said to her, panting my way through

the line I had rehearsed in case I caught up to her, "didn't you want to stay back there and be famous with Gene?"

For a long moment she stared, unsmiling, at me. The sounds of the party could still reach us, but they were nothing compared to the belching, trilling songs of frogs coming out of the surrounding darkness.

Then Marie turned to go, and I quickly called after her, "Wait! I'm sorry. I shouldn't have said that."

I hobbled after her and was soon at her side.

"Did he send you after me?" she asked. "That would be just like him. . . ."

"No, no. I came . . . I came on my own." Considering what I felt for her, those words seemed like a declaration of love.

"That asshole," she said, assuming we were both interested in discussing Gene Stoddard's character. "I told him not to do something like that. I told him he'd just make a fool of himself and say something that tomorrow he'd regret. But no. *Famous* . . . That's exactly what he thinks he is. Or should be. What a stupid *shit*."

"He's drunk—"

"Don't make excuses for him."

"I meant it as more of a question."

"He's drunk so often it's not even worth asking."

She began to walk away again, and now I noticed that she seemed to be favoring her right side. "Where are you going?"

"I don't know. Away from here. Home, I suppose."

The city and her house were miles away. "You can't walk. Let me give you a ride."

"I'm not going back down there." She nodded in the direction of the party and the rows of parked cars. From where we stood the largest bonfire was still clearly visible, its flames licking even higher than before. Someone must have found another source of fuel.

"You don't have to. My car's right over there."

As we moved through the trees, I watched Marie carefully. Yes, she was injured, of that there could be no doubt. She kept her right arm pinned tight to her side.

I pointed to her shoulder, which was slumped down and forward. "What happened? Are you hurt?"

"When I fell off Gene's car, I landed kind of hard."

I almost corrected her—*you didn't fall; you were pushed*—but I let it pass.

We arrived at my car, and I announced, "This is it. All mine. A graduation present."

Marie squinted through the darkness. "Pink? Is it *pink*?"

"More like a pale red. When it's washed, it'll be easier to tell the real color."

We both laughed at my defense of the car. "Okay. Have it your way. But it's a *very* pale red," she said.

I had another little clutch of fear when it occurred to me that the keys might have fallen out when I tumbled into the water, but they were still in the pocket of my jeans. I unlocked Marie's door and held it open for her.

"You'll get your car seat wet." She waggled her finger up and down in my direction to indicate my drenched condition.

"Oh well."

"You don't have anything to put on the seat? Gene always keeps a blanket in the car."

Her statement nicked me, but I loved her all the more for it, and in the process learned one more lesson about the inextricability of pain and love. And another lesson about my own character. Some other boys—most other boys?—in my place would have followed up Marie's remark with a wink and salacious question of their own—Yeah? What was the blanket for? And I have no doubt she would have answered.

"It's not like it's a new car or anything," I said.

When she entered the car, I noticed again how carefully she moved, and now she was supporting her right arm with her left hand.

"Is it your arm? Or your shoulder?"

Just the question was enough to make her wince. "Shoulder, I guess."

"Can you lift your arm?"

She made an effort, but it brought a gasp from her. "Not very well. It feels like something's grinding in there."

"Can I take a look?"

I stepped back, and she slowly, gingerly, extricated her right arm from the shirt. Once that was done, she sat back against the car seat to facilitate my examination.

Leaning over her, I caught the faint but unmistakable odor of Old Spice. I knew it so well because it was my father's aftershave, and I seldom stepped into the bathroom in the morning without smelling it. But I hadn't thought Gene used it. Finally I concluded that the white shirt must have been her father's, and the scent imbedded in the collar his.

Marie's breasts swelled above her swimming suit, the top of which had slipped down just enough to expose a line of paler flesh. . . . I forced myself, however, to attend to the duty I had volunteered for, and I concentrated on her right shoulder, which, even though she was sitting back, was still hunched forward.

The car's dome light was not very bright, and shadows extending from the hollow of her throat made it difficult to be certain, but it looked as though she had a distinct bump on her collarbone and perhaps the start of a bruise there as well.

"I should take you to the emergency room. In case something's broken."

That suggestion caused her to crane her neck in an attempt to look down at herself, and that movement brought only another grimace to her face. Then, in order to prove to me her injury wasn't severe, she quickly smiled and tried again to lift her arm. That failed too. "Shit," she said softly but angrily.

"Here. Let me try something. Can you take your shirt off all the way?"

If she was skeptical or suspicious, her expression didn't show it. Nevertheless, to demonstrate the purity of my motives, I stepped back again and looked away while she struggled out of the shirt. Once she was free of it, I took it from her, unrolled the sleeves, and knotted them together. I folded the fabric until it was in the approximate shape of a sling, which I then slipped over Marie's head. Now both the strap of her bathing suit and the sleeves of the shirt were looped around her neck.

"Try this," I said. "If it's too long or short, I can adjust it."

"Much better," she said, smiling her gratitude.

"All that Boy Scout training . . . finally good for something."

"You're a Scout?"

"Not really. Was. A Cub Scout. I quit after a couple years. The knot-tying always gave me trouble."

"I didn't think you were a Scout or an Explorer or whatever they call themselves. Troop 109 tried to make me their mascot or an honorary member or something. I think it was just a ruse to get me to go on their overnight camping trips with them."

"Can't blame guys for trying."

"Oh, no," Marie said, adjusting her sling slightly. "I never blame them for trying. Guys wouldn't be guys if they didn't try."

As I backed the Studebaker out of the cottonwood grove, it was with a gladdened heart and a relieved conscience.

When we arrived at the hospital, Marie insisted she didn't have to go in. Her shoulder felt better, she said, and she was sure her injury wasn't severe. To destroy her argument I only had to ask her to lift her arm. When she couldn't do that, I pulled into the emergency room bay.

I helped Marie from the car, and then said, "I'll park the car and be right in."

My father and mother wouldn't be waiting up for me—staying out all graduation night was a tradition that many parents honored—and Marie didn't have to worry about coming in late either. Her parents were out of town, and the older sister who was staying with Marie and her younger brother didn't care what time Marie came in. We were both free to spend as many hours at the hospital as might be required, hardly where either of us had believed we'd end up on that night.

As if in a concession to the lateness of the hour, the emergency room area was hushed and dimly lit. The only hospital employee I could see was a nurse behind a high counter, and Marie was speaking to her when I walked in. When I took my place alongside

Marie, the nurse, a sour-faced older woman with tiny eyes, stared intently at me. I must have made quite a sight—barefoot, clothes soaking wet, and wearing a smile probably rare in those surroundings. But then the other people who came into the hospital didn't make the trip in the company of Miss Marie Ryan. But I could clearly read the inquiry in the nurse's gaze: Who are you? Since I had no answer for the question, I simply grinned a little harder and tried to appear as though I was exactly where I belonged.

The nurse pointedly addressed Marie. "You can wait over there. Someone will be with you shortly."

We had barely sat down when Marie said, "His problem is he can't get out of his head the idea that something, *something*, good should come out of what his dad did. This stupid show he put on tonight—*God!*—that was just his latest crazy idea. Famous . . . He'll be famous, all right."

Since we'd left the river, Marie had not once spoken Gene's name.

"Yeah, they'll be talking about that for a long time," I said.

"I've tried to tell him, you're never going to forget what happened. Never. But you have to stop pulling the past up to the present. Let it stay back there. Let the days keep putting more distance between *now* and *then*." She shook her head and grimaced, and I couldn't be sure if her expression of pain came from her injury or this renewal of her frustration at trying to help Gene and failing. "You can see how much success I've had," she said ruefully.

She looked up at me, and I had the sense that she was waiting for me to confess my own inability to aid my friend through his life's worst period. What could I say? I have stopped short of openly professing my love for his girlfriend. . . .

"He'd be worse off without you," I said. "A hell of a lot worse off."

The height to which her eyebrows rose indicated that my words had failed to persuade her. I couldn't summon any enthusiasm, however, for extending the argument. Besides, the worsening pain in Marie's shoulder was commanding all her attention. Suddenly light-headed, she bent forward in her chair in order to lower her head and keep from fainting.

"Should I call the nurse?" I asked.

Marie shook her head, but just then the nurse came out from behind her desk to take Marie to an examining room. That didn't however, mean a diagnosis or treatment would be forthcoming. Hospitals today of course are staffed around the clock with emergency room physicians and support staff, but in 1962 Marie couldn't be attended to until a doctor on call was notified and an X-ray technician was wakened and summoned to the hospital. I saw both of them arrive. The tech, a sleepy, slow-moving, dark-haired, handsome young man not much older than Marie and I, showed up first, and not long after, Marie was ushered away, but more than an hour passed before the doctor appeared. I recognized him as Dr. DuFresne, an older physician famous in Bismarck for his elegance, his encyclopedic medical knowledge, and his vinegary disposition. He stopped just inside the door and took a last drag on the cigarette poised at the tip of his long fingers. When he thrust the butt into the ashtray's sand, it was a gesture performed with impatience. I worried that Marie would not be treated gently or compassionately, at least not in his hands.

Once the requisite medical personnel were in attendance, however, the wait for Marie was still long. And frustrating. Since we were both trapped in the hospital, why couldn't we be allowed to pass the time in each other's company?

At one point I leaned back in my chair and dozed off, an act that would likely be noted in fiction only because it would present an opportunity to reveal a character's dream. But in life we remember few of our dreams, and those we do recall are usually not tied to a time or a place. Dreams—and more commonly nightmares—create their own settings, and override our waking sense of our surroundings. But since so many of the moments of that time in my life have, as I recollect them, dreamlike qualities—unpredictable, emotionally intense yet ambiguous, imagistically vivid—I feel as though it's appropriate to make up a dream to accompany that scene in the hospital's waiting room.

I've been led into a ward with a long row of beds or gurneys, each separated from the next by a gauzy cloth curtain. I suspect that Marie is just on the other side of the partition, and soon that suspicion hardens into certainty. I can see her, albeit only in silhouette, but a shadow is enough for me to know it's her. She's moving around, dancing perhaps, and occasionally a part of her—her forehead, a leg, an elbow, her entire torso, especially her breasts—presses against the fabric, strains against it, almost as though she is trying to tear through. I don't understand whether I'm being invited to touch her through the cloth or whether she doesn't even know I'm there. My dilemma is complicated when I hear her voice. The sound of it is so faint that I can't make out any words, yet its murmur has a rhythm—rising and falling, louder and softer—that tells me she's speaking in sentences. But again, I don't know if she's talking to me. I'm paralyzed with the fear that if I reach out or speak to her, only to learn that her speech and movements are intended for someone else, someone whose shadow I can't see, I'll not only embarrass myself—something I'm willing to risk—but also frighten and alienate her when I'm revealed as an eavesdropper. Suddenly from over the top of Marie's side of the partition something is thrown—again, whether accidentally or purposely I can't know—over to my side. I can't tell what the object is, but it's right overhead, floating at first, then falling at great speed. I stretch out my hands to catch it, and in so doing startle myself awake.

Sunrise was less than an hour away when Marie finally reappeared. She was wearing a sling, just as she had been when she went in, but not the jury-rigged version I had knotted from her father's shirt. This one was made for its purpose. Canvas, it cradled her arm completely, and its work was supplemented by Ace bandages elaborately swathed around her, immobilizing her arm and shoulder. The elastic extended diagonally from the base of her neck to below her breasts and wound around her chest. To accommodate the wrap, the top half of her swimming suit was pulled down and bunched around her waist, while her shirt was draped around her shoulders.

She looked tired, but the color that pain had siphoned away earlier had returned to her cheeks. She smiled at me and asked, "Have you dried out yet?"

"Almost." In truth, only a little dampness remained in the creases of my clothes. "How about you? Can you leave or are they going to check you in?"

"No, I can go." Her glance over her shoulder made me wonder if she was escaping rather than being released.

Just at that moment Dr. DuFresne emerged from the small of-

fice behind the nurse's desk. "Remember, young lady," he said
sternly, "you're to check in with your family doctor next week.
He'll want to see how that bone's healing. I'm not convinced that
surgery isn't called for."

Marie nodded curtly at his admonition, and kept moving
toward the door. I rose and followed her, catching a glimpse, on
my way out, of Dr. DuFresne's look of disgust at my damp, di-
sheveled, barefoot appearance.

Marie's collarbone was broken, and if the combination of the
wrap and the sling didn't work, then it would be necessary, in Dr.
DuFresne's view, to knit the bone back together with a surgical
screw. For the next six weeks she was to use her arm as little as
possible and to keep that beautiful body tightly bound.

The hours she spent inside the hospital were not all devoted
to treatment of her injury. The first delay occurred because her
sister had to be telephoned and her permission given for Marie to
be treated. Her sister was willing to give that but wondered if she
should come to the hospital herself, something she didn't want to
do because their younger brother couldn't be left alone. Marie as-
sured her that wouldn't be necessary and that someone was there
who could bring her home. Next, both the X-ray technician and
the doctor were called away to attend to other patients. The first
was an old woman already in the hospital who fell attempting to
go to the bathroom on her own. The technician wasn't supposed
to read the X-rays, much less reveal what he saw on them, but he
told Marie that the old woman had broken her hip. Dr.
DuFresne, on the other hand, said nothing about the patient he
was called away to see, but he was even more curt with Marie
when he returned.

"Grumpy old bastard," Marie said as we drove away from the hospital. "Why would anyone who hates people as much as he does want to be a doctor in the first place?"

"How did it feel getting all trussed up like that?"

"It hurt like hell."

"Well, there's your answer."

We were both tired, Marie was in pain, and the eastern sky's night blue was already surrendering its darkest hue to morning's lighter tint, but Marie didn't want to go home. Not just yet. "Take the long way," she said.

I wasn't sure what that route would be. If I drove all around the city's perimeter, the trip probably wouldn't take more than fifteen minutes. Then it came to me. Marie wanted to be driven past Gene's house.

While I drove, Marie worried out loud about how her life would accommodate a broken clavicle. She was supposed to start her summer job at J. C. Penney's in the next week—would they want a clerk who could use only one arm and who would have to wear blouses with an empty sleeve? Who was going to change her Ace bandage and wrap her up again? Marie would prefer asking that favor of her sister rather than her mother, but her sister might attend summer school in Minneapolis. How often could she bathe? She wouldn't be able to wear a bra or shave her armpits for weeks!

She fell silent, however, when I turned up Keogh Street. Within the distance of a couple blocks—there could be no doubt about the direction in which we were headed—she raised the hand of her uninjured arm as if she were blocking traffic. "I want to go home," she said. "Now."

"Is something wrong?"

"Just turn at the corner."

I did as I was told.

By the time I parked in Marie's driveway and walked her to the door, doves somewhere overhead muttered their *ooh*s and *aah*s over the hour we were coming in, and there was sufficient light to read the address on the house across the street. That was the same test I had subjected dawn to on another occasion. This time I knew where Marie was.

I held the door to the garage open for her. "Will your sister be waiting up?"

"I doubt it. When I talked to her from the hospital and convinced her I was okay, she just told me to come in quietly."

Once again we were standing at her back door. Once again she thanked me for escorting her through a difficult time. Once again I thought of what it must be like to stand in this place and be more than Marie Ryan's friend.

Then, abruptly, she said, "Okay. Now."

"Now?"

"*Now* you can kiss me." She laughed at how her statement sounded like a regal command. "Said the queen."

"I'm not sure that would be such a good idea. Gene—"

"Forget about Gene. You must know that he and I are finished."

"He's gone through so much—"

She clapped her hand over my mouth. "Stop it. Stop defending him."

Her hand slipped away, but its sensation—softness, warmth, a faintly antiseptic smell from the hospital—lingered. Once I could form words again, I continued to try to talk my way out of the moment that I had desired more than any other. "Down at the river tonight . . . that wasn't the real Gene. He would never—"

"Don't you think I know by now who and what the real Gene is? And better than you? Now, are you going to take me up on my offer? You don't want to make a girl feel rejected."

Before I could answer, she hooked her fingers inside the collar of my T-shirt, pulled me close, and kissed me.

I had kissed a few girls before Marie, but her kiss, with its wide openmouthed intensity, its ability to at first be hard and then yield to pliancy, was astonishing. Because of her injury she had to withhold most of her body, yet her entire being still seemed behind her kiss.

Our lips came apart, and immediately I went back for more, to confirm both my good fortune and my physical impressions.

The next kiss was amazingly deeper, firmer, and softer than the first, and eventually I had to step back, breathless, unbelieving, and a little frightened that I couldn't match her passion.

"Whew!" was all I could manage, and with that, Marie laughed and sent me on my way, albeit with the admonition that I had best call her the following afternoon.

I parked the Studebaker in front of the house and was surprised to see both my father and mother hurry down the front walk to meet me. It was still too early for them to have gotten up, especially on a Saturday, so obviously they had been waiting for my arrival. The night before, they had cheerfully given me their permission to stay out as long as I liked, but as they approached, their expressions were drawn tight with anything but approval.

Just as sunrise's gradual light brings to view one feature of the landscape after another, I saw, dawning across my parents' faces, anger, worry, and relief, all within the span of seconds.

My father put his arm across my shoulders, an action that should have seemed an expression of affection; instead it seemed as if he were gently restraining me. On my other side, my mother also walked close, ready to block my movement in the other direction. Together they herded me toward the house, but neither said anything; that was left to Uncle Burt, who came out onto the porch as we approached.

Uncle Burt had driven down from Wembley for my graduation, and he had stayed the night. He too must have been waiting for me. His cigar had burned down to a stub, and the coffee cup in his hand was probably not his first of the morning.

He said, in that voice that was always a strange combination of delicacy and heartiness, "Your folks have been worried about you. As you might know, your classmates had a party down on the river last night, and there was an accident, a drowning."

I couldn't hear any more. I twisted away from my father's loose embrace and tore off across the lawn. I must have heard one of my parents—both of them—yell after me, "It wasn't Gene! It wasn't Gene!" just as I must have concluded, once I saw his car parked in front of the Stoddard house, that he could not have been the drowning victim, but I ran on and didn't stop until I came to that car and saw, faintly in the early morning light, the dusty outlines of footprints on the trunk, rear window, and roof, evidence of its having been used as Gene's stage. I ran my hand along the rear fin, not far from where Marie had fallen. I backed away from the Ford. In its wheel wells were traces of sand.

My mother had followed me down the street, and now she caught up to me. Gently she turned me back toward our house. "Sshh. That's okay," she said, as if I had been crying and needed to be quieted. "He's all right."

I certainly didn't argue with her, but I might have said, He is not all right, he is definitely not all right, and soon he will be worse. . . .

Back in the house, I allowed myself to be comforted and reassured. My parents were convinced that I had broken away out of fear and concern for my friend. In truth, what had panicked me *was* fear, and a familiar one. I had felt it on the night when Marie and I searched the branches of the trees for Gene's hanging body, and my fear then was that his death would preserve Marie's love for him. How much worse would it have been if on the night when Marie and I had exchanged our breaths, he lost his forever. She would never have recovered.

As it turned out, neither Bob Mullen nor Diane Burgie attended Carleton College in the autumn of 1962. Diane enrolled at Bismarck Junior College, and her decision to remain in her hometown was largely determined by her fragile emotional state at the time. And Bob? Diane's boyfriend and fellow scholarship winner was the young man who drowned in the Missouri River on the night of our high school graduation.

She blamed herself for what happened, and Bob likely would not have had it any other way. After I left the party in pursuit of Marie, after Gene slid off his car at the end of his act (as it turned out, his performance was mostly complete at the time of my departure), Diane was persuaded to drink a can of beer. The person who talked her into consuming alcohol for the first time was: A football player from Mandan High School; A trumpet player from St. Mary's Central High School; A farm kid from a small town west of Bismarck. All three accounts made the rounds, but probably the important detail, present in every version, was that this young man was someone who had been Diane's playmate in childhood. He had moved to another town or another neighborhood.

It doesn't matter. He was, as narratives so often require such a character to be, an outsider, the other. Diane was pleased to see him. Or at least she pretended to be. She and Bob had quarreled. He apparently had wanted to leave the party, but she had wanted to stay. The attention she paid the new boy, as well as the beer she drank (and another and another followed the first), was calculated to anger Bob and to demonstrate to him that she didn't have to shape all the contours of her life to his.

Her tactic worked. Or was it a tactic? Perhaps she allowed herself, under the influence of alcohol or not, to be attracted to someone other than Bob. Perhaps the occasion, an end and a beginning, prompted her to consider alternatives that she had previously barred from consideration.

Bob, desperate to win back her attention—or to garner the attention of others and in so doing demonstrate that he didn't need Diane's—began to do front and back flips on the sandbar. Bob was known for his conscientiousness, his seriousness, his intelligence; he was, in other words, someone who readily gained the respect and admiration of adults while he had few qualities that made him cool or popular or attractive among his peers. He wasn't an athlete, at least not in any of the sports that had audiences or followers. But Bob Mullen participated in gymnastics throughout high school, and it was that training that enabled him to impress the drunken crowd at the sandbar. In addition to his flips, he did a somersault off the roof of a car. But that was not his most impressive performance. He twisted through the air; he landed on the earth. But then he needed to bring the other elements into play. For fire, he launched himself over one of the bonfires, landing with a perfect roll on the other side of the flames.

Bob Mullen backed up from the river and then took a run at it. When his feet touched the waterline, he catapulted himself into the air, flipped, and came down right into the river's main current. Had he been heavier and less skilled at hurling his body, perhaps he would not have been able to propel himself so far from the sandbar. Had he been taller, perhaps he would have landed where he could touch bottom and still keep his head above water.

Almost immediately the laughter and shouts of encouragement that had accompanied Bob's attempt to entertain his classmates died when they saw him swept away—from light, the fire's flickering orange reflection on the water, to darkness, the river's true night face—the instant he splashed down.

And yet something—drunkenness, disbelief, all those years of parental warnings about the river's treacherousness, something—paralyzed the witnesses. A long moment passed before anyone stepped into the river for a rescue attempt. By then it was already too late. Most people said he vanished immediately into the black water, pulled under by a current that wouldn't permit him to surface even for a second to wave or shout for help. At least that's

what most people said. But Karen Conroy, who had been standing right at the river's edge, told me she caught one final glimpse
of Bob Mullen. She said she could see his pale form tumbling
through the water, as if he were still doing his somersaults and
flips while the Missouri rushed him off.

His body was discovered two days later, tangled in the driftwood and brush at a bend in the river fifteen miles south of Bismarck.

*Although Bob Mullen died with a mouth full of water, the
taste of dirt was on his tongue.*

The previous sentence appears in one of my journals, but the
line never found its way into a poem, story, or novel. For the insight—if it qualifies as such—on that sensation, I had my own
tumble into a Missouri River pothole to thank.

Why have I bothered to relate the Bob Mullen story when it
is a tributary that never joins the main narrative? Because while I
know—rationally, logically, sensibly, I *know* that Raymond Stoddard's deeds had nothing to do with that young man's drowning,
I can't separate them emotionally. Everything that occurred near
that place and time seems somehow to owe its causality to Raymond Stoddard and his murder of Monty Burnham. Raymond
Stoddard? He set the universe in motion.

The slain politician's son doesn't want to board the train.

*His mother and his uncle, however, remind him that being
sent away is not a punishment but a privilege, a reward for
being a good student and a respectful, dutiful boy who has
borne up under difficult circumstances. His mother kisses his*

forehead, and when she embraces him, he suddenly thinks he has a legitimate excuse for not getting on the train. He's ill! In his throat he feels that scratchy constriction that's often the first sign of tonsillitis. But that thought is enough to carry him back from the verge of tears, and with that retreat the sensation vanishes.

Just as he lifts his foot onto the step stool that will carry him into the train car, his uncle hisses into his ear, "Don't stay in the bathroom longer than you have to." Another passenger comes up behind him, so the slain politician's son doesn't have time to ask his uncle the question that seems so obvious: Why would I?

He walks down the train's aisle, looking for a seat on the side of the train that won't force him to look out on the platform where his mother and uncle will be standing, and as he does, his feeling of banishment is complete. He is being sent to a strange country whose customs, population, even food, will be alien to him. He is on his way to spend two weeks at Camp Way-Tah-Ga in northern Wisconsin, and he knows that the congregation of First Lutheran Church chose him to go, rather than a boy from a poor family as in years past, because the congregation, indeed the entire town, feels sorry for him. But why not leave, he thinks, since he is obviously no longer understood in his own land. Otherwise why would his mother, who has always been perfectly attuned to his likes and dislikes, his enthusiasms and fears, believe that living with boys he has never met would be anything but punitive?

Further evidence of this estrangement he comes upon two hours into his journey when he unwraps the ham sandwich his mother prepared for his lunch. The bread has been spread thickly with butter. Mustard—he likes mustard only. He dislikes butter on everything but pancakes and then only the thinnest film, which must melt completely. He folds the sandwich back into its waxed-paper wrapper and then tucks it inside the copy of Boys' Life *that he's already read. He lays both on the empty cushion beside him and tries to act as though they belong to the person who will soon return to his seat. If the sandwich has done nothing else, it has replaced some of his despondency with disgust. Adults—they act as though they understand, but they fall so far short you wonder why they even bother with the pretense.*

Once the slain politician's son actually goes to the bathroom, he believes he understands his uncle's warning. The toilet flushes with such swirling force and the water pours into the washbasin so swiftly that it's a temptation to linger, turning the water off and on, filling the sink and watching it drain, listening to the way the toilet's formless whoosh *contrasts with the train's rapid but still rhythmical rush. He feels as though he's on the edge of a discovery about the essential difference between liquid and machine, but remembering his uncle's words, he returns to his seat. By the time he next visits the restroom, his sorrow and self-pity have returned, and he no longer has any interest in insights or discoveries.*

When he disembarks in Wisconsin, he is met by a tall, sunburned, redheaded young man, a counselor from the camp who already has in his company a boy who rode the very same train as the slain politician's son. Jimmy Hogan boarded the train in St. Paul, but unlike the slain politician's son, Jimmy is an experi-

enced traveler and he roamed from one car to another, search-
ing for boys he remembered from his previous years at camp.
The slain politician's son saw the fat boy repeatedly waddle
down the train's aisle, but the slain politician's son was too shy
to speak to anyone.

Once they are in the station wagon that will take them the
thirty miles to Camp Way-Tah-Ga, Jimmy Hogan suggests to
the counselor that in the future the camp should send special
caps to campers, something that the boys could wear on their
way to Camp Way-Tah-Ga and in that way identify their com-
mon destination to one another. The counselor, a high school
senior or college student, the slain politician's son guesses,
doesn't acknowledge Jimmy's suggestion. Instead he lights an-
other Camel, which he keeps bouncing between his lips with his
vigorous gum-chewing.

Into the silence, the slain politician's son cautiously says to
Jimmy, "That's a good idea. The caps."

And with that, the two boys become friends. For the rest of
the ride, Jimmy tries to educate the slain politician's son about
the camp's culture and conventions. He begins, of course, with
the food. The hamburgers might look good, but they're usually
dried out and barely warm. The macaroni and cheese is okay if
you get a serving from the middle of the tray. The best breakfast
is French toast. The best dessert is the butterscotch pudding. He
advises the slain politician's son to arrive at the archery range
early when they have target practice, or else he'll get one of the
bows that's so tight he'll hardly be able to pull the string back.
Don't get in a canoe with the thirteen-year-olds because they
won't even let you paddle. Don't sit on the side of the campfire

*where the big trees are because the wind always blows sparks
and smoke in that direction. "Chapel" means the same thing as
"church." "Hike" and "nature walk" mean pretty much the
same thing. Don't wear shorts to play baseball or you won't be
able to slide. And whatever the slain politician's son does, he
should make certain he doesn't piss off Castle, the oldest counselor at the camp. Castle is always in a foul temper, but no one
is quite sure why. Some say it's because he's a junior high
teacher during the year, and by the time summer rolls around,
he's sick of kids. Another theory has it that Castle is an alcoholic who is kept from drink during the camp sessions. A more
forgiving, romantic explanation of Castle's dark moods suggests
that he once had a beautiful wife who was killed in an automo-
bile accident. As Jimmy finishes his list of admonitions, he
glances up at their gum-chewing driver, who says only, "Yeah,
Castle's a prick." The obscenity delights the boys.*

*The slain politician's son soon learns, however, that because of
the way the camp is set up, he and the redoubtable Castle are
unlikely to have much contact. Castle works mostly with the
younger boys, and the slain politician's son belongs with the
Wolverines (the ten- and eleven-year-olds), a group with whom
he quickly grows quite comfortable. Thanks to Jimmy, the slain
politician's son is assigned a bunk in Jimmy's dormitory, and
Jimmy introduces the slain politician's son to the other boys
their age and makes sure he is always gathered into the group
before any activity—flag races, hikes, swim instruction, candle
making, or woodworking—begins. The slain politician's son becomes so close to these boys that he wonders if he should reveal*

*to them how he is different from every one of them and always
will be. Finally he decides against it. He won't share with the
Wolverines his unique history, one that includes newspaper
headlines and reporters in the kitchen extinguishing cigarettes in
his mother's coffee cups. Indeed, though the slain politician's
son is the only Wolverine who has never before attended Camp
Way-Tah-Ga, his family owns a cabin on a small lake in North
Dakota, and in his mind the slain politician's son substitutes
those experiences for the not dissimilar ones the other boys have
had in previous summers. Ironically, it is Jimmy Hogan who believes he has an identity unlike anyone else's; Jimmy is not only
fat, he is left-handed and he has had his appendix removed.*

*Most of the boys have been looking forward to the day when
they'll be allowed to fish in the swift-flowing waters of the
Goose River. Since they arrived in camp they've been allowed to
fish only in the lake, and even then only with bamboo poles,
tiny hooks, red worms, and bobbers. They never catch anything
but crappies, bluegills, and sunfish. Today, however, they're
being driven to a location where the river suddenly straightens
its course and runs fast and frothy over and around a series of
big rocks. There the boys will be handed real fishing rods with
artificial lures and treble hooks and given instruction on how to
cast their lines into the pools and eddies where the big fish—
bass and walleye and northern and even muskie—lie. But before
any of them can wet a line, they must sit through fishing lessons, even if they've been doing this kind of fishing for years.*

*On that day, the Wolverines are divided and assigned to
other groups, and the slain politician's son is placed with five*

boys who will have—oh, shit!—Castle as their teacher. They gather near the pilings of a railroad bridge. The river there has shrunk back from the tree line, and they have a wide beach on which to line up and listen to their teacher's advice. The sand the slain politician's son sits upon feels simultaneously warm, soft, and damp, a new and peculiar sensation, and he adds it to the collection of never-felt-before that he has been compiling for the past seven months.

As it turns out, Castle, in spite of his profession in the non-summer months—it's been verified; he is a junior high school teacher—has no aptitude for or interest in instruction. He simply tells the boys, "Watch how I do it."

Next he performs a series of movements so rapid that none of the boys understands exactly what he's doing or why. He clicks something on the reel—the bale? Did he lock the bale back? Did he do something with the drag? He brings the rod back, then flings it forward, and the lure—a spinner with a tuft of fur attached to its end—whirs out across the water. Did he have a target in mind? How did he direct it there? Almost immediately after the lure splashes down, Castle reels it in swiftly, straightening the rod's tip from time to time. "The action has to be like this," he says, "so the fish will want to hit it."

The last thing the slain politician's son wants at that moment is to be handed the rod and reel and told to duplicate the instructor's act, but he doesn't have to worry. Castle has apparently forgotten both his charge and his charges. He's just a man fishing on a summer day, casting over and over again to that boulder-blocked expanse of water where the river seems to back up on itself.

Suddenly there is a small eruption right where Castle's lure splashes down. It looks as if sunlight has not just spangled the water's surface but burst up from beneath it. Castle jerks back on his rod, and then it's plain—he's hooked a fish and the fish is leaping into the air.

Castle hasn't addressed the boys, but even without being asked, they all rise from the sand and stand behind him. From the expressions on their faces it's obvious that none of them believed that today's lessons could truly lead to an outcome like this. That's a real fish, large enough to bend the rod and create its own wake as it fights across the current, the line, and Castle's strength.

The fish must lose of course, and by the time Castle has reeled it in close to the shore, it can no longer leap clear of the river or even shake itself on the line. And why, the slain politician's son wonders, would the fish try to escape in the first place by leaving the water for the air, the element it can't survive in?

One of the boys steps forward with the net, but Castle brushes him aside. Holding the rod in one hand, he steps into the river, bends down, and pulls the fish from the water. To the slain politician's son it appears that Castle grabs the fish by the lip, but that can't be. Fish don't have—Then he sees. Castle has hooked the fish again, this time with his finger, right under the fish's mouth.

A boy more knowledgeable about fish than the slain politician's son whistles softly and says, "A walleye!"

"What a pig!" Castle says. "That sonofabitch has gotta be twelve pounds."

The fish twists and wriggles so slowly in Castle's hand it seems as if it might be moving in the breeze rather than by its own muscle and will. Castle quickly and deftly unhooks the walleye, sets down his rod and reel, and holds the fish aloft with two hands. Its pale belly sags as if it were weighted with stones. Its eyes look as though they have been cut out of aluminum foil. "You pig," Castle says again, this time almost affectionately.

Castle finally acknowledges the boys who have been gazing at him as if he had been enacting a play for their entertainment. "One of you want to put him in the catch bucket?"

Like the other boys, the slain politician's son raises his hand and jumps into the air. He is sure that only he, however, has no interest in the fish. Instead he wants to do what no other boy has been able to do—to win Castle's approval and esteem.

And it is that purity of motive, the slain politician's son believes, that separates him from every other ten-year-old bouncing up and down on the sand, and that causes Castle to reach the fish out toward him and say, "Hold him tight. And watch out for the fins. They're sharp as razors."

Once the slain politician's son holds the fish, with its heft that doesn't match its light silver slickness, he can smell it, and that odor brings back his past—the family cabin, the heat that seemed to rise every morning from the lake's algae-choked shoreline, the grown-ups with their skinny pale legs bare the way they never would be in town, and their loud laughter, the hollow thunk of oar and boat, and the little panfish strung on a line as if they were beads run through with a sewing needle, and smelling like, like, like nothing else. . . . Is that past only a single summer removed from the slain politician's son? Is that possible? The memory seems as if it has to struggle an exhausting distance back to him. The walleye's gill yawns open so slowly it must be for the last time. For a moment the slain politician's son glimpses the fish's blood-red interior, and the sight appalls him so that by a laborious process—he slides the fish slowly across his shirt front—he shifts the walleye to his other hand and now holds the fish backward, its head and dead eyes and awful starving gills facing the other way.

While he wades into the water and opens the lid of the catch bucket, the slain politician's son has to squeeze the fish tightly but not too tightly, because he can feel how with just a little more pressure it could squirt from his hand.

The river water inside the bucket looks like weak tea, and for an instant the slain politician's son wonders if he is making a mistake. No, he is doing exactly what Castle asked of him, and there is no other way to gain the man's favor. He lowers the fish into the bucket.

It all happens so fast that afterward the slain politician's son can't be sure of the precise sequence—did Castle first cry out, "Not tail first! Not tail first!" or did those shouted words come after the fish, instantly revived when the cold water washed over it, with one sudden sinuous effort, burst from the bucket and escaped into the river's current?

No matter what the chronology, the consequence is unchanged. The walleye, a flashing golden shimmer, swims away, and Castle grabs the slain politician's son by the collar of his T-shirt and pulls him backward with such force that the boy lands heavily on the sand, his breath flying out of him so completely that he might as well have been shoved underwater.

"That was a trophy fish!" Castle shouts. "A goddamn trophy fish!"

He looms over the slain politician's son, who believes that the physical threat from Castle hasn't passed. The boy rolls across the sand until he can be certain Castle can't reach him, even with a kicking foot.

But Castle isn't interested in pursuit. He simply stares down at the slain politician's son in disgust. "Can't even put a fish in a bucket," Castle says. "Jesus. What a moron. What a little moron."

And then the slain politician's son makes the situation worse. He laughs, though his lack of breath soon causes his laughter to change into a fit of coughing.

It is the laughter that provokes Castle into grabbing the slain politician's son by the hair, shaking him, and then throwing him back toward the sand. It is the boy's helpless coughing fit that convinces the camp authorities that Castle's harshness can no longer be tolerated and that the man must be dismissed from working at Camp Way-Tah-Ga.

After the incident, the slain politician's son explains to his new friends why he couldn't keep from laughing. That was the summer of the "little moron" jokes—Why did the little moron throw his alarm clock out the window? Because he wanted to see time fly. Why did the little moron put his father in the refrigerator? Because he wanted cold pop—and when Castle insulted him with that very phrase, laughter bubbled uncontrollably from him.

In truth, the slain politician's son's laughter came from the sudden realization, insofar as such a thing can be realized by a ten-year-old boy whose bony ass is denting the sand of a river beach, that he had no special standing on this earth and that he *was therefore subject to the same vagaries of reward and retribution as every other human being. He was no different from any other Wolverine.*

⌒

This story came into being from an assignment of sorts. A friend, to whom I had been complaining of a personal publishing drought, suggested that maybe I needed to try writing fiction that was removed from my own life, times, and circumstances. "The Slain Politician's Son," which appeared in *The Stopped Clock Review*, was my attempt to follow that advice, and while it may not have seemed to most readers like such a radical divergence from my usual concerns, it was. I knew that Monty Burnham, like Raymond Stoddard, had a son, so I tried to invent a life for him. Believe me, any turn that took me away from the murderer's existence—and Keogh Street—and toward the victim's was a radical one.

⌒

I had ample opportunity to observe Diane Burgie in the aftermath of Bob Mullen's death because I was in two of her classes, biology and psychology, at Bismarck Junior College. But while she chose to stay close to home because her guilt-ridden, grief-stricken state left her too weak to stray far, I attended a community college in order to be close to Marie Ryan. By the end of summer 1962 she and I were going steady, and since she had a year of high school left, I decided that enrolling at the university in Grand Forks could wait. I say "I decided," but really, there was no decision to be made at all.

In fact I sometimes wondered why, since we were in classes together, Diane Burgie and I weren't used for an academic demonstration. The biology or psychology teacher—the demonstration would have worked for either subject—might have displayed both of us in front of the classroom and said to the other students, "Look closely at these specimens. They illustrate what love can do to a human being." Pointing to Diane, the professor might have noted the hair, once blond, bright, and shining, now lusterless and lank; the complexion, pocked and sallow; the expression, dour and despairing; the entire being, enervated and drawn inward. I, on the other hand, could have been used as an example of love's power to vitalize, to fulfill, to bestow happiness and hope. In fact, had my state of bliss not been so complete, Diane Burgie's doleful presence might have made me a little embarrassed over my great good luck.

Marie's broken collarbone did not require surgery, but it was slower in healing than originally projected. Not until the end of July was she able to remove for good the sling and elaborate webbing that had held her body tight to itself. By that time J. C. Penney's had assigned her to work in their credit department, so her temporary handicap didn't affect her ability to do her job. It did, however, have a strange effect on our burgeoning relationship.

It should go without saying that I could not get enough of Marie Ryan, yet her physical condition, coupled with my timidity, imposed a restraint on what we could do. While I could kiss her for hours, because of her Ace bandage binding, there was no possibility that we could go beyond kissing (or so I believed; I had a very clear notion of what should be the natural progression of sexual intimacies). Furthermore, she could put no more than one arm into an embrace, and my own passion had to operate with a governor on it—squeeze too hard or press too close and she might flinch with pain.

The eventual removal of the wrap and the sling freed Marie in ways that went beyond the ability to raise her arm or twist her torso or draw an unencumbered deep breath. After those weeks of control, her ardor could suddenly match mine.

The night of the day the doctor pronounced her healed we were parked on a hill west of Bismarck. The sun had barely gone down when the moon, full and antique yellow, rose to claim the sky. If we looked out Marie's side of the Studebaker, we could see the dark reflection of the Missouri unspooling itself far below. If we looked out my side, we could see the random cluster of the city's lights. Over the entire town the capitol building towered, each of its four sides presiding over a compass point. But notice I say "*If* we looked out, we could see . . ." Our eyes were fixed on nearer things. For the first time we were able to embrace with all the strength we owned, and we pressed ourselves together as if we were determined to seal our bodies to each other in spite of the resistances of clothing, skin, muscle, and bone.

During one of the brief moments when our lips and tongues were not twinned and twined, I mentioned how strange it was to feel Marie's actual flesh beneath her blouse rather than a bandage. Laughing, I added, "And you're wearing a bra for the first time!"

In response to a request I did not make, Marie unbuttoned her blouse and wriggled herself free of it. She twisted around so her back was to me. "I still have trouble reaching around," she said. "Unhook me."

My trembling, inexperienced fingers eventually managed to accomplish the task. Then, with a movement so subtle and deft I didn't quite understand how she performed it, Marie allowed her brassiere to fall off.

She turned back to me, her crossed arms covering her breasts. She let her hands fall away and at the same time reclined across the Studebaker's front seat.

In these pages are examples aplenty of my inventive powers (or deficiencies). There is evidence as well of how my imagination is as likely to lead to misapprehension and mistake as to truth and understanding. Let me merely say at this point that I could more successfully imagine my way into a murderer's mind than anticipate the wonder of Marie Ryan's perfect breasts exposed to my sight and touch.

Marie, however, had no patience with my awe. She extended her arms, beckoning me to lie down with her, and just in case I didn't understand the invitation, she whispered, "Come here."

The sight of the almost-naked Marie Ryan was intoxicating, but even more thrilling—and astonishing—was the feel of her. Her skin was warm and amazingly soft to the touch—silk right off the ironing board.

"*Now,*" she said.

When my kisses became too long and too intense, Marie turned her head to the side. As if to expand her body and its openness to pleasure, she extended one arm out under the dashboard and with the other reached up and pressed against the seat.

If the months-later occasion when we finally had intercourse was somewhat less ecstatic, mark it down to my overeagerness and awkwardness. The act occurred in the unfinished attic of Marie's parents' home. The attic entrance was through the garage, and we were frequently able to climb up there undetected. Under the slanting roof and the cobwebbed timbers, lying on our makeshift pallet (flattened cardboard boxes covered with winter coats and old clothes), we explored our bodies and their secret delights, and finally, on a warm April day that was warmer still in the attic, we went all the way. That was the phrase in currency at the time (and perhaps it still is), and while I felt its accuracy—I had plainly gone somewhere I had never been before —I also sensed its inadequacy: I knew there were further realms to travel to, and one journey was barely finished before I wanted another to begin. And gradually, with Marie's help, I overcame the ineptness of that first time. In sexual matters, she knew my nature better than I, and she taught me that the greatest pleasures came from being controlled by the moment rather than trying to control it.

Across from Marie's parents' home was an elementary school, and I remember being in the attic once when the shouts and laughter of children at play rose to our height. We had just finished making love, and while Marie still lay on our "bed," I rose and went to the high, small window to try to take advantage of what little ventilation it might provide.

The day, like so many on North Dakota's calendar, was breezy, and just enough air moved through the window to cool my sweating body. I couldn't see the children, but I could hear them, and the sound was enough for me to imagine their activity, their play. . . . What Marie and I had been doing was, of course, playful, yet just as certainly it was different. I didn't at that time have Frost's phrase—"play for mortal stakes"—but it applied. In our stifling garret Marie and I played together. Life and death depended on it. Whose, I couldn't be sure.

⁓

I didn't keep from my parents the fact that I was going steady with Marie Ryan, but neither did I go out of the way to advertise the relationship. I was concerned, a worry probably without foundation, that they might display an unseemly interest in what Marie might know about Raymond Stoddard. And though I say "they," I really mean my father. A year and a half after the murder-suicide he was still seeking the truth behind it. His quest was no longer very active, but he was not yet satisfied with any of the theories that might have settled the minds of others. My mother, as I said earlier, was content with the version that Ross Wilk had presented to my father.

But though I didn't want anyone else to try to take advantage of Marie for her inside information on the Stoddard family, I had no compunction myself about seeking to learn any secrets she might possess. I often questioned her about her memories of Mr. Stoddard and for any theories she might have had about his behavior. Marie, however, had little to offer, and not only because she had observed almost no examples of behavior that would lead one to conclude that the father of her then-boyfriend harbored murderous impulses.

As she made plain as far back as the day of Raymond Stoddard's funeral, she believed that the man was obviously deranged, if not legally insane. His acts were, ipso facto, evidence of that condition. The minds of such people couldn't be understood. Furthermore, pragmatic to her core, she thought it futile to try.

And though she wouldn't hold up any memory to explain Raymond Stoddard, she did tell me about an incident that corroborated her conviction that he was mentally ill.

Marie first met Raymond and Alma Stoddard when Gene invited her to a family picnic in September 1960. The day was windy, cold, and overcast, and to make matters worse the picnic site wasn't a Bismarck park but an unsheltered prairie hilltop north of the city. Mr. Stoddard, however, insisted that the spot, which he chose, was perfect. They spread their old wool blanket over buffalo grass so wiry and stubborn the stubble poked right through the fabric. Stones and the picnic basket weighted down the cloth at the corners and kept it from blowing away. The paper plates had to be heaped with food immediately, or the wind would tear them away like dry leaves.

And the food was not standard picnic fare. It was leftovers, and not particularly impressive ones at that. Chunks of cold (though previously overcooked) pot roast, unheated potatoes and carrots, apples (for weight, if nothing else), and buttered bread. Two thermoses—one filled with coffee and the other with milk.

Odder still was Marie's introduction to Mr. Stoddard. Shortly after meeting her, he wanted to know where she lived. When she told him, Mr. Stoddard said he knew the neighborhood well. When he first came to Bismarck, before he found an apartment for his family, he stayed with Mrs. Hills, who lived on Marie's street but had once lived in Wembley and was a friend of his grandmother's. Did Marie know Mrs. Hills?

Yes, she knew the old woman.

"How unfortunate," Mr. Stoddard said, "that she's no longer with us."

Marie didn't understand. "Not with us?"

"Why, she had a stroke," Mr. Stoddard said. "She passed away."

She wanted to make a good impression on her boyfriend's parents, but Marie Ryan couldn't allow this misinformation to stand. "No, she's alive. She lives just down the street from us."

"You're mistaken. She's no longer with us." Mr. Stoddard kept using the same phrase. No longer with us.

Another teenage girl might have backed down in the face of an adult's certainty. "She's alive," Marie reiterated. "Alive. I saw her recently."

Mr. Stoddard never stopped smiling or insisting. Mrs. Hills had had a stroke. She had passed away. He was sorry he hadn't attended her funeral.

Eventually, like the relentless prairie wind, he wore her down. Marie didn't submit to his belief, but she stopped arguing.

When Marie related this anecdote, I confessed that I didn't quite understand. So he had made a mistake; I didn't see how that was evidence of derangement.

Marie shook her head strenuously. It wasn't just that he was wrong—though that could have been a sign that he was delusional in his convictions—but that he wouldn't admit to doubt. He was so certain of the rightness of his belief.

That sounds, I suggested, as though you're describing someone religious.

"Okay," Marie said. "I don't have a problem with that. If you add 'zealot.' "

Yet for the most part, Marie resisted my efforts to pry from her any inside information on the Stoddard family, especially as such information might relate to Raymond Stoddard's pathology. In fact, she was critical of my curiosity.

I remember very well an evening when we sat in the darkened kitchen of her parents' house, facing each other across the table where the Ryan family ate their meals. I had been questioning her again about her memories of Mr. Stoddard and what Gene had told her about his father.

"Why," she wondered, "is it so important for you to know why he did what he did?"

One psychology class in high school and another in college provided me with a suitably high-minded and personal response. "If we can understand people like Raymond Stoddard—their, you know, their motivation—then maybe they can be stopped before they kill."

"Do you really believe *knowledge* can keep people from killing each other?" Marie had a gift for phrasing matters in such a way that the ground under your argument began to erode even before it was built. "Or that we can ever understand people like him?"

"Maybe."

"But there was only one Raymond Stoddard. And he did what he did. And he'll never do it again. Why not just let it all go?"

"Isn't it human to be curious? To want to know?"

"It just seems so pointless. Even if Raymond Stoddard had lived and he could tell us why he did what he did, we'd still only have a madman's word to go on."

I could never formulate an effective refutation to Marie's position, yet I never took that inadequacy to mean that my own beliefs were flawed. She was, I told myself, simply a better debater than I. So there was no reason for me to cease my interrogations, no matter how they might exhaust and exasperate her.

Let me offer just one more of Marie's memories of Raymond Stoddard, and I present it not as evidence of anything but simply to share an image that was lodged in her mind (and therefore in mine).

Marie never had that many occasions to observe Raymond Stoddard, and that was a consequence of the age as much as anything. In the early 1960s a boy might spend plenty of time at his girlfriend's parents' house, but she might never enter the interior of his. We all understood this, even if the *why* of it escaped us.

But Marie was there a few times (and if anyone was likely to defy the more idiotic strictures of the era, it was she), and on one occasion she and Gene were sitting on the living room floor in front of the black-and-white console television that I myself spent so many hours watching.

Mrs. Stoddard sat on the sofa and Mr. Stoddard was in his easy chair, but he was certainly not at ease. At one point he swiveled suddenly toward the living room window and the darkened night beyond and said, "Did you hear that?"

"Hear what?" Mrs. Stoddard calmly asked.

Suddenly embarrassed, Mr. Stoddard said, "Nothing. It's nothing."

Yet from where Marie sat, she had a clear view of him, and for the rest of the evening he seemed on alert, as if he were listening for that sound to repeat itself and its message that no one else could hear.

~

In the weeks and months after Marie and I started dating, not a word passed between Gene and me. From others I learned that for most of the summer and fall he was working out of town, continuing in the employ of his uncle's construction company. But Keogh Street was still his home, and occasionally I saw him drive by, now in a white Chevrolet convertible that he'd started driving about the time I acquired the Studebaker. His car was newer, faster, and cooler than mine, and he probably bought it with his own money. His job, according to all accounts, paid well.

Was I worried about how he would react to Marie and me being a couple? Yes. Was that worry intensified because he was Raymond Stoddard's son? Yes. And the worry played out on a daily basis as suspense, so while I was happy with Marie, happier than I had ever been, I was continually looking over my shoulder, constantly on the lookout for an attack from a wounded, enraged, drunken Gene Stoddard.

But Gene troubled my life in another way. As odd as it might seem, I missed him. He had been a part of my almost daily existence for years, while for only months had our friendship changed, so I couldn't quite adjust to the idea that now we were—what were we? Enemies? Rivals? Whatever term might have applied, the fact was we no longer had that regular, casual contact—*Did you understand that algebra assignment? Are you going to play touch football on Saturday? Do you want to get a burger at Jack Lyon's?*—that had for so long been a feature of both our lives. Are you going to play poker at Billy's on Friday? Do you want to drive or should I? Got an extra cigarette? *Want to know what Marie let me get away with last night?*

Perhaps, then, it was both a wish for reconciliation and a desire to eliminate the tension that I was living with that made me do what I did.

On the Friday after Thanksgiving 1962, snow began falling shortly after sunrise. By evening, close to a foot had fallen on the city. The snow was the dry, downy sort, so its effect was fairly benign. It was relatively easy to shovel, too light to snap branches or power lines, and since the wind was calm, flakes didn't stray far from where they fell. Still, even in a land as accustomed to winter's challenges as North Dakota, twelve inches of snow has an effect, and as I drove home late from Marie's, the streets were largely deserted. Snowplows had not cleared the streets, and I had to steer through the ruts left by cars that had earlier passed that way.

I had just turned onto Keogh Street when I saw Gene Stoddard trudging through one of those furrows. He had probably stepped out into the street because on that section of the block most of the sidewalks were unshoveled, the owners probably away for the holiday.

Could I have simply driven past? Certainly. And that option would have been in keeping with what our relationship had become. But as I said, the suspense had gotten to me, and this seemed an opportunity to address it, if not eliminate it altogether. Besides, he would recognize my car.

I stopped in the middle of the street and asked him if he wanted a ride.

Gene was hatless, gloveless, and wearing only a light jacket. His shoes must have been soaked through. Nevertheless, he hesitated before finally shrugging and climbing into the Studebaker.

"Remember Thanksgiving last year?" I said. "Sixty degrees." An innocuous remark about the weather seemed like a safe way to begin, even if it would allow him the opportunity to comment on how many other things were different a year ago.

"How about that time it snowed on Halloween? Who was the kid whose trick-or-treat bag got so wet it tore open and all his candy fell out? And then he went home crying, so we kept his candy?" Gene asked.

"Jerry Blessum."

"Jerry Blessum. Yeah." Gene was wearing aftershave or cologne, but its aroma was faint next to the stale but still over-powering smell of cigarette smoke and liquor. Was he drunk? Probably. "Fucking North Dakota. Snow on Halloween. . . . Why does anyone live here?"

What was I supposed to say—in order to be close to Marie? I changed the subject. "Where's your car?"

"Sitting in the driveway at Vicky Morhoeffer's. The battery's so fucking dead it won't even turn over."

For a moment I considered offering to drive him back there and help him start his car. In my trunk I kept, at my father's insistence, a set of jumper cables. They were there not only so I could get myself out of trouble, but so I could help others, as my father had done with the Stoddard vehicle on the second morning after Raymond Stoddard had hanged himself. I lacked, however, my father's Samaritan spirit. Indeed, it was hardly even an impulse to goodness that had prompted me to invite Gene into my car in the first place.

And in the general direction of that topic was where I ventured next, albeit with trepidation. "Vicky Morhoeffer, huh?"

"What can I say—she's a fucking slut. But she'll do anything. *Anything*. And her folks are hardly ever home."

I took that to mean that, unlike in a previous relationship, love was not involved. I understood as well that I was free to ask what Vicky Morhoeffer was willing to do. Instead, I headed for safer terrain. "She's a junior?"

"A junior? Yeah, I guess." We were on our block now, and he pointed toward his house. "Don't pull in the driveway. You'll pack down the snow, and it'll be harder to shovel in the morning."

I stopped under a streetlamp across from his house. I hadn't scraped the windshield very well when I left Marie's, and frost stars glittered on the glass under the light's glow. A few weightless flakes still floated in the air.

"Hey, you got any smokes?" Gene asked.

I reached into my shirt pocket for my pack of Chesterfields and handed it to him.

He shook out two cigarettes. "A couple to get me through the night?"

"Take all you need. Keep the pack, if you like."

Without warning, he grabbed my wrist.

I stiffened and that might have prevented Gene from pulling me toward him. But maybe moving me was not his intention.

Using my weight as an anchor, he drew himself closer to me. I could smell the rank, curdled odor of tobacco and whiskey on his breath.

Strangely, having my wrist in Gene's grasp didn't so much feel like a physical threat as it reminded me of a time in our childhood when we had taken each other's measure in quite a different way.

During one of the summers of our Little League play, Gene and I embarked on a strenuous program to improve as ballplayers. We practiced long hours, hitting fly balls and grounders to each other, pitching, batting (and sprinting after the batted ball), and with the help of instructional, inspirational articles in *Baseball Digest* and other publications, tried to strengthen our baseball muscles. Following the example of Hank Aaron's success, we tried to build stronger wrists by squeezing tennis balls and rolling weighted bars back and forth. To gauge our success, we were constantly calibrating each other's wrists, hoping to feel that increase in circumference that would indicate muscle growth.

Gene's grip on my wrist tightened, and when he spoke, the urgency of what he said seemed as much an appeal for validation as an expression of menace. "I had her first, you know. I had her first and I can have her back anytime I want. Any fucking time."

Fear might have motivated my reply. I was—I am—easily intimidated, and while I'm not eager to confess to cowardice, my commitment to honesty in this narrative won't let me back away from it. Nevertheless, I believe that something else was working on me. I felt sorry for Gene. And I leave to others the question of whether I betrayed Marie with my reply. Since I never reported this conversation to her, I can't report on her reaction.

To Gene I said simply, "I know."

He released me, and then he and my cigarettes were gone.

Lying in bed that night I felt none of the fear of Gene Stoddard that I had been experiencing for months. Instead what kept me awake was fear that flowed the other way. Would the day come when I, perhaps like Gene's father, could no longer live with the worry that someone was loose in the world who might at any time take my love from me? What was *I* willing to do to keep her close?

Those were my thoughts on a snowy night when almost nothing followed the path prepared for it.

As if to prove how fickle the climate of the northern plains could be, the next year's November gave us a day so fair it seemed a gift from the gods. The temperature was mild, the sky was a pale and limitless blue, and Marie and I drove right through the day's benevolent heart.

We had left Grand Forks, where by that time we were both students at the university, early on a Friday morning, and we were pointed toward Minneapolis. Marie's sister had extra tickets for a Brothers Four concert, and we planned to stay with her for the weekend. We not only had the concert to look forward to, we would have two days to take in the city's attractions, and if that weren't enough, there was also the possibility that Marie and I would be allowed to share a bed. For an entire night. The prospect was tantalizing, for while we were having sex often, we never had the chance to *sleep* together. To literally sleep through the night in each other's arms, head to dreaming head, took on an importance comparable to those earlier sexual milestones that marked the advance of our relationship. We both lived in dormitories at that time, but we were already making plans for the next school year. I was going to rent an apartment, and though I'd need a roommate or two to share rent, the apartment would provide a haven for Marie and me. Maybe she'd occasionally be able to check out of the dorm for a night or even a weekend, and we could truly live together.

As we drove through central Minnesota's gentle undulations—turn your hand palm-up and raise it to eye level and its contours should provide an analogue for that landscape, a relief after the pancake flatness of eastern North Dakota—Marie and I felt as though we could pass for husband and wife. We had stopped at a diner and refilled our thermos, and we passed the single cup back and forth. Marie lit my cigarettes for me. Our conversation was as familiar, comforting, and unrestricted as the sky. No longer living under our parents' roofs, our lives seemed completely and happily our own. Had we passed a highway sign announcing that the road we were traveling on would go on forever, it would have only deepened my contentment.

But what we passed, at intervals just regular enough to be puzzling, were cars pulled over to the side of the road. Eventually, I slowed for one, and the sight of the family inside, with identical expressions of confusion and grief on the faces of father, mother, and three children, alerted us to the possibility that something might be happening in the world that had nothing to do with conditions along Highway 10.

Marie snapped on the radio—and it was never off again

when we were in the car—and we learned what in the instant of knowing it suddenly seemed strange not to have known: The president had been assassinated.

Did I steer the Studebaker onto the shoulder of the road? I must have. Yet the force of the radio news seemed sufficient to propel the vehicle's tons without any help. That same force moved Marie and me into an embrace.

For a moment we debated whether we should go back to Grand Forks, or perhaps even drive to our hometown. Certainly Bismarck would find this news especially upsetting, considering its own history of assassination. But not every vehicle had pulled over. Cars and trucks continued to whiz past us, and Marie and I thought we had already learned the lesson. Deliveries had to be made. Appointments had to be kept. Rituals had to be observed. Leaves had to fall. Clocks had to tick.

In fact, America was still unsure, in the autumn of 1963, what it should do and what it should postpone. The Brothers Four concert was canceled, but the National Football League played its scheduled games. Of course, before the decade was over, the country would have its protocols for post-assassination behavior well established.

Marie and I were allowed to sleep together that weekend, at least after a fashion. Her sister kept her bedroom and her bed for herself and gave Marie the couch. I unrolled my sleeping bag on the floor next to her.

As we lay in our makeshift beds, Marie reached her hand down to me. I took it, though I didn't pull myself up toward her or tug her down to me. Her sorrow, I assumed, canceled her desire to make love. I was well aware of the line that ran from sex to pleasure. I even knew of the connection between sex and pain. But of the power of sex to heal or affirm, I was ignorant and would remain so for years to come.

During the drive back to Grand Forks on Sunday, Marie was quiet. She was no doubt thinking about what had happened in the nation in the days just passed and how unsettled and unsettling the future now seemed. And perhaps that uncertainty caused her to question other matters—how many of us in those days of late November suddenly let go of assumptions and never picked them up again? So Marie may also have been given over to contemplation of what life would be like in the company of a boy—a man—who could not guess her need. And wouldn't ask.

After the assassination, however, Marie and I were no different from most Americans: We resumed the lives we'd expected to lead and acted as though the future was once more in our control. We continued with our studies, Marie as an education major who hoped to teach elementary school, and I as an English major with the intent to teach as well. My ambition to write I kept to myself.

Just as I had planned, at the start of my junior year I moved off campus. I found a dark, damp, two-bedroom basement apartment close enough to the university that I could walk to class. For the necessary roommate I recruited Rob Varley, an acquaintance from Bismarck. Rob was quiet, solitary, and dedicated to his studies. A chemical engineering major, he spent almost all his spare time either at the university's new computer center or in a laboratory. His focus on the future rendered the past of little interest, so we seldom reminisced about our hometown or our high school years. As I recall, Rob made only a single comment about Monty Burnham's murder. The entire episode in the city's history was, he said, "stupid," an unsurprising assessment from someone who was interested only in problems that had solutions. When Rob was home, he was sleeping or studying, usually in his bedroom with the door closed.

In other words, Marie and I had plenty of opportunities for privacy, and though the university had a regulation prohibiting female students from visiting men in off-campus housing, the apartment's entrance was on an alley and was blocked from general view by a garage and a shed, allowing Marie to come and go undetected. She probably spent as much time at the apartment as Rob, and she was responsible for whatever touches the place had that made it feel like something other than an underground cell. She hung curtains on the tiny windows that looked not so much out as up. She found a bookcase at a yard sale, painted it white, and arranged Rob's and my books on the shelves. She threw a blue checked tablecloth over the lopsided, rusting table at which we ate our morning cereal. On the wall above the sagging couch she hung framed prints of Alpine scenes. As part of her dormitory contract she could eat in a campus dining hall, but she often prepared meals for us in the apartment, using the groceries we shopped for together at the local Piggly Wiggly. From those years two images dominate because of their frequency. The first— Marie, walking away from my bed after lovemaking, heading for the bathroom with a sheet awkwardly wrapped around her, her lovely back and backside exposed. And Marie and me on the couch, both of us reading; she's lying down, her skirt is above her knees, her legs are across my lap, and I am absentmindedly rubbing her feet.

We were so comfortable and established as a couple that we could, like real husbands and wives, presume permanence in our relationship without discussing it. So it was only natural that Marie should walk into the apartment one October day and announce, as a wife would to a husband, "I think I'm pregnant."

Here is what I should have done. I should have turned off the radio (the Yankees were playing the Cardinals in the World Series), walked over to her (she was standing at the entrance to the tiny kitchen, one hand on each side of the door frame, as if she were bracing herself for my reception of the news), taken her in my arms, and said, Wonderful. Terrific. Let's go talk to Pastor Shoup over at Christus Rex right now and tell him we want to get married. You don't need your parents' permission, and I know I can get either my mother or my father to say yes without any trouble. And then we'll go on with our lives and nothing will change except we'll be married and that's what we're going to be anyway. No attempts to be clever or eloquent. Just simple, straightforward talk, without pose or artifice.

But though Marie's announcement should have come as no surprise—we had always been inconsistently careful about birth control, and during the previous year we had become even more lax about the matter—I was shocked. In my contentment I had become complacent to the point of intransigence—I liked things just the way they were. Fittingly, I remained seated while Marie stood less than two yards away. In attempting not to demonstrate that I had been jolted, I tried for cool.

I asked the question that men have asked for millennia, and, next to "Is it mine?" it must be the one that women hate most to hear. "Are you sure?"

Her shrug said that she would try for a nonchalance to match mine.

There was still time for me to say or do something that would help close the distance between us. But there was another reason for my cool, and it came out in my next question. "Is this any different from before?"

Marie cocked her head quizzically. "Before?"

"You know. With Gene. What happened that time?"

Now it was Marie who stepped closer, but while she sat down across from me, she kept her arms and hands off the table, perhaps to prevent me from reaching over and touching her.

"That time?" she asked warily. "I'm not sure I know what we're talking about."

"Hey, it's okay. I know all about it. He told me on his mom's wedding day. Asked me if I'd be his best man. He wasn't exactly overjoyed at the prospect of being a father, but he was ready to do the right thing."

"Was he?"

"So when did you realize you . . . you know, that you weren't pregnant. That time."

Marie pointed to my cigarettes. Instead of just taking one from the pack, she said, "May I?"

"Help yourself."

For the next few moments Marie did nothing but bring the cigarette to her lips and inhale and exhale, directing forceful plumes of smoke toward the low ceiling. I suppose I might have said something, but it seemed as though the right of next comment had been reserved in her name. Throughout this silent time she often stared right at me, and rather haughtily it seemed to me, something I was prepared to note if a quarrel broke out.

She eventually looked away—into the cracked and chipped soup bowl we used for an ashtray—and that was the moment when she began to speak.

"It took me a moment to remember when the wedding was . . . when you say Gene told you. But it's coming back to me. Yes, I was once late with my period, and that could have been the time. That was unusual for me. And I'd been having pains and problems with my period. Something that still happens from time to time, not that you've noticed. I had an appointment to see a gynecologist. So Gene must have let his fear override his brain. After all, he was accustomed to things going badly in his life. But he knew where babies came from, so he had to have known I couldn't have been pregnant. *Could not have been*." She leaned over across the table, and the urgency of her words seemed to lift her from her chair. "Do you understand? *Not possible*. He should have known that . . . that we hadn't done anything that could result in pregnancy. But maybe he had some confused notions about human anatomy or reproduction. Maybe he believed in virgin birth. Maybe he was simply making up a story just for you, something to impress you. Or depress you. But I do recall that for a few days he wore this look like his world was about to end. Not unlike the look you have right now." She sat back down.

"The Yankees are losing. Maybe that's what you see."

"That's very funny."

I lit a cigarette of my own.

"But all jokes and sports talk aside, I have to make sure: You understand what I'm telling you, don't you? I could not have been pregnant. *I could not have been.* Not then. Not anytime Gene and I were together. It was not possible. We did some things . . . and we would have done more if he had had his way. God knows he tried. But you were the first. Do you understand? The first. The *only.*"

"All right."

"Maybe you need to know what Gene and I did? What happened that might have let him think—wrongly, stupidly—that I could have been pregnant?"

"That's okay."

"No, that you wouldn't want to know, would you? Instead of the truth, you'd rather have your own version of things. Your own fantasies. After all, you could have asked me anytime. God knows you've asked me enough questions about the past. But you've always cared more about what was impossible to know than what you could know. You're as haunted by the past—part of the past—as Gene was. But *his* ghosts were forced on him. He didn't choose them."

If it weren't for that remark, I might have allowed myself to be chastened, and, repentant, I might have done exactly what the moment called for—apologized and asked for Marie's forgiveness. After all, I believed her. There was never a moment when I didn't believe her. Never. But when she compared me to Gene, I became angry.

"Okay. So now I have two versions of the past. Another chance to choose."

She crushed her cigarette out so forcefully the bowl jumped

and skidded across the table. Long after the cigarette was extinguished she kept jabbing the butt into the ashes. When she finally looked up, her eyes were flaring with fury, and even her tears had no power to put out the blaze. "You know what?" she said. "Fuck you. Just *fuck you.*"

Before I could make a move to stop her, she pushed violently back from the table, and stood, toppling her chair in the process.

Earlier I mentioned images that branded themselves on my memory because of their frequency. Here is one I carry because of its singularity: The apartment is tiny, but Marie manages to gain running speed as she heads toward the door. Although her progress is nothing but forward, away from me, her shoulder-length hair—brown in her first few strides but closer to red as she dashes through a shaft of sunlight that has found its angled way through a ground-level window—waves from side to side as she runs. Similarly, the motion of her plaid wool skirt is lateral as she runs.

Wounded pride and self-righteous anger kept me tethered to the apartment for an hour or two, and then I left in search of Marie.

~

Because of what happened at his tenth high school reunion, Raymond Stoddard did not want to attend his twentieth. But in the first week of January, the representatives of Wembley High School's class of 1941 sent out invitations to their forty-six fellow graduates, and Raymond's wife, Alma, immediately marked off on their calendar the days in August when the reunion would take place. Raymond knew he could do nothing to dis-

suade her from making plans for them to attend, or to make her understand why he didn't want to go.

Right from the start everything about the ten-year reunion had been wrong, wrong, wrong. First of all, the planners decided to hold the event in conjunction with the Catholic high school's reunion, and in the process ignored the fact that the two schools had been rivals, not allies. Next, the band, such as it was—piano, bass, drums, and trumpet—played music popular during the war years, neglecting the obvious fact that in the spring of 1941 the United States' entry into the war was seven months away. Over the course of the evening, Raymond noted renditions of, among others, "Don't Sit Under the Apple Tree," "You'd Be So Nice to Come Home To," and "They're Either Too Young or Too Old." His fellow classmates, however, applauded those songs as if the songs had actually furnished the score to their high school years. Twice the band played "Skylark." Raymond knew that song had come out in 1942, because he remembered exactly where he was when he first heard it. He had left Wembley on the train with a small group of friends and acquaintances, new recruits like himself, and all of them bound for Kansas and basic training. The train had a stopover in St. Paul, and Raymond got off to stretch his legs. He had never ridden a train for that distance before, and he had never been that far east. He walked up and down the platform, never straying more than three cars from his own, breathing in the odor of diesel fumes, and listening to a song that came from somewhere inside the station. Its melody was both melancholy and expectant, and in that regard served as the perfect signature for his state of being. He would hear the song often enough in the future that he would soon know its name and composer, and the versions he favored. While he stood on the platform listening, a thin, cold rain fell, and Raymond felt as if he were already in a foreign country.

It was raining on the night of the ten-year reunion dance too. The preceding week had been exceptionally warm and the summer of 1951 exceedingly dry, so when the rain began, it was treated as another cause for celebration on a night when most people's spirits were already high and their moods festive. The dance was held in the high school gymnasium, and not only the gym's doors but the school's outer doors were thrown open to take advantage of the rain-cooled air. In fact, couples almost immediately began dancing their way out of the gym and into the cooler, darker school corridor, often swaying in time to the music right next to the double doors propped open to the night.

In Raymond's view the weather was to blame for what occurred that night, though he was willing to concede that things might have ended as they did even without the rain.

Throughout the evening, in dance after dance, partner-switching had been customary. Not only men but women too felt free to cut in on other couples, and the intent behind this activity was often to restore couples who had dated in high school. The husbands and wives who were not from Wembley, and the unmarried men and women, good-naturedly went along with the constant realignment of couples.

For most of their high school years, Alma had dated Monty Burnham, the most popular boy in school. Their relationship was so long and durable that their classmates assumed that Monty and Alma would someday marry. But the romance foundered, for the rumored reason that Monty "got too serious." And though they each went on to marry other people—Raymond and a girl from Grand Forks—there still seemed something fated about them—the class president and the prettiest girl—being together.

That would certainly explain why, when Monty cut in on Raymond, laughter, cheers, and applause spontaneously erupted from their classmates.

Playing to the approving crowd, Monty danced off with Alma, whirling, spinning, exaggeratedly swinging their arms, moving them off together with speeded-up, elongated steps, as if they were waltzing around a nineteenth-century ballroom, though Monty paid no attention to the rhythm of the actual music. The song in fact was, as Raymond remembered well, "Begin the Beguine," one of the few instances when the band accurately matched the music to their high school years, though not to the year of their graduation. Alma's expression—her unrestrained smile, her astonished laughter—made it plain that she enjoyed being part of the show.

Once they exited the gym, they kept right on going, into the night, into the steady rain. Other couples followed their example, and soon half the reunion crowd was dancing exuberantly on the high school's soggy lawn. Out there they certainly couldn't hear the music anymore, but it didn't matter. Their laughter would have drowned out the band anyway.

Raymond stood in the doorway, dry and watching it all. Or trying to. The rain was a heavy veil that made it difficult to tell one dancing couple from another. He thought he was able to keep track of Monty and Alma, but he couldn't be sure—so *many of the men wore dark suits and white shirts, and Alma was one of three women who came to the reunion in a light blue dress, and that blue turned dark when it became wet.*

Finally, Raymond turned away. He didn't want to do what he felt like doing—running out into the rain, grabbing Alma by the arm, and hauling her away from Monty Burnham and the entire reunion. Behavior like that would only reveal him to be more or less what he was—a humorless, jealous fool.

Instead, putting on an expression that he hoped would be read as sophisticated nonchalance, he strolled back to the gym, shaking his head in amusement over his classmates' antics.

He walked to the refreshments table. There, two identical punch bowls were set up. One container of pink liquid, however, had been spiked with Everclear, and Raymond assumed this was the nearly empty bowl. He hadn't had anything to drink all evening, but now he scooped out a full cup, lit a cigarette, and waited under the backboard of one of the gym's two baskets for his wife to reappear. The net had been removed from the rim, and Raymond wondered if that had been done just for this occasion or if it had been taken down for the summer. The crêpe-paper decorations that had been hung the length of the court had gone limp from humidity.

At the other end of the gym stood a cluster of men talking, Raymond was sure, about the war and their roles in it. Raymond was entitled to join the group, but he had tired of war stories and their distortions before the war was even over. On more than one occasion he had listened to accounts of battles on the very day they'd been fought, battles that Raymond himself had been in, and he invariably found those reports, like the songs played at the reunion, false. Yet those storytellers weren't necessarily lying; they were simply trying to make sense of the senselessness they'd lived through, and in the process warped the truth for the sake of their tales.

His cigarette burned down to the filter. Raymond had been willing to flick his ashes onto the gymnasium's floor, but he didn't want to crush out the butt on the varnished hardwood. He considered returning to the outside door. There he could throw his cigarette out into the rain and hope that it might seem his only reason for going there. Instead he walked over to the water fountain outside the locker room door and deposited his cigarette there. There must have been twenty butts already sticking wetly to the porcelain.

Monty and Alma were by now the only couple who had not yet returned from their dance in the rain. Raymond surveyed the gym for Mrs. Burnham, wondering if she was as troubled and curious over her spouse's absence as Raymond was. She, however, was involved in a raucous conversation with four other women, one of them so pregnant she looked as though she might give birth at any moment. In what must have been a joking reference to her condition, the woman opened her eyes wide and puffed out her cheeks. The other women laughed uproariously.

The band began to play its rickety rendition of "Moonlight Serenade," another of the few examples of songs that really were popular when they were in school, though Monty and Alma would have been more likely to dance to it than Raymond and Alma.

And just at that moment Alma entered the gym. Her dress was soaked, and while its skirt was wrinkled and shapeless below her waist, the fabric above clung shamelessly to her torso. Her hair hung down in wet tendrils. Alma wore a bewildered expression, and perhaps she'd been crying, but then again the rain might have created that effect. In each hand she carried a shoe. Raymond made no move to approach her or signal his presence.

Eventually of course Alma saw him standing under the basket, and she began to hurry toward his end of the gym. Alma had not been a cheerleader in high school, but she ran across the gym floor just as she might have after leading a cheer for the home team. And Mrs. Burnham and the other women in her group regarded Alma as coolly as high school girls might have watched a cheerleader for a rival team.

Before Alma reached him, Raymond decided that she had allowed Monty Burnham to fuck her somewhere out there in the rain. When she came close to him and stood on her tiptoes to kiss his cheek, Raymond looked over her shoulder, examining the back of her dress for mud or grass stains, evidence that she had been lying on her back on the wet ground. The fabric was only wet, but Raymond told himself that didn't mean anything. She and Monty might have done the deed in the backseat of a car or leaning up against the school's bricks. Not that it mattered. . . . In his mind Raymond had moved into the realm where neither logic nor fact was necessary for belief to be sustained.

Because she might admit it, he didn't ask Alma if she had

just had sex with Monty Burnham. And he didn't ask her because she might deny it. From that moment forward, Raymond Stoddard would live as a man of faith.

A few minutes later, Monty entered the gym. He stood at center court, gazed expectantly up at the ceiling, and turned up both palms. It seemed to Raymond that men especially found Monty's act humorous.

For ten years Raymond did nothing in thought or action that might alter his conviction about what had happened between his wife and Monty Burnham. Indeed, he learned how he could make practical use of it, particularly in his sexual relations with Alma. If he felt no desire for her he could justify his rejection of her by reminding himself that she had been unfaithful to him. And when that same thought—Alma being fucked by another man—oddly stirred Raymond, he could make love to his wife with a passion that was equal parts passion and anger. Have sex with him, will you—take that, and that, and thatthatthat. . . .

So of course Alma wanted to attend the twentieth reunion. What other opportunity would she have, since they had left Wembley and moved to Bismarck, to renew her relationship with her former lover? And of course Raymond was determined that they not go. He could not face the possibility that another man would once again dance off with his wife. Yet without speaking to Alma of his belief, what could he possibly say or do that would explain his unwillingness to reunite with his classmates?

For months he worried the problem. Then, one night while he was watching an episode of Peter Gunn, *a solution came to him. He had been drinking beer since he'd come home from work, and alcohol in any form often allowed his thoughts to travel into orbits they could never reach when he was sober. It was so simple, really. He could get a gun, Raymond reasoned, and kill Monty Burnham. The notion had barely formed itself when he laughed out loud at its ridiculousness. Alma heard him and came in to ask him what was so funny. Raymond gestured vaguely in the direction of the television.*

Barely a week later that coldly murderous thought revisited Raymond. He was sober this time, and though he laughed once again, after a few seconds his laughter halted as abruptly as if a hand had clutched his throat. The next time, he didn't laugh at all.

———

This story could be read as another chapter in the lives of the Monty Burnham and Raymond and Alma Stoddard that have been revealed through the other fictions in these pages. Indeed, those fictional characters perhaps have more substance than the real people. The stories allow access to their inner lives, something that life generally won't offer. But notice that "Reunion" (published in the magazine *Windsong*) says nothing about Killeen, Texas, and what occurred in the fictional bathroom of a fictional hotel between a fictional Monty Burnham and a fictional Alma Stoddard. It contains no reference to a wartime confession or a confrontation between two soldiers, and of course I have no evidence that either event occurred. In fact, the narrative has no basis in any reality I'm aware of except that Raymond, Monty, and Alma graduated from the same high school in the same year.

But I suspect that the story had its origin in the emotions I experienced that October when Marie vanished so suddenly from my life.

~

After Marie ran from my apartment, I looked everywhere but couldn't find her. Not in the library, not in the student union. Not in the registrar's office, where she had a work-study job. Not on the banks of the English Coulee, where she sometimes sat and watched the water's slow swirl and flow. I phoned Blackmore Hall, Marie's dorm, but was told she wasn't in her room. I called Jackie Rickinger, Marie's friend from Bismarck who lived in another dormitory. She hadn't seen Marie since their Educational Psychology class that morning. I went to Neville Hall, the home of the education department, and walked up and down the corridor where the faculty had its offices, believing that she might be conferring with a professor. After I made all those rounds, I went back and visited or called each site again. And then again.

In spite of my search's futility I was confident that I'd find Marie and sure that she would accept my apology. Because he had once meant something to both of us and because of his hard-luck history, I had always been careful to temper any remarks I made about Gene Stoddard. But no more. As part of my contrition I would gladly portray him as a lout and a liar. Further, I was certain that I could convince her, because this was now my belief, that I regarded the news of her pregnancy as cause for celebration. If I found her soon enough, I'd propose that we commemorate the occasion with a steak dinner at the Bronze Boot.

But when the curfew for women arrived at ten o'clock (men

had no restriction on their hours), I was pacing the sidewalk in front of Marie's dormitory, and I still hadn't seen her or heard from her.

The receptionist at Blackmore Hall was in my Shakespeare class. Phyllis. Stout, stringy-haired, earnest Phyllis Orr . . . After flattering her with questions about *King Lear* and the upcoming exam, I finally persuaded her to reveal that Marie had checked out of the dorm hours earlier. On the form where she signed out, she listed her parents' address and phone number as her location until Sunday afternoon at five o'clock.

Marie had no car. No train ran between Grand Forks and Bismarck, and the bus left much earlier in the day. It seemed unlikely that anyone with whom Marie could ride would leave for Bismarck on a Thursday afternoon or evening. Those factors helped me decide: I wouldn't drive to Bismarck that night—no matter how hard I pushed the Studebaker, I wouldn't arrive before three A.M.—but if I didn't hear from Marie before morning, I would leave then.

I slept little that night, so when dawn came, I didn't waste any time. I tossed a hastily packed suitcase into the trunk and hit the highway. Less than five hours later, I was in Bismarck, and before I went to my own home, I drove to Marie's.

As soon as Mrs. Ryan answered the door, I immediately knew my being there was a mistake. I had not only Marie's accounts but the evidence of my own eyes to know how Mrs. Ryan had struggled with alcohol over the years. A nervous, high-strung woman, she used her worries, real or imagined, as her justification for drinking, so when I asked if Marie was there and Mrs. Ryan's eyes widened with her answer—"Isn't she in Grand

Forks? With you?"—I realized that I simultaneously had caused her to be apprehensive about her daughter and had given her a reason for pouring herself a stiff drink. Stammering, I tried to say something that would allay her concerns. "I-I'm sure that's where she is. But when I told her I was coming to Bismarck for the weekend, she said maybe she'd follow me here. I was sure she was joking, but I thought I'd check just to be sure. I'm sorry I bothered you." Mrs. Ryan habitually chewed her fingernails to the quick, and before I backed away from the door, she had the tip of her little finger between her teeth.

My mother too was skeptical of my reason for coming home. "I needed a little break," I told her. "You know, sleep in my own bed. Eat a home-cooked meal."

By that time my parents were living apart, and my mother had perhaps developed the ability to read the signs of a troubled heart in the faces of her family's men. "Are you and Marie having difficulties?" she asked.

I couldn't manage a response any more convincing than, "Nothing serious. We'll work it out."

Throughout the day I drove by Marie's house, hoping I'd see her in the yard, in a window. When I wasn't driving, I was back at my mother's house or in the phone booth next to the Mobil station, calling Grand Forks—Marie's dorm, Jackie Rickinger's room, my apartment. I gave my roommate my mother's telephone number and ordered him to phone there immediately if Marie, if any female, should call. Finally, late in the afternoon, self-conscious of my many circuits of the Ryans' block, I parked a short distance away and continued my watch from the car.

I'm not sure how long I sat there but it was with no sign of

Marie. In the gutter in front of his house a neighbor of the Ryans' burned a pile of prematurely fallen leaves. The air was still, and since the block was canopied with trees, the leaf smoke didn't rise very high. It hovered over the street until evening dusk arrived, and then, mingling, the smoke and the dusk completed the task of bringing autumn darkness to the block. I drove away in defeat.

Since it seemed as though it had lately become my habit to distress mothers and mothers-to-be, I decided to risk disturbing one more. After parking my car in front of my mother's home, I walked down to the house that would always be the Stoddards' to me.

Alma Stoddard—I could never get used to her as Mrs. Mauer—answered the door, and I had barely uttered a word of greeting, much less offered a reason for my visit, before she embraced me and ushered me inside.

The living room was little changed from the room I had spent so many hours in as a child. The console television was now a color set—*The Wild Wild West* was on—and on top of the TV, Gene's graduation portrait joined his sister's. In place of the wing-backed chair where Mr. Stoddard used to sit there was now a Naugahyde recliner. This was where Gene's mother insisted I sit. She pulled up a footstool and sat at my feet.

She was even thinner than when I had last seen her, and the vestiges of her beauty had vanished with those pounds. Her dark hair was shot through with gray, and her eyes were sunken and dim, like a votive candle's flame guttering in its own liquid before it goes out. Creases ran down from the corners of her mouth. The smile she struggled to shine on me, however, seemed genuine, and genuine too seemed her interest in my college career.

After I told her about the courses I was taking and my possible plans for graduate school or law school (no longer a serious ambition but one I still occasionally expressed, especially on Keogh Street), she said, "I hope Gene changes his mind and applies for college one day."

"He still has time. There's a woman in my Modern Drama class in her sixties."

"I remember when the two of you used to sit at the kitchen table and work on your arithmetic together. . . . He's certainly smart enough to attend college. . . ."

"Sure, he is."

"But he doesn't have the discipline. And you need discipline, don't you? Brains and discipline?" She bent toward me, eager for confirmation of her theories on educational success.

"I suppose. . . ."

"A chemist. I always thought Gene would make a good chemist."

"He would. . . ."

"But when he and the Ryan girl broke up, something went out of him. He just couldn't get himself back on track."

Her sense of causality was off. Gene's derailment coincided with his father's suicide and subsequent notoriety, but I didn't correct her.

Mrs. Stoddard turned and gazed toward the kitchen, remembering perhaps the hours Gene and I had spent hunched over our homework there. Her choice of subject was appropriate; while math problems stubbornly resisted my efforts to solve them, numbers gave up their secrets quickly to Gene. Then she sat up straight on her stool and coolly said, "And your life is on track, isn't it?"

"I guess."

"Completely on track. Of course it is. College. Plans for the future. A girlfriend. She's still your girlfriend, isn't she?"

Although at the moment I was unsure of that fact, I nodded.

"He kept calling her. . . . My God, how long did he call her, trying to talk her into taking him back?" She looked again in the direction of the kitchen. Their telephone, I recalled, hung on the wall next to the cupboard. "It reached the point where I thought of calling her myself. Can you imagine that? I don't know what I would have said. . . . And I even suggested that he call you, his old friend." Alma Stoddard turned a mirthless smile in my direction. "But he wouldn't do that."

I couldn't think of anything to say in my defense.

"Only later did I realize how foolish that suggestion was. Because you weren't his old friend anymore, were you? You weren't about to help him with *that* problem, were you?"

I stood abruptly. "I have to go, Mrs. Stod—Mrs. Mauer. I'm home for the weekend, so I thought I'd see if Gene might be here. Does he have his own place here in town?"

Alma Stoddard didn't rise. She cupped her chin in her hand as if she were bracing herself. "He's living in Minot now. Working for his uncle's construction company up there." She quite deliberately did not look at me.

I thanked her and without escort left the house. Keogh Street in those years was largely treeless, yet just as in Marie's neighborhood, someone in the vicinity was burning leaves. I could smell the fire, though I couldn't see smoke or flames. Why that smell is regarded so fondly is beyond me. It is, after all, the odor of endings.

The following day, Saturday, I was once again on the road soon after sunrise, driving up Highway 83 from Bismarck to Minot. The early start was necessary. I wasn't sure how I'd find Gene, but I was prepared to drive up and down every street in the city until I sighted that distinctive white convertible of his. And when—or if—I came upon it? Then I would seek out its owner, and determine if he had recently driven to Grand Forks in response to a call from a Miss Marie Ryan, who required rescue or refuge from the fool who had fathered her child.

As it turned out, Gene was not nearly as difficult to locate as I'd feared. I stopped at a gas station on the south end of the city, opened a telephone directory, and there it was: G. Stoddard, 1705½ Arapaho, KL5-2232. The station attendant provided directions to an avenue on the city's hilly north side.

We were no longer friends, Gene and I, but our lives continued to parallel in odd ways: We both continued to live in North Dakota, not in our hometown but in cities in the state's northern half, and we had both rented basement apartments. His white Impala was parked in front of a stucco house that had a covered apartment entrance built into its side like a chute.

The convertible's top was down, and when I peered into its interior, I guessed that it had been left down all night. The day might have been warm for October, but the night had been cool and the car's dashboard and upholstery were, at that late morning hour, still beaded with dew. Gene must have had matters more important than his car's welfare on his mind when he pulled to the curb.

With my palm still wet from where it swiped a path through the moisture on the car door, I marched on. The leaves littering the stairwell clattered like castanets as I kicked through them on my way down the steps to the apartment. I had not quite reached the door when I tried to formulate a plan that good sense would have said I'd needed well before I got that far.

If Gene admitted that Marie was inside—or if his denial was unconvincing—I was prepared to push past him and . . . and what? Haul her bodily from the apartment? Carry her to my car and transport her back to Grand Forks against her will? I could as well put what love she might still have for me on a chopping block and butcher it before her eyes.

But I had gotten that far, and I heard in the apartment's interior someone moving toward the door in answer to the buzzer I had already pushed twice and was about to lean on again.

It was probably not my desperate, bloody thoughts that somehow showed in my features and frightened the young woman who came to the door. More likely it was simply the sight of a stranger.

"Yes?" She peered around the door she was willing to open only inches. I guessed her to be close to Gene's and my age. Her blond hair was tousled, she wore no makeup, and her eyes were still heavy-lidded from sleep.

"I'm looking for Gene, Gene Stoddard?"

Nothing in my manner apparently conveyed goodwill, because she didn't open the door any wider or alter her guarded expression. "He's at work?"

"I saw his car. . . ."

"Len picked him up? Like always?"

She made every sentence into a question, a mannerism I adopted as well. "I'm a friend of his? From Bismarck?" In my case, however, the tone matched my dubiety.

Either the word "friend" or "Bismarck" convinced her of my harmlessness. She opened the door and stepped back, an invitation for me to enter.

My mission to Minot was completed. Marie and this young woman could not have both been at 1705½ Arapaho. Nevertheless, I felt too foolish at that point simply to walk away. I stepped into Gene Stoddard's home.

His place was not furnished any better than mine, but without Marie Ryan's touch, it had nothing to raise it above the level of slovenly, threadbare utilitarianism. The couch was covered with newspapers. Empty Hamm's beer cans littered the top of the coffee table. A bent coat hanger served as an antenna on the television that sat on a chair. The room smelled of cigarette smoke and motor oil—Gene must have been operating heavy equipment for his uncle's company.

The young woman reached out her hand. "I'm Joy?" After we shook hands, she stepped quickly back and folded her arms across her chest, self-conscious because nothing covered her ample breasts but her pink cotton pajama top. Her plaid pajama bottoms didn't match the top and barely reached her ankles. Joy and Gene slept together. In the same bed. All the night through. Head to dreaming head.

Joy had a pretty round face and a plump, shapely figure. She was self-conscious about her hair, but whenever she made a tentative move to reach up and pull her fingers through the tangles, she had to quickly bring her arm back down to cover her breasts.

"Are you from Minot, Joy?"

She nodded eagerly. "I work at First National? Bank?"

"And Gene's working for his uncle?" Raymond Stoddard, I recalled, also once worked for the construction company owned by Alma's brother.

"He really likes it? He says it reminds him of when he was a kid? Digging in the dirt with his toy Caterpillar?"

His play must have been solitary. I had no recollection of the two of us on our hands and knees pushing dirt around.

"What will he do when winter comes?"

Her shoulders rose as automatically as the ends of her sentences, an embarrassed shrug that made me think she and Gene didn't talk much about the future.

"Well. Winter. It's not here yet, is it?" That mention of time, though it was to a season rather than the hour, provided me with the opportunity to make my exit. I pretended to look at the watch I didn't wear. "I have to hit the road. I was just driving through Minot, and I thought I'd take a chance and see if I could catch Gene."

"He'll be sorry he missed you?"

Yes, that was open to question.

I was halfway out the door when I realized I had left something unsaid. "I hope you and Gene have a very, very happy life together."

That sentence I had no difficulty ending on a dying note of conviction.

Upon the new planks and between the freshly painted columns, my father stood, hands on hips, a happy man on the porch of the house he and his brother had worked so hard to restore. His smile was as wide as any I'd ever seen cross his face, and though it was turned in my direction, I would learn soon that I was not the reason my father was beaming as if lit from within.

The highway that led from Minot back to Grand Forks ran right through Wembley, so I'd phoned ahead and asked my father if I could stop there and spend the night with him and Uncle Burt. Of course, of course, he said; it would be wonderful to see me and hear firsthand how I was doing in college.

While I carried my suitcase up the front walk, Uncle Burt came out too, and both brothers watched me approach. Whether it was Burt or my father who was in charge of preparing their meals, the food must have agreed with my father. Since he and my mother had separated, he had gained weight, and now the brothers truly looked brothers—a matched pair of tall, smiling, balding big-bellied men. There it was, I thought, the body of my future.

My father and uncle were both eager to show me the work they had done on the house, but before we went inside, we had to walk around the outside of the house so they could show me what was *not* there but had been in their youth—the outhouse, the poles that first brought electricity and then telephone service to the house, the huge garden whose harvest fed them throughout the year, the pit and the barrel in which the family burned much of its trash, and the barn where their father stabled his horse and the small buggy it pulled through the streets of Wembley.

Upon entering the house, I was immediately taken on another tour, and as we moved from room to room, the brothers continued to take turns telling me about the remodeling work. They had even tried to furnish the house according to their memories.

My father, who had never shown the slightest interest in the way my mother decorated our home, now boasted about how the iron bed frame in the largest bedroom was just like the one that once held their parents' mattress, which had also been covered with a blue coverlet. The rocking chair in the parlor was a duplicate of the one their father had sat in while reading the *Wembley Daily News* after working all day at the drugstore.

Then, once I had been shown the claw-foot bathtub, the wainscoting, the newel post, the coved ceiling, the brass door-knobs, and the leaded glass windows, the three of us sat down at the dining room table (its mahogany surface gleaming like a mirror). For the first time in my life, my father offered me a beer. I accepted, and then as we three men who shared a last name raised our bottles of Budweiser, my father revealed that he and his brother had at long last solved the mystery of Raymond Stoddard's motivation for murdering Monty Burnham, or so they believed.

Raymond's father, I was reminded, had worked for the railroad, a job that didn't make him wealthy but provided a steady income and a comfortable life for his family. In fact, they were sufficiently well fixed that the senior Mr. Stoddard was able to purchase a vacation place, rare indeed among North Dakotans of that generation. Their little cabin was on a lake in northeastern North Dakota, not far from Wembley.

I recalled that Gene often lamented having to spend two weeks of his summer at Lake Liana. It meant he had to miss part of the Little League season, and to make matters worse, there was nothing he particularly liked to do at the lake. Fishing didn't appeal to him, and that was the activity his grandfather and father engaged in from dawn to dark. Whenever Gene's grandmother saw him idle, she would put him to work, doing everything from hauling water to picking blueberries. His grandparents were strict and insisted that the lights be turned out early every evening and that everyone go to bed in order to rise early the following morning. For Gene, the time spent at the cabin was more punishment than vacation.

Gene's feelings about the place were not, however, the family's feelings. Everyone else loved the cabin, no matter how dilapidated it was or how primitive living conditions were there. After his retirement from the railroad, the senior Stoddard managed to spend as much time there as in Wembley.

Until, that is, his and his wife's health began to fail. She developed a heart condition that made even walking across a room a venture that taxed her to the limit. His bones became brittle; he fell and broke a hip. A coughing fit cracked a rib. He shrunk and stiffened; bending down or raising an arm overhead was next to impossible. Then, as if to make his diminution complete, his wife died, and his spirit shrunk to match his body.

Given those circumstances, his beloved Lake Liana might as well have been on the far side of the moon, so inaccessible was it to him. Others now spent vacations at the cabin that he had worked to make livable, and upon their return he had to listen to their reports on how many fish they'd caught, how many glorious sunsets they'd witnessed, how bracing was the morning air.

His health worsened. Pneumonia put him into the hospital, and as he lay in the room he believed he might never leave alive, a visitor came and presented Mr. Stoddard with a business proposition.

Since the old man would never again cast a line into Lake Liana or spend a night under the cabin's roof, and since he could not divide the place equally among his sons and daughter, who were in any event liable to squabble over the property after their father was dead, wouldn't Mr. Stoddard prefer to sell it himself and thereby exercise some control over the cabin's future? If you sell it to me, the visitor argued—pleaded—you can be sure that the cabin will be as well cared for—as loved—as it has been with a Stoddard as owner. The visitor even shed a few tears as part of his petition.

The old man was sufficiently selfish and grudging that this appeal worked on him. From his hospital bed he signed the papers that deeded the cabin and the waterfront land on which it sat to his visitor. The salesman—swindler, some might have it—who talked Mr. Stoddard into this transaction paid the dying old man exactly what the original purchase price had been.

When Raymond learned of the sale, he was furious, but though plenty of people told him he could have the deal nullified—an enfeebled old man in a hospital, for God's sake!—Raymond refused to do anything. If his father was going to be that petty, then he, then the entire family, would have to live with the consequences.

Like his father, Raymond had loved the cabin, and as long as his father was alive, Raymond blamed him for what he had done. Once the senior Stoddard died, however, Raymond transferred his rage to the man who had talked the old man out of his property. That smooth-talking son of a bitch was none other than Monty Burnham.

My father sat back, and then it was left to my uncle to explain the sources and the evidence that they had uncovered and relied on in piecing together their story.

Their research started, strangely enough, on the occasion of my high school graduation. Burt had been at our home when the news came of Bob Mullen's drowning at the river, and the tragedy brought back to him his own graduation celebration. It too had been held by a body of water, though one much more benign than the Missouri River. The family of one of his classmates had a cabin on a lake about forty miles from Wembley, and they convened there for a night of bonfires and beer drinking. Burt could recall many of the specifics of that evening—including an altercation between two classmates—but for the life of him, he couldn't remember whose family owned the land that was the site of the celebration. Ordinarily he might have been able to live with his curiosity unsatisfied, but for some reason this little mystery nagged at him.

He went for long drives in the country around Wembley, searching for the cabin or the lake. Finally, on the shores of tiny Lake Liana, he found what might have been the site of his graduation night celebration. The cabin, however, looked much different from the way he remembered it, and he might have marked that down to another of memory's inaccuracies, except that memory usually tricks us by enlarging the buildings of our past. We return to our elementary school classroom or high school auditorium, and we're shocked to discover how small it is. Then Burt realized what had caused the disjunction between memory and reality. The cabin had recently been remodeled and was almost doubled in size because of an additional story having been added.

Dorling was the little town nearest Lake Liana, and a gas station attendant there was able to tell Burt who owned the cabin. It was the Burnham family. Of course—that made sense. After all, Monty was in the same graduating class, so it would stand to reason that the Burnham cabin could have been used for the party. Burt had a vague memory of Monty on that occasion—was he involved in that fight with another classmate? Burt also seemed to recall that it was Monty who departed early from the party. But he wouldn't have left his own family's cabin, would he?

But Burt had to live with these uncertainties and inconsistencies until quite recently when he had a chance encounter with another member of the Burnham family. Monty's cousin, Irv Schmitz, came into the pharmacy to have a prescription filled, and Burt asked him what had happened with the cabin. Oh, it was still in the family, Irv said; Monty had been so proud of the deal he'd made to acquire the cabin that no one would ever consider selling it. Monty's sister and her husband had completely remodeled the place, and all the branches of the family took their turns vacationing at Lake Liana. Not much questioning was needed to get Irv to divulge the particulars of Monty's negotiating coup. "There was nothing," Irv said, "that old Monty appreciated more than talking someone into or out of something."

At that point Burt pushed his chair back, just as my father had earlier when he'd finished his portion of the narrative. And there the brothers sat, two aging fat men finally contented that yesterday was fixed, its mysteries solved, its story complete. Of course any explanation for Raymond Stoddard's behavior that had him acting to avenge the loss of an ancestral property would be especially satisfying to those two. They were, after all, living in their own reclaimed, restored past.

Darkness, which on dwindling autumn days hasn't much patience anyway, could wait no longer and now filled the room. As if any movement required enormous effort, my father partially lifted from his chair, reached up, and twisted on the light above the dining room table before sitting heavily back down. For a moment, we squinted at one another in the sudden illumination as if we were verifying the company we kept. The brothers smiled at me to see that I was one of them.

With the same abruptness but none of the violence with which Marie rose from my table only days before, I stood. "I have to go," I said. "Back to Grand Forks."

"You're spending the night," my father said. It was not a command but a gentle reminder. My suitcase already stood in the bedroom that had always been reserved for guests.

"I can't stay."

The brothers regarded me quizzically. I hadn't time to concoct an excuse because I had nothing more than a spontaneous impulse to flee. Yes, the more time that passed with no word from Marie, the more my fear and concern increased, but something additional was working on me—in me—and trying to push me toward the door. I hadn't sufficient time or maturity or wisdom to absorb the lesson Marie had tried to teach me, but perhaps without her recent angry words on the subject I wouldn't have sensed anything wrong in how those brothers lived.

I repeated my words, "I have to go," and both my father and my uncle looked at me strangely, an indication, I hoped, of what I was to them, a stranger, not their kind, not someone who dwelt in the past, whether refashioned or otherwise.

"We were thinking," Uncle Burt said, "that we'd walk downtown for supper. Get some steaks at the Windmill." He spoke so calmly, so mildly, that he must have perceived me to be in an agitated state.

"I can't. There's . . . there's a . . . ." I started to explain, to *try* to explain, that a girl was out there somewhere, a girl I had to find. But I stopped short when I realized that I was speaking to men unlikely to understand. My father had left the woman he loved—didn't he? didn't he still love my mother?—for this, this boy's life. And Burt? Well, in the previous few minutes I had suddenly moved much farther down the road toward comprehending my uncle's nature, something that I wouldn't have full understanding of for years to come.

"I can't stay."

The brothers looked at each other again, and maybe in that instant they both recalled something about youth that they had forgotten, no matter that they were living in the house where they must have first felt youth's passions. "I'll get his suitcase," Burt said.

Or perhaps Burt left us alone so that we could have a father and son talk, during which I would disclose what was troubling me. But I was not interested in anything that might delay my departure.

My father was the one to snap the silence stretching tauter between us, and he did it with the question that was always his easiest substitute for intimacy. "Do you need any money?" He stood and reached for his wallet.

That question might have been my entrée to say, Money? I do

indeed need money, and lots of it. I'm getting married and soon. But I had already determined that the distance I had closed that day between my father and me was for nothing more than traveling convenience. "I'm okay," I said.

"Gas? I believe the only station open today is the Conoco you passed on the way into town."

"I filled up in Minot."

He nodded. "The Studebaker still does well on mileage?"

"Almost as good as your old Rambler."

His faint smile told me that I had pleased him by recalling one of his vehicles. His pleasure would have been diminished if I'd told him that I remembered that car, would *always* remember that car, because it had been parked in the Stoddards' driveway on that day. I hadn't a single image in my memory cache of his emerald-green Rambler in front of our house.

Burt clumped into the room with my suitcase, I took it from him, and my father and I walked out into the October evening's chill. I opened the trunk and lifted the suitcase in.

"That theory you have about Monty Burnham cheating old Mr. Stoddard out of his cabin . . . did you tell Mom about it?"

"That subject wouldn't be . . ." He paused, as though his concern for the precision of language was coming back to him. "An area of interest for her. Not any longer."

When I drove away, my father was gazing up into the bare branches of a maple tree that overhung the house and no doubt dropped a good many of its leaves onto the roof and into the rain gutters every year. If that tree had been there when he was a boy, it couldn't have been more than a sapling.

Back in Grand Forks I resumed my search for Marie, phoning, driving by, and looking into all the places I had tried only a few days before. I even tried some new locations. Since it was Saturday night, I checked a few bars, though Marie disliked them and their atmosphere. There were undoubtedly parties throughout the city, and while Marie was not averse to attending them, I had no way of knowing where they might be held.

It was well past midnight when I gave up and returned to my apartment. My roommate was not there, but that was not unusual. Somewhere on campus there was a laboratory he could get into and study in, no matter what the hour. I checked the kitchen table and the stand the telephone sat on to see if he had left a note informing me that Marie had called. There was nothing.

For many of the hours since Marie had run out, I had been in motion, and that had enabled me to keep my anxieties under control. But once I stopped moving, with no destination or mission but to get up the next morning and begin again, my fears leaped to the fore, and though they had no specific form, that didn't mean they didn't have the power to rattle me right to the core. I didn't believe that Marie would try to harm herself. A quarrel like ours would never be enough to shake her love of and commitment to life. Similarly, she would never contemplate ending the life inside her, even if that had been possible, and, need I remind you, in 1964 abortions were not only illegal but generally unavailable. And while those beliefs might have had their birth in her Catholic background, it wasn't the church that sustained them. She and I had both forsaken the religions we grew up in, and besides, Marie's strongest faith had always been reserved for the values and certainties of her own character. But my fear didn't need sharp definition. I had only to imagine the permanence of what was presently true—*Marie was lost to me*—to experience a dread unlike any other.

During the days and hours and minutes of my futile hunting for Marie, I had begun increasingly to feel like a failure, not as a searcher but as a lover, a mate. I was sure of my love for her, yet I questioned its power—shouldn't it have been strong enough to lead me to her, no matter where she might be?

On Sunday morning I added a new location to my search circuit. I drove past Saint Michael's Cathedral, making sure I passed when crowds of congregants were exiting. No luck. I had tried libraries, bars, and churches, hometowns and old boyfriends; I had staked out her family and her dormitory, and nothing, not the personal or the institutional, had yielded results. By midafternoon the October sky had darkened to a stony gray and a cold autumn wind had begun to blow. I decided to go back to my apartment to try the telephone for a few hours.

And there she was. In my kitchen.

Marie Ryan was sitting in the same chair that she had knocked over in her haste to get away from me. On the table in front of her was an educational psychology textbook. A cigarette was burning in the ashtray, and an open Coke was near at hand. She was wearing a floral print blouse and tan corduroy slacks. She had kicked off her shoes.

"Rob let me in," she said. "And I helped myself to a Coke. I hope you don't mind."

I had driven her away by failing to respond as I should have to the news she had brought me, and now I was failing again and knew it even while it was happening. She had brought herself to me—back to me—and rather than overturning the table—or any other obstacle standing between Marie Ryan and me—and wrapping her in my arms, I remained where I was across the room, noting her brand of cigarettes, the angle of her shoes under the table, the pallid green of the Coke bottle contrasting with the living green of her eyes. In my life there have been so many times when, rather than like a hand opening and reaching, I have been a fist, closed and tight. I have never told my writing students this, but I have long known there are two ways to make use of yourself in your fiction: You may stand back and notice, as Saul Bellow says is our human purpose, or you may live fully and store up experiences that may one day find their way into your art. The cigarettes were Pall Malls. The toes of her loafers were scuffed because when she sat in a chair, she usually folded her legs under her, with her toes touching the floor.

At least I had the good sense—or was it so?—not to immediately demand where she had been or to try to shame her with all the searching I had done.

"Look," I said, "I'm sorry. I've had time to think about it. And really, it's good news, you being pregnant, and we—"

She waved off my little speech. "Forget it. My mistake. False alarm. Aunt Bertha's back." It was a phrase Marie and her friends used as their euphemism for menstruating.

"You're sure?"

"Please. Give me some credit. Yes, I'm sure." She crushed out her cigarette and closed her textbook. "Relieved?"

And I knew enough not to answer that one. "I was worried about you."

"I know, I should have called you. I was pissed off. What can I say? I've just been so on edge lately. I think it's that statistics class—it's *killing* me."

"So where were you?"

"A girl down the hall from me was driving to Minneapolis, so on a whim I said I'd ride with her. I stayed with my sister."

I hadn't thought to call there. "I was worried. . . ."

"I should have called. I *know* that. I'm sorry."

We might have continued like that, mired in my guilt-inducing expressions of worry and her subsequent apologies, but Marie saw a way out. She walked over to me, looped her arms around my neck, and kissed me vehemently enough to loosen—slightly—my clenched self.

If you have never experienced simultaneous passion and relief, I recommend it; the concoction is powerful and obliterating. It mattered then only that I was holding her again.

After a few moments of breathless kissing, I turned Marie around 180 degrees and pulled her tight to my chest. She reached up and back and again put her arms around my neck. This exposed her exactly as I wanted, allowing me to unbutton her blouse and caress those magnificent breasts. Gradually I ran my hands down the concavity of her stomach and dipped my fingers inside her waistband. Since her slacks rode low—hip-huggers, in the parlance of the day—that move brought me very close to where I wanted to be.

When I reached down a little farther, however, Marie dipped and twisted her torso, and I had no choice but to pull my hands away. "Huh-uh," she said, and between quickened breaths added, "I told you. I have my period."

She spun around another 180 degrees, kissed me again, and asked, "Or was that a test?"

"I forgot. For a moment."

"You have a very short memory." She tugged at my belt. "We could do something else. . . ." Now it was her hand squeezing its way inside my waistband.

"That's okay."

"What's the matter—afraid of accumulating debts you can't repay?"

Oh, how well she knew me! "I'm just happy to have you back."

"I can feel how happy you are," she said.

Since early childhood, the existence that has held the most appeal for me is one of unruffled routine, and almost immediately after those sirens came wailing down Keogh Street, I wanted things to revert to what seemed to me the calm of what had been. Taking the wrong lesson from those tumultuous days, I wanted—or so I believed—a return to a life in which I could take certain things for granted. This desire for placidity is perhaps too strong in me, and as a consequence I have often convinced myself it's present when in fact something is still roiling below the surface.

Nevertheless, it seemed to me that once Marie came back from her brief trip to Minneapolis, our lives quickly returned to what they had been, and it seemed that that was what we both wanted. We soon resumed having sex, although for a few months we were a bit more cautious. We were both busy with work and our studies, but we were together as often and, if questioned I would have said, as happily as before. When the semester ended, we packed up the Studebaker and drove together back to Bismarck for the holidays.

Where I promptly fell ill with strep throat, and for a few days I lay in bed with a fever and a throat so sore I could barely swallow. By Christmas day I felt better, but I still used my sickness as an excuse not to attend church with my mother and sister. After church they would go to the Christmas luncheon held every year by the Burnett sisters, another ritual I was pleased I could pass on. For a few hours I would have the house to myself.

I poured myself a cup of coffee, lit the first cigarette I could smoke in days, and, still in my pajamas, sat up in bed with the copy of *The Short Stories of Ernest Hemingway* that Marie gave me for Christmas. (The book, the Scribner's paperback edition priced at $2.95, is still on my shelf.) I had barely begun to read when someone knocked on my bedroom door. I'd thought I was alone in the house, and I hadn't heard the doorbell, but I wasn't startled for long. The door eased open, and there was Marie's smiling face.

"Are you feeling up to company?"

"Yours—yes."

She was skipping out of church too, she said, and when she took off her coat, I could see she was dressed for mass in a wool skirt and a turtleneck.

"I think God will forgive me," she said, "if I spend the morning tending to the sick."

"Not necessary. I'm feeling much better. Really."

Throwing back my blankets, I started to get up, but Marie pushed me back onto the bed. "I told you. I'm here to nurse you back to health." She took my cigarette from me, inhaled, and then put it out.

"The first thing I have to do," she said, pulling my T-shirt off, "is make sure your lungs are clear." She put her ear to my chest, but any pretense of listening soon fell away as she covered my torso with kisses.

She sat up. "Your heart *seems* sound, but I wonder . . . can it stand up to a little excitement?"

"I'm willing to risk it."

Without any more talk, Marie kicked off her shoes, pulled her sweater off over her head, unhooked her brassiere, wriggled out of the girdle that she needed only to hold up her nylons, and stepped out of her panties. She made no effort to fold or neatly stack her garments, but left them all lying in a small pile on the floor. Then, wearing nothing but her skirt, she climbed onto my narrow bed.

I reached for her, but she brushed my hands away. "We can't have you exerting yourself. Not in your weakened condition. You lie still and let me"—she pulled her skirt up to her hips and straddled me—"take care of you."

What was happening in that bedroom that had been mine when I was a boy was of course a boy's fantasy—a beautiful girl enters his room and gets into his bed. Inevitably I remembered when Marie had come to my room in quite a different way and for quite a different purpose—the night when, scratching on my screen, she woke me, and we went out together to search for her boyfriend. And suddenly through that tiny fissure of memory Gene squeezed his way into the bedroom.

But only for an instant.

With Marie moving rhythmically above me, her eyes half-closed, her breasts rising and falling, how could I think for long of anything but her? She leaned forward, pinning down my wrists and reminding me that I wasn't to grab or touch. Then she sat back, putting her hands on her own buttocks. When she bent down again her hair fell forward over her face and mine, and within that tent every breath I took was full of her heat and essence. Then, arching back up, she tossed her head and shook her hair back over her shoulder, but in the room's furnace-dried electric air, a few strands still floated free. Having taught me what I must not do, Marie now caressed her own breasts. The winter wind gusted hard and rattled the storm window in its frame, and when I came, it was with the same kind of shudder and gasp I might have displayed had I been dropped naked into snow. Marie's orgasm was a less dramatic trio of softly uttered *oh*s.

My memory of what happened is reliable, but occasionally my brain tries to put something *before* when in fact it was *after*. The mind performs these reversals or alterations no doubt because it has a narrative sense that life lacks and wants its stories to be as dramatic, harmonic, emphatic, and orderly as possible.

For example, I keep wanting to remember that it was on that Christmas Day that Marie, lying in my arms, us sharing a post-coital cigarette, announced that she was transferring to the University of Minnesota. But I know that wasn't so. I know it. She received notification before Christmas that she had been accepted into a special, experimental program that would allow her to seamlessly combine the completion of her undergraduate degree with teacher certification and admission to graduate study. When I traced my finger along her naked clavicle, feeling for that tiny irregularity where the bone broke, I knew—we both knew—that a separation lay ahead for us. We had already had our discussions of the difficulties that would pose, but we always concluded those conversations quickly with assurances that our love would overcome any problems.

And I know that when we made love in that narrow bed it was not for the last time. I know that. Just as I know that our relationship didn't end that day. But perhaps because the mind wants the symmetry of a story that would both begin, as this one did, and end on Keogh Street, it tries to force my memory to delete the remaining six months of our relationship. Maybe I misremember the end of our life together so I can make Marie's educational opportunity responsible rather than my own behavior on the day when she told me she might be pregnant. And maybe something in the way Marie and I made love that day—made love and made memory—tinged it with valediction, a farewell fuck for each to remember the other by. It may have been nothing more than what seemed a game that day—*don't use your hands!*—but perhaps it was in fact Marie's wish, still unconscious at that point, not to be contaminated by my touch.

But however false my memory tries to play some facts, it situates precisely in time and place—Christmas Day 1964, my bedroom—what Marie said after she rose from my bed and unself-consciously dressed in front of me. The little tale she told had probably been thrust to the forefront of her consciousness by the nearness of the Stoddard home, just across the street and down the block. Had she opened the curtains and looked out, she could have seen it from my window.

"Did you know," she asked me, "that Gene didn't call your father immediately after discovering his father's body?"

"Yeah. He tried to phone Marcia first. And then when he couldn't reach her—"

Clasping her brassiere, Marie shook her head. "There was a little time between those calls. Did you know that? What he did before he called your dad?"

"I don't believe I do."

She adjusted her breasts within the brassiere's cups. "First, Gene got two pans from the cupboard, one he filled with hot water and laundry detergent and the other with hot water and Pine-Sol."

When Marie pulled her sweater over her head, static electricity again gave her hair a will of its own, and the strands stuck out in a way that reminded me of the graduation night party when she tried to coax Gene down from the roof of his car, and the bonfire backlit her and gave her hair that same look of coppery filament. Once again she lifted her skirt, this time to pull on her panties and shimmy her girdle into place. "Mr. Stoddard had . . . When he died he . . . wet and soiled himself, and Gene wanted to clean up his father and the garage before anyone else came on the scene."

She adjusted her nylons, smoothed down her skirt, and stepped into her shoes. "He did a decent job on the garage floor, and the tires his father had stood on Gene just threw into the backyard. He couldn't clean his father's trousers, though, and for a minute Gene considered taking them off and finding a clean pair of pants. But in the end he just couldn't make himself do it. He couldn't undress his dad."

Marie put on her coat, gold wool and double-breasted, and buttoned it to her throat. The heat our bodies had made had cooled. She pulled her collar as high as it would go. I reached for the T-shirt she had pulled off me. Christmas services were over. Marie had her own family dinner to attend.

"You're right," I said. "Gene never told me that story."

"Why would he?" she asked on her way out the door. "He wasn't trying to seduce you."

In addition to the Hemingway collection, Marie also gave me a Rooster tie and a copy of *The Freewheelin' Bob Dylan,* the album with the cover of Dylan and Suze Rotolo arm-in-arm in the middle of a slushy New York street. I have that album still, like the Hemingway, although I no longer own a turntable to play the record on. I hadn't asked for the album, the book, or the tie, but Marie was well enough attuned to my tastes and desires that it would have been reasonable for me to expect any of those gifts.

And while I didn't expect the little anecdote she told about Gene, in a way it too was a gift. Here, she might have said, I know this is something you'll like. And in giving it to me perhaps she was trying to get rid of it—Here, I don't want this and I know you do. I present it to you, confident that you'll never lose it and that one day you'll find a use for it.

Yes. How well she knew me and my desires. And perhaps since she could not face a life with a man who would never stop hungering for exactly what she wished to divest herself of, she had to choose a life apart from his. I've often wondered—did Marie Ryan ever tell the man she eventually married anything about Raymond and Alma Stoddard? About their son, Gene? About both the boys who once lived on Keogh Street? It would not surprise me to learn that she didn't. Nor would I blame her.

~

Since Marie W. remembered the past with such clarity, she wondered why its appearance in her dreams was so muddled and confused. Even by the surrealistic standard of dreams, hers seemed to operate on the far edge of unreason, especially in matters of chronology.

For example, no matter how many decades had passed since she'd lived under her parents' roof, her dreams never played themselves out in the home she currently lived in—nor in any house or apartment she had once called home—but in the Bismarck, North Dakota, dwelling she grew up in. No matter how old her four sons were, they were almost always infants or, at most, grade-schoolers in her dreams. Her parents, of whom she never dreamed when they were alive, once deceased appeared to her regularly. They were alive and in the fullness of health in those dreams, yet they commented often on the inconveniences of being dead.

Marie's own age fluctuated in her dreams but within a narrow range. She was always an adult, no matter the age of her parents or children, but she couldn't find any means, not her appearance, not external events, that enabled her to locate her age precisely.

But the greatest confusion came from three males, a

boyfriend from high school, a boyfriend who followed the first and with whom she had a relationship that began in high school and went into her college years, and her husband. These three were as different as could be. The first was a brash, opportunistic, unpredictable boy. The second was sensitive but shy, brooding and often remote. And her husband was a confident, ebullient, unshakably cheerful man. Yet these three freely changed identities in her dreams. She might be driving somewhere with her husband and their children only to find, upon arrival, that it was her first boyfriend who lifted her son out of the backseat, and her second boyfriend who held open the door to the house they were visiting. The oddity wasn't, however, that all three males were present. There was only one man but with an identity that wasn't fixed. One would suddenly become another, and with no discernible transition, and no matter how strange these shifts were to her waking mind, within the dream they were unremarkable.

Of course the reason for this shape-shifting, this identity swapping, was within Marie, yet she had no idea what curl or twist in her brain or psyche might be causing it. Any explanation she came up with seemed pedestrian and inadequate. Yes, these were three males to whom she had professed love. Yes, she'd had sexual relations (but not intercourse) with all three. Nothing in those facts, however, explained the phenomenon. She didn't pine after former boyfriends or even possess much curiosity about them. She didn't feel she had made a mistake in severing her relationships with them. She loved her husband and lived a contented life with him. She had a forceful, well-defined personality—others said it of her, and she felt its truth as well—

and she had never sublimated her own identity to any male, not to her father, her husband, her sons, or to an old boyfriend. In the end, no amount of self-analysis brought her an answer or decreased the frequency of the dreams.

Then Marie received notice of her high school's twentieth reunion, to be held in Bismarck in mid-August. Both those boyfriends of her youth graduated in the same class as Marie, so though it was by no means a certainty, it was possible that if Marie and her husband attended the reunion, the three men who exchanged identities within her dreams might be in the same room at the same time. She'd had no interest in attending her ten-year reunion, but now it seemed to her that this social ritual had the potential of correcting the confusion of her dream life.

As soon as her husband came home from the Minneapolis clinic where he had his pediatric practice, she presented the letter of invitation to him. "What do you think?" Marie asked. "Feel like driving to Bismarck in August?"

He laughed, but something in her demeanor must have told him she was serious. "Why not? Will I get to meet your old boyfriends?"

Marie had told him nothing of her dreams, and though his question, both eerie and prescient, jolted her, she tried not to show it. Instead, she attempted to match his jaunty tone. "Get to? I'll insist on it."

He rubbed his hands together in gleeful imitation of a scheming silent movie villain. "At last—I'll find out if you always made that little mewing sound when the back of your neck is kissed, or if that's only for my benefit."

She took the invitation from his hand. "That's just for you, baby. Just for you."

In truth, Marie came into the marriage with little in the way of sexual history, especially compared to her husband's, but what she had, or hadn't, done before they met was of no consequence to him. Had Marie told him about her dreams, she was sure he would find them only amusing. He was not a jealous man, nor was he given to angst or introspection, and until the dreams began, Marie had always felt her spirit was a match for his.

The first of the reunion weekend's events was a mixer at the Sheraton hotel. Marie and her husband were staying at a Holiday Inn on the city's opposite end, and once they settled their sons in their adjoining room and reminded them they were limited to a single Spectravision movie, the couple set out for the evening.

In the parking lot, Marie's husband tossed her the car keys. "You drive," he said. "It's your town." And then he launched into a falsetto rendition of the J. D. Souther song. "It used to be his town, it used to be her town. . . ."

Her town . . . yes. A town whose streets and avenues were once as familiar to Marie as the halls and rooms of her own home, yet that night she had trouble finding the hotel. Over the years, the city's hotels had changed hands; what was once a Sheraton was now a Radisson, and the new Sheraton was on a street that had been changed to a one-way. Eventually, Marie had to park two blocks away because she couldn't figure out how to negotiate her way to the hotel's block.

As they walked toward the Sheraton, a solitary man kept pace with them on the opposite side of the street. He was wearing a white shirt, dark slacks, and cowboy boots, and though Marie didn't recognize him, she assumed he was on his way to the reunion too. Why couldn't he be one of her former boyfriends? Twenty years was more than enough time for bodies to shrink and expand, for hair to grow out or fall out, for features to flesh out or seam in ways that would make people look nothing like their yearbook portraits. Why did Marie believe she would know either of those boyfriends on sight? Did she think that the intimacies of love were a kind of imprinting, rendering her able to identify them by instinct? Or was she counting on them to recognize her and then announce themselves? For that matter, what process had her mind followed to make those boys appear as men in her dreams? Did her unconscious have a talent, Marie wondered, like a police sketch artist, to produce accurately aged portraits of someone she knew two decades before?

Once again, her husband seemed to know her thoughts. "Now, those old boyfriends," he said, "any chance there might be some residual bad feelings? Should I be ready to defend your honor or fight for the right to take you home?" He bobbed and feinted and threw phantom jabs into the night air.

Marie laughed in spite of herself. If nothing else, this little display of his demonstrated how different he was—with his buoyant spirit and his always-ready willingness to take himself and everyone else lightly—from her previous too-serious boyfriends, and she wondered again how it was possible that they could be confused or conflated, even in a dream. She felt a sudden rush of love for this man she'd married, and she stepped inside his boxer's stance, raised up on her tiptoes, and kissed him on the long, clean line of his freshly shaven jaw.

He dropped his hands, running them languorously down her back. When he reached her buttocks, he squeezed and pulled her tightly to him. "Or should I"—he assumed his comic British accent—"find other ways to demonstrate my rights of conjugal primacy?"

"You're doing a pretty good job of that right now."

He squeezed harder, and she pivoted away from his embrace. "Before we go in there," she said, "maybe we should set up signals. You know, if we need to be rescued from someone boring, or if the whole evening is just too excruciating."

"Good idea," he said. "How about an erection? If you see that I've got a hard-on, you'll know that means we've got to get back to the hotel right away."

"I was thinking more along the lines of a tug on the earlobe."

"A page from the Carol Burnett playbook. Okay. I like mine better, but the earlobe tug will work, too." He pushed open the door of the hotel. "Let us go among them."

The mixer was being held in a large banquet room, and Marie hesitated before its open doors. The room was dark but for candles on tables, and the flickering light gave everyone inside a spectral presence as they moved in and out of the wavering shadows. Marie had no more than glanced inside when her heart instantly misgave her, and she was ready to give up on the *entire enterprise. But what could she say? Minneapolis was 450 miles away, their night's accommodation had already been paid for, and her husband was standing expectantly by her side.*

A plump scowling woman who must have been from Marie's class but whom Marie did not recognize sat at a long table just outside the doors. With obvious consternation, she said, "They haven't provided me with any of the registration materials, so just write your name on one of these labels and stick it somewhere on yourself."

Marie's husband, for whom any unsmiling countenance was a challenge, said, "Any place visible, you mean."

She looked at him blankly.

"Because I could stick it on my chest," he said. "Under my shirt." He reached inside the gap between his buttons and tapped his fingers in imitation of a beating heart. He bestowed upon her the irresistible smile that he swore he never practiced.

Grudgingly returning his smile, she said, "Someplace visible."

He pretended to slap the label onto his forehead, and the plump woman allowed her grin its full release. She asked him the question she never asked Marie. "Do I know you?"

He pointed to his wife. "She's a senior. I already graduated."

As they walked away from the registration table with their names pasted onto their clothes over their hearts, Marie asked, "Must you charm everyone?"

The question's petulance surprised Marie—it had leaped from her before she could stop it—but her husband seemed not to take offense. "I must! I will not cease from my labors until every man, woman, and child is charmed!"

At the bar, Marie ordered a white wine and her husband asked for a light beer, and while they stood with the sweating containers in their hands, two couples approached them. Marie wasn't sure how it happened, but almost immediately after the introductions were made an invisible partition descended on the group. The men drifted off, talking, as near as Marie could tell, about the brown suits Ronald Reagan wore, and Marie was left in the company of two women she only vaguely remembered from high school but who now pretended as though they had all been closer than they really were.

Neither of the women had aged well. Rhonda Veach, now Rhonda Schneeberg, had been a raucous, overweight tag-along in high school, and while she was still heavy, she apparently believed her pounds now worked to her advantage. She had squeezed herself into a tight, low-cut dress that revealed an embarrassing abundance of cleavage. Janice Schmidt, née Kalsow, with whom Marie had been closer in elementary school than in later years, was also wearing a low-cut dress, but she was so thin and darkly tanned that the skin of her neck and chest looked, even in the poor light, like paper that had been crumpled and then smoothed out.

While they were catching up—an activity that largely consisted of an enumeration of children's names and ages—another woman joined them. Peggy Pilquist and Marie had been good friends, and their embrace was spontaneous and genuine. Peggy looked disturbingly similar to the way she'd looked in high *school—pretty in a wide-eyed, well-scrubbed way. Her blond hair was still carefully waved around her face just as it was in her graduation portrait.*

The group's talk soon became a recitation of notorious high school incidents—the cow smuggled into the gymnasium, the bowling ball rolled down the stairs, the principal's car pelted with eggs—that challenged no one's memory. When they began to speculate about certain individuals—the boy arrested for stealing tires, the girl pregnant at prom, the algebra teacher and the phys ed instructor found out in an affair—Marie felt herself tested. But her memories seemed to coincide with everyone else's. The conversation gave her no reason to believe that the confused identities in her dreams had anything to do with a general disorientation about the past. Perhaps if Marie could separate Peggy from the others, Marie could ask her if she ever dreamed about old boyfriends or if the present and the past ever exchanged themselves in dreams.

And just at that moment an old boyfriend stealthily approached. For a good portion of high school Janice Schmidt had dated Randy Oslund, and that was exactly who now loomed behind her. Randy's index finger in front of his wide grin warned Marie and Peggy not to give away his presence.

Randy was over six feet tall, and even thinner than he'd been in high school. He had close-set eyes and fine blond hair that looked windblown even indoors, and when he raised his arms over Janice Schmidt, he looked like a predatory bird. His white shirt and dark trousers gave him away as the man Marie had seen earlier walking toward the hotel.

Janice must have sensed he was there, because she whirled

about. When she saw who it was, she shrieked, and instantly they fell into each other's arms.

No, not a bird. A vampire, for Randy Oslund pronounced, in his Transylvanian accent, "I haff come for you, my darling."

Their embrace went on so long that Marie imagined they were giving their bodies a chance to remember the sensations of the past. Even when they broke their clinch, they still kept their arms around each other.

Janice pretended to punch Randy in the ribs. "And where were you planning to take me?"

"The Haystacks, of course!" That was an area north of town whose dirt roads and isolated groves had once provided teenagers a private place to park. Marie had spent her share of time in cars with fogged windows out at the Haystacks, and on one occasion her and her boyfriend's passions ran so hot that as their bodies pressed and undulated against each other, they didn't notice that her glasses had slipped from the armrest and gotten trapped under them. In the car's muffled silence the snapping of the plastic frame made a sound like a breaking bone. Marie had no trouble recalling the incident or the boyfriend in whose arms she'd rolled around on the car seat.

Laughing, Janice said, "I'm ready to go. But won't your wife wonder where you are?"

"Hell, we'll be back before she knows I'm gone."

"So, Speedy Gonzales, I guess that hasn't changed."

Randy Oslund affected a stricken expression and clapped his hands over his heart, but Marie could tell Janice's remark caused him no real pain.

In spite of the jokes, Marie recognized that their feelings for *each other were genuine, though the emotion likely had more to do with history and nostalgia than with still-fresh desire or affection. The intimacy of their display, however, no matter that it was feigned or performed for an audience, shocked Marie. Was there a door to the past that she had somehow left open, and did that explain her dreams? Or had the dreams pushed open the door?*

But while Randy and Janice shocked Marie, she also envied them. She could easily imagine her husband acting like Randy Oslund with an old girlfriend. And inviting Marie over to meet the woman. Unlike Marie, he talked openly about women with whom he once had relationships, even to the extent of describing their sexual behavior. Marie had once accompanied her husband to an Austin, Texas, medical conference, and he introduced her there to a woman he had dated during his first year of medical school. A neonatologist, she soon excused herself to attend a seminar, and then Marie's husband told Marie about how the woman had never seemed to warm to him during their time together, and how she'd preferred to make love on all fours, a position that no doubt suited her because it didn't require her to touch him or look at him. And that anecdote reminded him of another woman who, from that same position, would reach back and grab his testicles, a move that once brought a yelp of pain from him that she mistook for ecstasy.

Even when such frankness embarrassed Marie, she knew it signaled his confidence with her, and she had to admit it was preferable to a husband who hoarded and cherished his memories of other women.

Her husband detached himself from the group of men and

returned to Marie's side. "Babe, I'm going to join these gentlemen up in their room. Someone needs a physician's second opinion." He pressed the tips of his thumb and index finger together and, bringing them to his lips, inhaled audibly. Although he had, in deference to his status as a physician and a father, stopped buying marijuana years ago, he could not turn down an invitation to smoke someone else's.

"Be careful," Marie said. "Please."

As he walked away grinning, he said, "If you can't trust the class of '63, who can you trust?"

Rhonda, Janice, and Randy also walked away, leaving Marie with her old friend.

Peggy leaned close, bringing with her the scent of cigarette smoke and hair spray. "Guess who's here—and he's looking for you?"

Marie felt herself blush. "How can anyone be looking for me? How does anyone know who's here and who isn't?"

"Okay, asking. He's asking if you're here."

"I have no idea."

"Just think for a minute. I believe you know."

"Oh, please, Peggy. This isn't junior high. Just tell me."

Peggy smiled coyly. "I don't believe I will. Anyway, keep standing right here. I'm sure he'll find you." As if she were enacting an exit she had rehearsed, Peggy bowed and backed away.

One of them was looking for her. . . . Marie tried to determine which former boyfriend that was likely to be. She couldn't believe that shy young man would seek her out. Instead, he would stake out a position, just as he had on that winter night *when he'd stood on a street corner and watched the house—was it Peggy's?—where Marie was attending a slumber party. It was after midnight when someone saw him out there and told Marie. She stepped into her shoes and ran out to him in her pajamas. While they both stood shivering under a streetlamp, he explained that it wasn't that he hadn't trusted her when she'd told him she'd be there, but his worry caused his faith to tremble. So perhaps he was watching Marie now from some dark corner, waiting for her to notice him, then approach him, and say, "I've been dreaming about you."*

When Marie finally severed the relationship with him, both he and she shed tears. Finally, however, his moodiness, his inaccessibility, and his passivity wore her out. She felt she expended so much energy in closing the distance between them, in sending out signs of affection so he could learn through imitation to match them with his own, in fulfilling the needs he could not or would not articulate for himself, that she was losing too much of herself. Simply put, he exhausted her.

Yet he was not the likeliest candidate to be searching for her. No, if someone was sorting through the assemblage, checking name tags and staring into faces until he found Marie's, it was probably her first boyfriend, that smiling, intense, determined-to-get-what-he-wanted-at-any-cost young man. Why wouldn't he cross identity boundaries in her dreams? He could seldom be restrained in the time he and Marie were together.

When Marie was sixteen, she traveled with her family to a Minnesota lake for their summer vacation. Marie hadn't wanted to go. Although the summers of her adolescence seemed long, two weeks apart from her boyfriend was a deprivation too much to bear. She wrote him twice a day, and she promised him, almost to the minute, when they would be reunited. Her father pulled into the driveway, and Marie jumped from the car. She ran into the house, heading for her basement bedroom from where she would telephone her boyfriend and tell him she was back— Come over right away!

But he was already there, waiting for her just inside her bedroom door.

Once Marie's fright subsided, her joy at seeing him—after fourteen days and nights!—took over and she launched herself into his arms. In the busyness of unloading the car and unpacking suitcases, Marie's parents didn't notice that her boyfriend was already there when the family arrived; they assumed he had hurried over in record time to see Marie.

Over the next few weeks, Marie learned that that had not been the only day he'd taken the key from under the pot of geraniums and let himself into the house. He confessed that he had been in there almost every day, and as evidence he had hidden little notes throughout her room. She put her hand under her pillow and found a note; she opened a drawer and found another. He put one in her jewelry box and tucked another inside a high school yearbook. None of the notes said anything more than "Hi there!" "It's me!" "Surprise!" and initially Marie found them endearing. But when she came across one taped to the back of a framed photograph of her parents, she suddenly felt a chill. The site of that note—"It's me again!"—was certainly more innocent than the drawer where she kept her pajamas, nylons, brassieres, panties, and slips, but the note on her *bureau changed everything that surrounded it. Suddenly Marie's room felt less like hers; it had been transformed into a space anyone might occupy. The bedroom door fit poorly in its frame and only with great effort could it be pushed or pulled to shut tight, and even then the door had no lock. Not that it mattered. As those little scraps of paper—"Guess who!"—demonstrated, Marie had no threshold she could cross where the world wouldn't follow. When Marie broke up with him a few months later, she told him it was because they were becoming too serious, a phrase that back then almost always meant the girl no longer knew how to restrain her boyfriend's sexual demands or how to keep her own desire from duplicating his.*

Marie hadn't finished her glass of wine, but she made her way back to the bar. From there she thought it would be easier to not only see someone approach but also to read the history in any face's features.

In fact, Marie had barely reached out her glass to the young bartender to ask for a refill when a man unexpectedly thrust his face in front of her and demanded, "Why'd you break my heart?"

Startled, Marie pulled back, and when she did, she saw who was confronting her. Fortunately, she caught herself before she made matters worse and spoke the words that came first to her tongue. Oh, Terry, it's only you.

Instead, Marie greeted that pop-eyed, mock-belligerent face with, "Hello, Terry. It's nice to see you."

"Why? So you can rip my heart out and stomp on it and finish the job?"

They both knew what he was jokingly referring to. Throughout their grade-school years Terry Bart had had a crush on Marie. He plagued her on the playground, following her everywhere, teasing her, making her his special target in dodgeball; he went blocks out of his way just so he could walk past Marie's house after school. Finally, when they reached junior high, he became bold enough to ask Marie if she would go with him to a school dance. "I'm sorry," she told him, "but I'm going with Danny McCabe." Danny was an eighth grader and someone with whom Terry knew he could not compete. In the next few years Terry learned to make a joke of the rejection, but Marie knew his sense of defeat and disappointment had been real. In high school when she was briefly between boyfriends, Marie consented to attend a party with Terry, and though she tried to make it clear to him that he would never be more than a friend, he still tried, drunkenly, roughly, persistently, to kiss her at the party. Marie eventually pushed him away and left the party, walking home through four inches of fresh snow in kitten heels.

"Do you still live in Bismarck, Terry?"

"You mean you haven't kept track of my every move? Denver. We've lived in Denver for the last seven years."

"We?"

"My wife. We met at Augustana. She's right over there." Terry pointed across the room, but in the dim light his direction was useless. *"Can you wait right here? I'll go get her. She'd love to meet the girl who broke my heart. God knows she's heard enough about you."*

The idea of being introduced to Mrs. Bart in that context

held no appeal for Marie, and as soon as Terry left, she slid
away from the bar. She wanted to head toward the door and
then wait for her husband over by the elevators, but that meant
stepping into the light. Anyone looking for her, whether an old
boyfriend or an aspirant like Terry, would find her easier to spot
if she left the banquet room's shadows.

She circled behind the bar, back by the troughs of iced beer
and soda and the stacked boxes of inexpensive wines and
liquors. One of the bartenders, a young man not much older
than Marie's sons, looked at Marie and raised an eyebrow con-
spiratorially in her direction. Just as Randy Oslund had done
earlier, Marie raised her finger to her lips, and the bartender
smiled and nodded in understanding. But what, Marie wondered, did the young man believe he understood?

What if Terry Bart, and not one of Marie's ex-boyfriends,
were the anonymous seeker Peggy had told her about? Wouldn't
that make sense? Terry was there; he had obviously been looking for her. Perhaps Marie was fleeing from a rendezvous she
had already had. . . .

Ceiling-to-floor draperies encircled the room, and Marie
moved close to the heavy dark fabric. She had no idea what the
curtains were for, but she was ready to adapt them for her own
purposes, to step inside a fold or opening and vanish from sight.
As unobtrusively as possible she began to move around the
room, all the while glancing back at the entrance so she
wouldn't miss her husband when he returned.

As soon as he came into view, she planned to run to him
and tell him they must leave immediately, that it had been a mistake to come there, that she wanted nothing to do with the past

and certainly wanted none of its scenes enacted ever again. It wasn't feasible to leave Bismarck tonight, but she'd insist they leave first thing in the morning. She couldn't bear the thought of being in the city in the full exposure of daylight.

Just ahead a small knot of people stood in Marie's path. She could try to go around them, a move that would necessitate leaving the available cover and possible escape route of the draperies; she could go back in the direction from whence she had come; or she could stop right where she was and wait, hoping she wouldn't be noticed and that they would soon disperse and clear the way ahead. She stood still.

Someone in the group ahead must have said something funny, because every one of them either threw their head back or bent over with laughter. Almost as if they were in on the joke, the people at the table nearest her also began to laugh uproariously.

Suddenly, through the sounds of all that merriment and beneath the room's general din, came a voice, barely more than a whisper, and from right behind her. A man said—she thought she heard him say—"Would you like to go to Paris with me?"

Marie didn't recognize the voice, but given the room's noise and its poor acoustics, how could she? It could have been her husband speaking to her and she wouldn't have been able to identify him.

And perhaps the man wasn't even addressing her. If she waited for just a moment before turning around, he would certainly repeat his question and then she would know exactly who was there and why.

The question never came again, but eight years later, when

Marie stood on the Pont des Arts with the man she loved, she was sure that, in spite of her dreams' efforts to confuse her, her decisions in life had been the right ones. At that moment in Paris, however, who was beside her seemed of less importance than the fact of the May sun warming her back and lighting the gilt of a building that looked to her like a wedding cake.

Although the relationship-cancer that eventually put an end to the us that was Marie and me may well have been in place on that Christmas Day when she came to check on my health—indeed, maybe it was present from the very beginning—we continued to see each other after she transferred to the University of Minnesota. I drove to Minneapolis, she rode the bus to Grand Forks, or we met in Bismarck when we both went back there for one school vacation or another. But in none of our meetings, letters, or many telephone conversations did we ever make arrangements for permanence, and eventually the simple fact of the 315 miles between us may have been too much to overcome. When we each began to find excuses not to make the journey—an exam to study for, a paper to write, a lecture to attend, a party not to be missed, a snowstorm predicted, a car with a fussy carburetor—our life together was all but over. We both decided to attend summer school at our respective institutions (one of us, I don't remember who, must have been the first to make that choice, and the other no doubt followed suit out of spite). Our breakup, like my parents', was not the result of a single explosive incident but more a gradual loss of the energy relationships use for fuel. By autumn of 1965 we were finished.

At first I told myself that was all right. My pride had been wounded—Marie didn't have to transfer to another school. Then another girl briefly captured my interest. A creative writing professor overpraised my poems and stories and told me I could be admitted to the University of Iowa's MFA program. He was wrong, but the damage was done; my head was turned. When I graduated, I, like Marie, left North Dakota for an adjoining state, but she headed east and I went west, to the University of Montana and its new graduate writing program. Once there, I was, I told myself, exactly where I wanted to be and ready to begin realizing my deepest literary aspirations. The mysteries of the human heart could be known, and I would devote my life to the careful search for words to convey that knowledge.

Then on a winter morning, after three days of warm Chinook winds rolling down the Rockies, after a night of drinking in a Missoula, Montana, bar with a group of students who shared my naïve ambitions, I woke with a profound hangover and a refrain running through my brain as if on a perpetual circuit: *I need Marie, I need Marie, I need Marie, I need Marie, I need Marie . . .* the vowels—*eye ee ah ee eye ee ah ee eye ee ah ee*—sounding for all the world like the siren of a Parisian police car. The words may not have come to me previously in quite that form, but the emotion that underlay them, I realized, had never left me and never would. That feeling, as if it too had been covered in snow, surfaced in January's thaw.

Sunk though I was that morning in self-pity and despair, my sense of irony was still intact. When Marie and I were together, I used to worry that someday I would lose her to Gene because, while I could make and state the case that I *wanted* her, he could make the stronger claim by asserting that he *needed* her. Now, however, it was too late for both of us. I had lost touch—*wonderful phrase!*—with Marie, and though this is another sequence I can't be entirely sure of, she may have already found the man she would marry, a man who, unlike the boys of Keogh Street, would answer *her* wants and needs.

As long as my mother was alive—and it took many years before her two-packs-a-day habit caught up to her—I returned to Bismarck every year. Once I married (more of that soon) and eventually started teaching, largely because I needed to find work that provided benefits and brought in a paycheck larger and steadier than the erratic royalties and option money that came my way, those annual returns to my hometown were usually in the summer. At decade-long intervals, however, I made *certain* that those trips were in the summer. Specifically, I made it a point to be in Bismarck during the days when the class of 1963—Marie's class—held its reunion.

But as far as I knew, she never returned. And why would she? In the late 1960s Marie's father was transferred, and her family moved to Illinois, and even if Marie had had enough pleasant memories of the city and her time there—enough, that is, to over-power her association with the lurid, tragic Raymond Stoddard affair—she had never been attached to the past. A writer I revere, William Maxwell, once said, "I don't think I have outlived any part of my life, it all seems to coexist," and while I could say the same thing about my life, that sentiment was never Marie's. Remember her advice to Gene? He had to "stop pulling the past up to the present." Besides, had she come back to Bismarck, for a high school reunion or any other reason, what good would it have done me? She would have been in the company of the man she'd married, a doctor she met in Minneapolis when she was in graduate school and he was interning. To this day they live in Edina, a Minneapolis suburb, with their four sons.

(Incidentally, my informant on matters Marie has usually been the wife of my college roommate, Rob Varley. After earning a master's degree from the University of North Dakota, Rob returned to Bismarck to work for a utility company, and he married Karen Holmes, a former friend of Marie's. Karen was the secretary of their high school class, and she's been in charge over the years of keeping track of classmates and issuing invitations for reunions.)

For many years that wife I mentioned earlier accompanied me on trips to my hometown. A native of Billings, Montana, she was a nursing student when we met in Missoula. A soft-spoken, sincere, pretty woman, it would never have occurred to her trusting nature that on any occasion when we were in Bismarck, I was constantly scanning the streets in the hope that Marie Ryan might also be back in town and I could catch a glimpse of her. A glimpse. I told myself that I wanted nothing more. Just something to satisfy my curiosity, to see if she was as lovely as ever (and as lovely as Karen, who visited Marie in Minneapolis, said she was). She was my first love, an adolescent obsession. Many such youthful infatuations stay with men and women. Sometimes for years. They're normal. Harmless. That was what I told myself. Then, just when I thought I had convinced myself that all those things were true, the refrain would begin again, its vowels wailing through my brain—*eye ee ah ee eye ee ah ee eye ee ah ee. I need Marie, I need Marie, I need Marie, I need Marie, I need Marie. . . .*

During the years of our marriage my wife never suspected that I was in love with another woman. Why would she? I never lied to her about where I was or who I was with. How could I love someone I hadn't seen for five years . . . for ten . . . for twenty? When our marriage inevitably ended, it wasn't because I had been caught in an affair. But my emotional remoteness, my inaccessibility, finally exhausted my wife.

I remember the occasion when the end came. We were in the car together, running errands or going out for lunch. The circumstances don't matter. I might have said something, but it's more likely that I didn't. My silences were more common, and more wearing, than any speech, even of the wounding sort. She suddenly let her head fall back against the headrest, and said, without a trace of anger or vitality in her voice, "I've had it with you."

Indeed she had. Caring for the sick or injured was more than her profession; it was her natural disposition. For months, for years, she had tried to revive our marriage, willing to do almost anything to bring it back to health. "What do you want from me?" she used to ask. I didn't take advantage of her invitation. What was I supposed to say—*be someone else?* And since I was unwilling to be anyone other than who I was—joyless and remote—our marriage expired.

Even when I was no longer making those annual pilgrimages to Bismarck in the company of a wife, I was usually not traveling alone. We had twin daughters, and the divorce didn't diminish their willingness—their eagerness—to make the trip to Grandmother's house and to the city that had been their father's boyhood home.

When the girls were nine or ten, I decided to take them on a tour of the state capitol and its grounds. One of our first stops was the building's legislative wing, the art deco Great Hall where Raymond Stoddard murdered Monty Burnham. I planned to show them the banquette where the senator had been sitting when the assassin approached, the floor that had once been stained with blood, its red swirling into the marble's pattern. I intended to give them a lesson in history. . . .

I couldn't do it.

While the scene and the story probably would have been to them nothing more than a bit of gruesome Bismarck trivia, I couldn't take the chance. What if a detail—as slight as the bullet-pocked stone floor or as large as the connection to Keogh Street and their ancestry—lodged in my daughters the way the details had made a home in me? Of some matters ignorance is preferable to knowledge.

I've brought the matter of Raymond Stoddard and his motivation about as far as I can. If I haven't made the choices clear, let me present them one more time. You might choose to believe, as my mother did, that Raymond Stoddard killed to avoid a scandal involving his job with the state. You might side with my father and think that resentment and anger over the Stoddard family's being cheated of a dwelling and acreage was enough to make Raymond buy a gun and use it. It may be your conviction that murder always proceeds from a deranged mind whose purposes are never available to us. Your character, your experiences, your values, your worldview—all these will cause you to favor one theory over another. Have you ever succumbed to an irrational impulse? Could jealousy corrupt your soul? Have you ever acted with nothing but bitterness behind the behavior? My own hypothesis doesn't require much beyond what's known of the principals' lives—that and the knowledge that nothing has a power quite like love to tilt us toward murder and self-destruction.

I imagine—and it hardly seems appropriate to term this theory the product of imagination, so plausible does it seem to me— *that Raymond Stoddard had always known that his wife loved another man before she loved him. For years, this was a source of satisfaction for him. He regarded himself as blessed that Alma Shumate chose him; he had a special pride that he possessed what others wanted. In economic terms, her value increased according to how strongly she was desired by others. However, just as the rich man worries that he will lose his treasure, so Raymond Stoddard's anxiety eventually outpaced his happiness.*

Maybe Raymond's doubts needed nothing to grow but his own insecurities, and maybe they began with a casual remark, a comparison his wife made between him and other men. It might have been a perfectly harmless observation. Why, Alma asked her husband when he reached for his money to pay the restaurant bill, do you always carry your wallet in your jacket pocket? Every other man I've known—my father, my brother, Monty, Pastor Lundgren, Bill McCutcheon—carries his in the back pocket of his trousers. Monty. Only a first name was necessary.

They both knew of whom she was speaking. Or maybe it started with Monty Burnham's rise to prominence. One evening he was featured on the news, a brief segment showing him at the dedication of the Lewis and Clark monument overlooking the Missouri, and Alma leaned farther forward than she ever did for an act she liked on The Ed Sullivan Show *or with more interest than she showed in any episode of* The Loretta Young Show, *her favorite program.*

And that was all it took.

She still thought of Monty Burnham. She knew Monty Burnham, knew him and his habits well enough to recollect without effort how he carried his wallet. He wasn't only part of her past; he was in her present. She might be looking out a window, but she wasn't seeing the snow falling or the wind sweeping away the fallen leaves, she was thinking about Monty Burnham. He was more real to her than the sunset pinks and lavenders of the horizon.

Who is to say where worry crosses over to fear and then hardens into agonized belief? We either have the ability to talk ourselves out of our fears or we don't. And Raymond Stoddard reached the point where he suspected that anytime Alma left the house it might be for the final time. Her suitcase was packed, and around the corner her lover was waiting. Of course he forgot that Wednesdays were her days for working at the church or that she had told him that she was walking over to Mrs. Morton's house for coffee or that she said she'd stop at Super Valu; he believed that anytime she left the house it was for another assignation.

Over the years Raymond Stoddard had tried various mea-

sures of self-treatment to salve his perpetually wounded pride or to alleviate his misery. He had always drunk, but at some point the act become purposeful, determined. The benumbed man, after all, feels no pain. Anger too can be a narcotic, and though he was never able to use it as successfully as bourbon, the few times his rage burst forth, Raymond found himself oddly released from pain. For that matter, his own reveries could sometimes offer him relief, even when the object of contemplation was his wife in the arms of another man. He pictured so vividly the scenes of Alma in bed with Monty Burnham that Raymond was briefly taken outside himself; he was no longer a man in agony, he was an impersonal creator, a visionary, a vehicle for his own lurid imagination.

None of his strategies for relieving his pain lasted for long, however. It always returned, and frequently redoubled. Finally in January of 1961—and how many residents of the northern plains have come to a life-altering conclusion in deepest winter, as though something in their brains could crystallize and take form just as their breath does in the frigid air—Raymond Stoddard concluded it all had to stop, even if his own life was subsumed within that "all."

Marcia Stoddard's semester grades arrived, and they were not good. A C in Introduction to Drama. A C– in biology, and they went down from there. A D in Spanish, and an F in Educational Psychology.

Her father was furious. "She had to attend the university," he said, slapping the printed grade form down on the kitchen counter. "She had to graduate early from high school, and then junior college wasn't good enough for her. Oh, no. It had to be the university. And I'm shelling out good money for grades like these?"

Alma tried to calm her husband and to keep his ranting from being overheard by her son and his friend watching television in the living room. "Shhh. You know she was struggling. She said so at Thanksgiving."

"This isn't just struggling. See this. F. That's failing. Not struggling. Failing."

"She promised she'd do better. It was a bad semester."

"She promised. And does she know how she'll do better? I'm going to have a talk with her."

"What do you think that will accomplish? She's let us down. She knows that. She's let herself down."

"If she doesn't have a plan for how she's going to improve, I might have a few suggestions for her."

"I really don't think that's what she needs to hear right now."

"What she needs . . . Maybe what she needs isn't the important thing right now. Maybe—just a minute. Are you telling me that I shouldn't speak to my own daughter? Is that what you're saying? Because—"

"Oh, for God's sake. Will you stop? You're not going to solve this with a talk. You've never bothered talking to her before, about her grades or anything else. You . . . you're barely a father to her."

Because Raymond couldn't quite comprehend what his wife had said to him—he wasn't Marcia's father?—he looked elsewhere for assistance. The boys in the living room—if they'd heard Alma's statement, surely they would register its shock, *wouldn't they? What the hell? Dad isn't—? Mr. Stoddard isn't Marcia's father? And Raymond's son was rising to his feet—was he coming out to the kitchen to demand the truth of his paternity? But Gene merely walked to the television set and with a half turn of the horizontal hold stopped the picture from rolling. His friend never took his eyes off that week's episode of Gunsmoke. Was it Raymond who had misunderstood? Had his wife merely offered a comment on him as an insufficiently attentive, barely engaged father, and in that regard not very different from every other father? That interpretation was certainly available.*

Yet Raymond rejected it and chose instead to take Alma's blurted remark as revelation, the confession he had dreaded and longed to hear.

His wife had not just loved another before she loved him— that he could handle and indeed in some moments could even gloat about—but she had had sex with that man. That was harder to bear. Of course she had never stopped thinking about, caring about Monty Burnham—the reminder of him, of them and their love for each other, was constantly present in Marcia. Their child. And that was, quite literally, a fact he could not digest. He bolted from the kitchen on his way to the bathroom, but when he saw his son and his son's friend, Raymond turned around. He ran to the garage and there he lurched to the trash can just in time: He vomited onto the sack of garbage that he had put there only an hour earlier.

What was he to do? He thought he had known what his darkest worry was—that Alma constantly, secretly compared him to another man and found her husband wanting—but Ray-

mond realized now that even in his bleakest, most pessimistic self-pitying moods he had not imagined circumstances as black as these.

With the new year, the legislators invaded the city for their biennial session, and soon their plans to create or thwart new laws became the news that dominated local and state media. Newspapers and television news programs could be counted on to carry articles and interviews in which senators and representatives lobbied, through the press, for or against the projects and issues closest to or furthest from their hearts. Monty Burnham was a rising star in the Republican party, and whether he sought the attention of the cameras or the cameras looked for him is irrelevant; he was a reliable media presence, as close to famous as any North Dakotan was likely to come during the first cold, snowy days of 1961.

On its six o'clock nightly news broadcast, Bismarck station KFYR televised a brief interview with Senator Burnham on the contentious subject of the state's property tax, and as it happened, Raymond Stoddard, who usually favored the news on KXMB, the CBS affiliate, was watching KFYR during the Burnham segment. Had Raymond's wife been in the room at the time, Raymond might well have turned to her, pointed at the screen, and issued his ultimatum: Him or me—which is it? Right now, make your decision. No deliberation, no discussion, no denials, no explanations, no lists of pros and cons. Right now—him or me.

But the only other person in the room was the teenage boy who lived up the block, waiting for Raymond's son so the two of

them could attend that evening's basketball contest—Bismarck
High School versus its in-town rival, St. Mary's. They wanted to
leave early enough to be in time for the junior varsity game as
well.

But what if Alma had been there? It wouldn't have mattered. Raymond knew what she'd say. He was foolish, imagining things. The past was past. She might profess her love for
Raymond, depending on whether he'd angered or touched her
with his accusation. But Raymond Stoddard now lived in a
realm where neither protest nor proof, nor protestations of love
or innocence, could reach him. Nothing of the usual life of humans could affect his faith. Alma loved another man, and Raymond knew it. The only thing left was to leave this life with
nothing behind but this message to his wife: I know.

Raymond tried composing a suicide note to Alma, a letter
that would make it clear that he was aware that she loved someone else and always had. But every attempt to write this communication failed. Sheet after sheet he tore up or crumpled and
tossed aside. He couldn't get the tone right. He wanted to sound
noble, self-sacrificing, yet he also felt that he was entitled to be
angry and aggrieved—her contempt for him finally became too
much to bear. He wanted to outline the relevant background to
his suicide, yet any attempt to go into the past enlarged the
scope of his note and soon he was writing page after page of
personal history. He didn't want to write an autobiography. Indeed, any account of his life only served to emphasize how
undistinguished it was. Yet he had to find a way to leave a message for Alma, something that would tell her that he knew

about her feelings for another man, and that he could no longer go on living with this knowledge.

He purchased a .45 automatic, the make and model of sidearm that he and Monty Burnham trained with during the second World War. In the privacy of the basement laundry room Raymond filled the clip to capacity with cartridges, slammed the clip into place, and pulled back on the automatic's slide to chamber a bullet. Then he clicked on the pistol's safety. Although he hadn't picked up a gun since his years in the service, the feel of the weapon in his hand was so familiar that he thought its loading and operation might well belong in the same category as riding a bicycle—once learned, never forgotten. He put the .45 into the pocket of his overcoat—first wrapping it in a dish towel so its shape wouldn't give itself away—and each day he carried it to work with him. That was the extent of his plan; the rest would be improvised as chance presented itself. He couldn't be sure when he'd see Monty Burnham, but Raymond knew when the senate was in session and where the legislators were likely to be when they were not in chambers. Raymond made it a point to visit the legislative wing frequently.

The day soon came when he saw Monty Burnham sitting on a red leather banquette outside the senate, which was in recess. Raymond wished the man had been alone, but he could hardly afford to let the opportunity pass. Who knew when he'd have another? He returned to his office and put on his overcoat with its familiar weight on the right side. Into his left pocket he placed the envelope containing the folded, signed confession that he had typed days before. That communication he had had no trouble composing; it came out exactly right the first time, and he was quietly proud of its straightforward—yet still slightly enigmatic—uncomplaining acknowledgment of guilt.

His decision to say nothing about his motive before shooting Monty Burnham was governed by the same logic, if it can be called that, that decided Raymond against leaving a note for Alma. He didn't know what to say because he didn't know what not to say. But if the act itself was going to tell her everything that needed to be said, then the sight of the .45 pointed at Monty Burnham would have to be sufficient explanation for the senator.

Only the actual sound of the gun going off was Raymond unprepared for. That long hall, those high ceilings, the walls and floors of stone—the .45 boomed and echoed like none ever had during his years of training and combat. He knew the gun would jump in his hand and send a jolt all the way up his arm—he was heedful to aim his second shot as carefully as the first—but the noise, the noise! For a moment his hearing was affected, and shouting and screaming reached Raymond's ears as if they came from a much greater distance than from the men and women scattering around him. Then, as his hearing gradually improved, the noise from those same people grew louder, as if they were now coming closer, when in fact everyone wanted to move away from the man with the gun.

After shooting the senator, Raymond walked away calmly—his calm was a pleasant surprise—away from the scene, away from the man twitching and jerking and clutching at his throat as if his death couldn't come fast enough and he wanted to choke off his last breath, away from the blood-smeared stone

*floor, away from the panicked onlookers who weren't sure of the
direction in which to run. At an even pace, Raymond exited the
building through the south door, and not until he was negotiating the icy steps leading down from the building was he even
aware that he was still holding the gun, and even then his awareness wasn't of a weapon, an instrument with which he had just
committed murder, but of weight, and that awareness led to another: He was a fugitive, fleeing a crime, and fugitives needed
neither the extra weight nor evidence connecting them to the
crime. No matter that Raymond Stoddard had no expectation of
escape from capture or incrimination, as he walked away from
the capitol, he instinctively lightened his load by flinging the gun
away, and when it landed in a snowdrift, it had not only its
weight to help it sink through the snow but also the heat it still
held from Raymond's hand and from being so recently fired.*

*Raymond Stoddard's Ford was not the only car leaving the capi-
tol's parking lot. As he waited at the stop sign for his turn to
pull out onto Fourth Street, he counted five cars ahead of him,
all employees who had probably heard—or heard about—the
shooting and were driving away from the grounds as quickly as
possible. Surprises kept multiplying. He was shocked and somewhat indignant that he could make his escape—although he hesitated to think of it in that way; after all, he had no hope, no
desire, of a permanent getaway—with so little difficulty.
Shouldn't the entire capitol building and grounds be sealed as
quickly as possible to prevent the assassin's flight?*

*He drove the few blocks to his home, and once he arrived
there, he pulled into the driveway and automatically got out to*

*open the garage door in order to park the car inside. Then he
stopped himself, remembering that he needed the garage's empty
space for what lay ahead. He entered his house through the
front door, walked unhesitatingly through the living room and
kitchen, and exited into the garage.*

*The tires were piled in a corner, waiting to be put on the
Ford once winter's snow and ice melted from the roads. Raymond reached inside the dark well of the heaped tires to bring
out the coiled clothesline rope. He tested again the knot that he
had tied days before. It held tight, as he knew it would. The
knot was a variation of one he tied in fishing line when he was a
boy. Seven twists and then circle through—it looked more like a
noose than the actual noose would. He threaded the other end
of the rope through the loop but left an open circle. When he
reached up to gauge whether it was large enough to fit over his
head, he knocked off his hat, which under the circumstances
struck him as hilarious, the setup to a joke without a punch
line: Did you hear the one about the man about to hang himself? He forgot to take off his hat. . . .*

*Continuing to move quickly yet deliberately, Raymond un-
folded the stepladder and climbed high enough to toss the rope
over a crossbeam, a process he repeated a few times. He wanted
to make certain the rope wouldn't slide from side to side. The
other end of the rope he anchored by tying it to one of the legs
of a built-in workbench. With the stepladder still in place he
brought the tires over and stacked them under the knotted rope,
the height of which had to be adjusted one more time. The ladder would enable him to climb up to the top of the pile of tires.
He'd loop the rope around his neck—making sure to take off*

his hat first!—and then he could push the ladder and send it crashing to the floor. He'd have to balance only long enough to kick the tires out from under him, and only two would have to fall away to guarantee that his decision would be irrevocable.

Once all these preparations were in order, Raymond went back inside the house. He didn't have a lot of time, but he could have one more cigarette and warm up a bit. Working in the garage had been almost as cold as it would have been to work outside. He sat down at the kitchen table. He took the typed confession from his pocket and put it under the ashtray. No need to remove his hat or overcoat. He wouldn't be here long.

One small matter was still plaguing him. Those failed attempts to write a suicide letter—had he thrown them all away? Raymond was sure he had. But had he only crumpled them up before tossing them into the wastebasket, or had he torn them to pieces? Had he emptied that basket into the garbage can in the garage? He thought he remembered taking those precautions, but if he hadn't, someone could retrieve those sheets— some of them containing no more than a few words, others filled with clumsy crossed-out sentences that were supposed to explain his life and why he chose to end it as he did—smooth out the paper, decipher his scrawled handwriting, and believe they had the answer to Raymond Stoddard.

Well. Let them try. If the papers were there, they were there. Raymond didn't have the energy to walk down the stairs and climb back up again. Not when he still had those ladder steps to negotiate. And now he heard the sirens that he had been listening for, though he couldn't determine if they were moving toward him or if they were still speeding toward the capitol

building. But if they weren't coming his way yet, they would be
soon.

He wondered from how far away they could be heard. Or,
put another way, how far his fame had already traveled. If Raymond could hear the sirens from his kitchen, certainly they
could be heard in the homes of his neighbors on Keogh Street.
People in the older houses and apartments in the center of the
city could probably hear them. And farther away? Could they
hear the sirens in those expensive homes on the western hills? In
the run-down houses south of the tracks? In the offices of his
brother-in-law's construction company out on Airport Road—
could they hear them there? In the Frontier bar on Main Avenue? His wife and son—could they hear them? And was
everyone within earshot asking, as people so often do at the
sound of a siren, what's happening? What's wrong? Raymond
hoped they were heard everywhere and that to every ear they
would inspire the same questions, not just today but every day
hereafter. What happened? What went wrong?

He had just lit his second Old Gold when Raymond heard
the front door open. He had an impulse—an absurd, ridiculous,
impossible impulse—to rush to the garage to complete his mission before Alma or Gene—no one else, not even the police,
would enter without knocking, ringing the bell, or shouting
their presence—discovered him, but then Raymond relaxed. He
still didn't have to hurry. Not yet. The garage was his domain;
he could walk out there at anytime and neither his wife nor his
son would have any curiosity about what he might be doing out
there on a winter's day.

It was his son, his son and his friend who lived up the

street, their faces red and their noses running from their walk home from school. Before Gene could ask his father why he was sitting at the kitchen table rather than at his desk in the capitol, Raymond put a question to his son. "Where's your mother?"

"I'm pretty sure she works at the church library on Wednesdays."

Raymond nodded. "Wednesday. That's right. It's Wednesday." In his mind he added to the day a calendar notation, calculating the date that would for years after bear his mark and name more than his birthday ever had. "What time will she—"

But Gene was already turned to the refrigerator, reaching inside for the milk he would swig from the bottle. The neighbor kid, however, kept watching Raymond, and with the gaze of someone who doesn't recognize what his gaze fixes upon.

And perhaps Raymond did look different. He was, after all, someone he hadn't been the last time these two young men had seen him. Why wouldn't his appearance be altered—what identity had more strength and power than "murderer"? For that matter, Raymond hadn't, he realized, looked at himself since he'd left the capitol. Perhaps before he went into the garage he would seek out a mirror for a quick self-inspection, just to see if he could see what this kid saw. Then again, why bother? He had never known who he was better than at this moment.

He tilted his hat back and took a last drag on his cigarette. Look all you like, kid; Raymond Stoddard will never be anything but a mystery to you.

Since my mother's death, and instead of those regular visits to her and my hometown, I've been making a very different journey. As a result of my friendship with a French editor, I'm able to live for a few weeks in Paris. His apartment is in the Latin Quarter, my Montana home is near a number of first-class trout streams, and because he is a fanatic fly fisherman, he is more than happy to swap residences every summer.

His apartment, in a building dating to the seventeenth century, has much to recommend it. Rue Xavier Privas is a quiet street, but only steps from the Seine, the Saint-Michel Metro stop, Notre Dame, and from wonderful bridge views. Boulevard St.-Germain is close enough that I hear those distinctive French police sirens regularly. Shakespeare & Company is nearby, and I browse its shelves frequently. Two or three evenings a week I eat dinner at Chez Pento, a wonderful tiny restaurant that has been feeding diners for over a hundred years. But those are the attractions that Jerome might list in a brochure if he were interested in subletting to any American. Only to me might he mention the slanted ceilings with their exposed beams . . . which remind me of the attic where Marie and I first made love. I can stand at the window, and though I am looking down at a cobbled courtyard where children play and my neighbors greet one another, those sights are not as poignantly real as the remembered image behind me. After lovemaking, Marie lies unashamedly naked on our makeshift mattress, and the late afternoon sun slants through the window, lighting her just so and revealing the sheen of perspiration that covers her from head to foot. She glistens. She shimmers. She shines. She glistens. She shimmers. She shone, shone, shone. . . .

ACKNOWLEDGMENTS

For their advice and support I am deeply grateful to my agent, Ralph Vicinanza, and my editor, Bruce Tracy. I am fortunate indeed to work with these consummate professionals and to count them as friends. For the information and insights they provided about the past, heartfelt thanks to Bruce and Barb Evanson and to Mark Miller. Special thanks to Eben Weiss and Bara MacNeill. Thanks also to Jennifer Hershey, Laura Ford, Beth Pearson, Ryan Doherty, and everyone else at Random House for their expertise and enthusiasm. Finally, for her love and inspiration I owe a debt that can't be repaid to my wife, Susan, who is present on every page of this novel.

SUNDOWN, YELLOW MOON

LARRY WATSON

A Reader's Guide

A CONVERSATION WITH LARRY WATSON

Random House Reader's Circle: You tell the story through a timid and unnamed narrator. Was he modeled after anyone? At times he is likeable, yet ultimately he betrays his best friend. What relationship did you have with the narrator while writing? How do you think the reader should react to his actions?

Larry Watson: I'm strongly tempted to duck this question, because the narrator—timid and traitorous, as the question suggests—is based on me. We grew up in similar neighborhoods in Bismarck, North Dakota. We both lived within view of the state capitol building, and in childhood came to know that distinctive structure well. We both graduated from Bismarck High School. (He's from the class of 1963; I'm from 1965.) We both attended the University of North Dakota, and we both became fiction writers. Each of us in adolescence fell in love with a girl who had been dating our best friend. In fact, the narrator is one of two characters in the novel with a real-life counterpart. Anyone who knew my wife, Susan, when she was younger (or, for that matter, who knows her now) will almost certainly identify her as the model for Marie Ryan. I seldom base my characters so closely on people from life, but these two characters in *Sundown, Yellow Moon* are exceptions.

I suppose I could console myself because the question also applies the word "likeable" to the narrator, but I've already read reviews, met with book clubs, and heard from readers who have said they find the narrator unlikeable. I can live with those opinions, and I understand why readers respond to the narrator in that way. He lives too much in his head and too much in the past. He is calculating and self-absorbed. But he is also punished for his failings. The man who looks back on his life and tells this story—these stories—is haunted and anguished. I, of course, escaped his unhappy condition. I never broke up with my Marie Ryan; my wife and I have been happily married for more than forty years. There are other essential differences. I never had a neighbor who was an assassin and committed suicide, or had a friend who was a murderer's son, and no matter the extent to which fictional characters might be based on real people, they can't be the same people when their experiences are different.

This is a long way of saying that the narrator is and isn't me. Even when a writer works from the actual, the very act of writing produces an aesthetic and an emotional distance that guarantees the written version will differ from its real-life analogue. The narrator and I also share a reverence for the writer William Maxwell who wrote in *So Long, See You Tomorrow* that "in talking about the past we lie with every breath we draw." That strikes me as a little strong, since "lie" to me suggests an intent to deceive. It would be more accurate, in my view, to say that our memory always lies to us. But then fiction is a lie to get at the truth.

RHRC: The entire town of Bismarck, North Dakota, becomes obsessed with Raymond's murder and suicide and, of course, his motives. You grew up in Bismarck. Was it how you portrayed it in the book? Was there an instance in your youth that inspired this story? What is it about this landscape that you wanted to bring to the reader?

LW: The correlation between the Bismarck of the novel and the "real" Bismarck is similar to the correlation between the narrator and me. I wrote about a place that resembled a real place but whose true existence was in my imagination. For the purposes of the novel I altered a few facts about the city, and I'm sure my memory altered others. Nevertheless, the real Bismarck of the early 1960s was, I believe, comparable to the Bismarck of the novel in that they were both fairly conservative, largely middle class, and somewhat repressed homogeneous communities, removed in many respects from the rest of the nation by climate and geography. One of the ironies of the novel is that Bismarck is brought out of its isolation and anonymity by an act of violence. There have been, unfortunately, too many real-life instances of communities made famous, however briefly, by the violence that has occurred within their borders. In that regard, it should be noted that *Sundown, Yellow Moon* takes place not only in a small city on the northern plains but also in America. From the political assassinations of the 1960s to last year's insane slaughter on the Virginia Tech campus, Americans have had event after gruesome, grievous event that have forced us to ask again and again who we are as a people and why we live in such a culture of violence.

RHRC: First loves, first lovers, childhood friendships, and people's past relationships are big themes in this book. How do you think each relationship affects the next? Which relationship in the story was primary for you? Which one did you feel contained the crux of the story?

LW: I do believe in the power and durability of first love, but whether that early relationship lasts, as my wife's and mine has, or doesn't, it's still capable of forming a template that many people apply to subsequent relationships. These people spend a good part of their lives seeking to find a partner with whom they can recapture the passion, purity, and intensity of a youthful love affair. This is the predicament of the narrator of *Sundown, Yellow Moon*. Because of that, I regard his relationship with Marie Ryan as the crux of the story. To the end of his days the narrator will long for something he once had but can never have again. And he knows it.

RHRC: Raymond Stoddard's motives for the murder of Monty Burnham and his suicide are never revealed. Do you believe there is a single motive? Did you write it with a clear answer in mind? The protagonist seems to believe it was jealousy. Do you agree? Do crimes always need motives?

LW: I didn't write *Sundown, Yellow Moon* with an answer in mind as to Raymond Stoddard's motive. I never doubted that he would have one, or more than one, but the desire to know what is ultimately unknowable—what was going on Raymond Stoddard's heart and mind—obsesses not just the narrator but other characters in the novel.

Jealousy is plausible as a motive, but of course, the narrator is drawn to that as an explanation because he himself is prone to jealousy. I had hoped that one of the ways readers would participate in the novel would be through examining their own personalities and by speculating on how that examination would lead them toward certain explanations. But it would be a brave, introspective reader willing to do that.

Yes, I believe that crimes always have motives, no matter how irrational, crazed, twisted, or inadequate they may be.

RHRC: *Sundown, Yellow Moon* contains many short stories written by the protagonist, who is a writer himself. How did you come up with the idea?

LW: Almost immediately after the murder and suicide, the narrator struggles to comprehend what has happened. Such acts are beyond puzzling; they're inexplicable. But that doesn't stop people from trying to understand and explain them. Reason won't provide answers, so the narrator tries to imagine his way into lives that are otherwise closed to him. At first this activity takes place only in his mind, but that signals the beginning of his life as a writer. It made sense to me that he would continue to do that throughout his life, though, as for any artist, at some point the aesthetic demands of making a good art object—a short story, in this case—takes precedence over the personal stimulus that initially moved him toward making that object in the first place. Artists are, in my opinion, people finally more interested in making than knowing. The narrator of *Sundown, Yellow Moon* has a dramatic past that provides him with all the raw material he needs for a lifetime of stories. I thought that, by including his stories in the text, readers would be able to see how his imaginative mind works. Do we know him any better through reading those stories? I believe we do.

RHRC: When you began writing this story, what were you hoping to accomplish? What did you want to find out or share with your readers? You also speak directly to the reader. What did you set out to accomplish with this technique?

LW: I could never be classified as a postmodernist, fabulist, or metafictionist, but anyone who writes fiction as long as I have is bound to notice some self-consciousness about the practice creeping into his thoughts. And while I'm dug in too deeply in the realist trenches (and am too devoted to story) to write a novel that is entirely a self-reflexive riff on the nature of narrative, I am interested in conducting fictional experiments and in attempting to see whether I can challenge the borders of fiction—without losing readers in the process, of course. In *Orchard* I tried a nonchronological form. And in *Sundown, Yellow Moon* I tried to address some fundamental questions about stories, such questions as Where do stories come from? Why do humans need them? What uses do we make of stories? How do fictional truths differ from other varieties? What is the relationship between memory and imagination? So in the writing of *Sundown, Yellow Moon* I was aware that I was a writer remembering and imagining his past and in the process writing about a writer remembering and imagining his past. But I didn't want this to be an exercise in academic theorizing or in navel-gazing; I wanted, as I always want, a story that would engage, entertain, and move readers, and in the process provoke some thought. Addressing readers directly was a way, I hoped, to indicate that they and I were in this together.

RHRC: Do you have a writing routine or any rituals surrounding your work? How long was it after you first had the idea for this story before you started writing it?

LW: I don't have routines or rituals that must be followed—no necessity for twenty sharpened pencils or a pot of Earl Grey tea. I can work in any place and at any time as long as I have the materials at hand. But I do make sure that I work on a novel— producing new material, not just reworking old—every day. I will probably also make a journal entry, and I might work on a poem, an essay, or a short story. But I must work on a novel every day without fail. I began writing *Sundown, Yellow Moon* almost as soon as the idea came to me.

RHRC: What are you working on now?

LW: I've been working on a novel set, once again, in the early 1960s, and for this novel, whose working title is *The Doctor's*

Boys, I've returned to Montana. A teenage boy has become infatuated with a woman a few years older than he. In pursuing her, he finds himself in competition with a charismatic, powerful man, a doctor in the community.

QUESTIONS AND TOPICS
FOR DISCUSSION

1. What does *Sundown, Yellow Moon* say about the nature, source, and durability of young love?

2. Of the available possible explanations for Raymond Stoddard's actions, which do you favor and why?

3. Each character seems to favor a particular explanation. What does that preference reveal about his or her character?

4. Does the explanation you favor reveal something about your character and experience?

5. The narrator writes stories to explain and understand what happened in his neighborhood. Is that a universal human response, or does it stem from his personal nature?

6. Does *Sundown, Yellow Moon* say that storytelling is a basic human impulse?

7. The narrator doesn't emerge as an entirely likable character. Why? Is he made less than sympathetic because of what he says and does, or because of what he thinks and feels? Or because of what he writes?

8. What does *Sundown, Yellow Moon* say about the nature of memory? Of memory and imagination?

9. In some respects, the narrator is stuck in the past. What prevents him from living in the present?

10. How is the setting, both the time and the place, important to the action in the novel?

11. Because of the many stories within stories, it's not always possible to determine what "really happened" in the narrative. How does that uncertainty figure in the novel's themes?

12. If you knew the narrator based only on the stories he's written, would you characterize him in the same way you would based on his behavior, speech, thoughts, and emotions?

13. Do you have a favorite character?

14. There have been many assassinations and attempted assassinations of politicians in the United States. How does this novel comment on the social, psychological, and cultural response to such events?

15. What does *Sundown, Yellow Moon* say about violence in America?

LARRY WATSON is the author of *In a Dark Time,
Montana 1948, Justice, White Crosses, Laura,*
and *Orchard.* He has won the Milkweed Fiction
Prize, a National Endowment for the Arts fellowship, the Mountain and Plains Booksellers Association Regional Award, and numerous other
literary prizes. He lives with his wife in Milwau-
kee, Wisconsin. Visit www.larry-watson.com.